THE MISSING MASTERPIECE

THE MISSING MASTERPIECE

A Dorothy Martin Mystery

Jeanne M. Dams

This first world edition published 2017
in Great Britain and the USA by
SEVERN HOUSE PUBLISHERS LTD of
19 Cedar Road, Sutton, Surrey, England, SM2 5DA.
Trade paperback edition first published
in Great Britain and the USA 2017 by
SEVERN HOUSE PUBLISHERS LTD

British Library Cataloguing in Publication Data
A CIP catalogue record for this title is available from the British Library.

ISBN-13: 978-0-7278-8718-4 (cased)
ISBN-13: 978-1-84751-825-5 (trade paper)
ISBN-13: 978-1-78010-893-3 (e-book)

This is a work of fiction. Names, characters, places and incidents
are either the product of the author's imagination or are used fictitiously.
Except where actual historical events and characters are being described
for the storyline of this novel, all situations in this publication are
fictitious and any resemblance to actual persons, living or dead,
business establishments, events or locales is purely coincidental.

All Severn House titles are printed on acid-free paper.

Severn House Publishers support the Forest Stewardship Council™ [FSC™],
the leading international forest certification organisation.
All our titles that are printed on FSC certified paper carry the FSC logo.

Typeset by Palimpsest Book Production Ltd.,
Falkirk, Stirlingshire, Scotland.
Printed and bound in Great Britain by
TJ International, Padstow, Cornwall.

AUTHOR'S NOTES

I have invented some of the procedures at the Scriptorial and the Abbey. I have also altered parking regulations to suit my own purposes. And those who know Mont-Saint-Michel and environs will, I hope, forgive me for making small changes to some hotels and restaurants and cafés and so on, and running up a few new ones. My intent was to depict the atmosphere of that remarkable place, not to be literally accurate in every detail.

My favourite teacher in high school, more than fifty years ago, was one A.T. Krider. (We students never knew what names lurked behind the initials.) Mr Krider was much more than an English teacher in my senior year. He taught me critical thinking and gave me confidence in my own abilities. I was devastated when he died during my first semester in college. The character going under his name in this book does not particularly resemble my revered teacher; I used his name because I like to think he would have been amused at playing a role in a mystery novel.

I owe particular thanks to Barbara Maitland, who patiently corrected my French, gave me tips about the food and culture in Normandy, and helped me keep my computer running – a lady of many talents.

This book is dedicated to Patricia Kearns, of Keynote Web Design, who designed and has maintained my website for many years. Patty, you're super and I love you!

ONE

I ignored the phone. My mobile was on the coffee table, and with two cats in my lap, not easy to reach. Everyone knows, of course, that disturbing a sleeping cat is NOT DONE. The cats will forcibly remind anyone of that who attempts this gross breach of manners.

Alan knows the rules. He put down his book, got up, and picked up my phone just as it stopped warbling. 'Gilly,' he said, looking at the display, and handed it to me.

I called back. 'Sorry, love, I couldn't make it to the phone in time. What's up?'

'Oh, Dorothy, the most wonderful thing!' I held the phone a little farther from my ear while she went on. 'You'd never guess!'

'You've sold one of the big pieces. *Diana*, maybe?' Gillian was a young sculptor whose fame was spreading. In defiance of current trends in art, she did absolutely beautiful figurative work, and the buying public loved it. She had recently completed a life-size bronze of Diana the huntress, complete with bow and a wreath of oak leaves in her hair.

'Better than that! I'm doing a show in May, and you'd never guess where!'

'I give up.'

'Bayeux! You know, in Normandy?'

'I have a vague idea. I saw the Bayeux tapestry about fifty years ago, but I don't remember much about the town. Is it big enough to make a show there worthwhile?'

'Only about the size of Sherebury, but masses of tourists come to see the tapestry. A new gallery opened about a year ago, and they've had such great success with paintings that they're branching out into sculpture, and oh, Dorothy, they chose me for their first major sculpture show!'

'Shows their good sense. May, you say? That's doesn't give you a lot of time, does it?' I looked at the crackling fire and the dog asleep on the hearth rug. Outside the sky was dark grey, the trees black leafless skeletons. January was being its usual grim, depressing self.

'I have tons of small things ready, and three big ones in the clay. You haven't seen those. There's a gorgeous David, and a really ugly Goliath to go with him, and an Eve. I haven't started work on Adam yet, but I'll have time to do a maquette before the show.'

'Biblical themes? That's new for you, isn't it?'

'Our new bishop preached that really great sermon about the Old Testament – remember? – and got me interested. Gosh, there are enough really great characters there to keep me going for years. Samson and Delilah, Moses, Abraham and Sarah and Isaac – the lot. I know they've all been done before, but not the way I'll do them!'

'You're very brave to take on David. There've been a couple of pretty good takes on him already.'

'I can't compete with Michelangelo. Nobody can. But I've never honestly liked the Donatello or the Bernini. The one's too smooth and effete, and the other's too fussy. No, you wait till you see mine! And that's why I called, actually. Not just to blether on, I mean. What I really wanted was to beg you and Alan to come with me. My French isn't wonderful, and Alan's is terrific. But it's more than that. The people at the gallery speak really good English. But I want someone to – well – just be there for me.'

'Your parents . . .' I began.

'They can't come!' It was nearly a wail. Gillian was in her twenties, and a proudly independent young lady, but she adored her parents and remained very close to them. 'Dad's off to Mumbai next week for a year. He'll be a consultant to their security bureau, and Mum's going with him. He's going to be frightfully busy and doesn't think he can get away, even for a little while. He's tried to persuade Mum to come for the opening, but she's not about to let him be without her. She worries about his health.'

'Oh, dear! Nothing serious, I hope?'

'Dad says not. He's just a bit rundown still from that bout of flu last month. That sort of thing always hits him really

hard, poor dear. So you see, I really, really need someone to
hold my hand, and you're sort of my honorary grandparents,
so you will come, won't you?'

Alan, who had heard every word of her excited narrative,
reached for the phone. 'Gilly, Alan here. Of course we'll be
happy to come with you. I've wanted for years to take Dorothy
to France, and Bayeux is a perfect place to begin. A fascinating
city in itself, and quite near Mont-Saint-Michel. And then
there's Monet's garden at Giverny, and Honfleur, and Rouen
. . . altogether an embarrassment of riches. We're delighted
for you, Gilly. We'll work out travel details when we're nearer
to the time, shall we?'

'Yes, but I'm going to call the gallery right this minute and
have them book a room for you at the same hotel they've
arranged for me. The seventeenth May; put it on your calendar
now!'

I smiled at Alan as he put down the phone. 'Gilly's twenty-
four going on twelve. She's as excited as a kid at Christmas.'

'She has a right to be. A solo show at her age is a major
accomplishment. I hope you don't mind my agreeing without
consulting you.'

'Don't be silly. I'm excited, too. I don't remember a thing
about France, and it seems silly that we've never been there,
when it's so close. We'll have a wonderful time, and the kids
will get spoiled to death by Jane. Won't that be nice?' I petted
Emmy fondly. She yawned, gave Sam a half-hearted swat, and
went back to sleep.

TWO

The older I get, the faster time seems to pass. The weeks
between mid-January and mid-May seemed endless
looking forward, but they passed so quickly we barely
had time to make all our arrangements. We'd fly to Paris, and
then Gilly would go on to Bayeux, a few days early to get the
show set up. After a brief, tantalizing glimpse of Paris for

the American who hadn't been there for over fifty years, we'd hire a car and drive to Bayeux.

I was just getting excited about the whole thing when the blow fell. Three weeks before we were to leave, Alan broke his left ankle. It was Watson's fault. Our big, lovable mutt is getting on in years, and has become a bit deaf. Snoring away near the Aga, he didn't hear Alan come into the kitchen until he was quite near. In an excess of doggie enthusiasm, he got to his feet and leaned his considerable bulk against his adored master. Alan, ready to step over the dog, was off-balance. Down he went, one foot sliding under the stove in his effort to avoid Watson. He heard the crack, he said later, as the bone went.

I wasn't home at the time. Gilly had persuaded me that I needed some new clothes for the trip. I was in a fitting room at our small local Marks and Spencer, hoping that the lovely sweater I'd set my heart on would fit me, when my mobile rang. Alan, sensibly, had first called for an ambulance and then phoned our next-door neighbour, Jane Langland, who called me.

I was far more upset than Alan, who took it all calmly enough. 'Not the end of the world, darling,' he told me from his hospital bed. His voice was a little slurred; the pain meds were beginning to take effect. 'It'll heal quickly if I do as they tell me, which I have every intention of doing.'

'It's the end of our trip, though,' I said, trying not to snivel. 'Not that it really matters, as long as you're going to be all right. But Gilly will be so disappointed.'

'There's no reason to disappoint her. You two can go.'

'Oh, no! Not without you! Your French is the reason she wanted us, and I couldn't possibly manage alone.'

'Mmm,' was his only reply as he slid into drugged sleep.

The argument continued when he woke up in the morning, and Gilly joined in on Alan's side. 'The people at the gallery say almost everyone speaks some English, at least, and they'll help if we can't manage.'

'What about Paris? I'd be alone there, and I can't say the idea thrills me.'

'You'll love Paris, dear heart, and it's only for a few days.

And I'll join you just as soon as the doctor gives me permission. It won't be long.'

It was Jane, our next-door neighbour, pet-sitter and dear friend, who finally persuaded me, though. 'Non-refundable bookings,' she said. 'Far too late to change. No travel insurance?'

Well, no. We hadn't thought the insurance necessary.

'One flight's not too bad. Fifty pounds or so?'

'About that.'

'All the flights, hotels, trains – a tidy sum to lose.'

It was a valid argument. Alan and I aren't impoverished, but we're not rolling in wealth, either. Dropping a whole bunch of money for nothing isn't in our DNA.

So I went ahead with plans, though dispiritedly. Travel with Alan is fun. Travel alone, not so much.

Really, though, it hadn't been so bad, I mused as I sat in my hotel in Bayeux. Paris was pretty much what I had expected. Noisy, crowded, fascinating. Once Gilly had left, I'd explored the city in my favourite mode, afoot. I'd bought a really good French phrase book before I left Sherebury, along with a detailed map of Paris, and was able to get around reasonably well. My English friends had told me to expect Parisians to be rude, and some of them were, but no more so than the residents of most big cities. It helped that I tried to speak French, even though I did it badly. At least I was making the attempt, and most of the people I dealt with seemed to appreciate that.

It was all a bit exhausting, though, and I looked forward to my nightly phone calls to Alan, so I could carry on a real conversation. I was careful to stress the high points – the Louvre, the market stalls on the Left Bank, the exquisite food – and downplay the annoyances. Once I started talking about Bayeux, though, it was easy to be enthusiastic.

'I can't *wait* for you to get here! The gallery's wonderful, and the people are really nice. And oh, my, the hotel! Several notches above our usual, Alan. You're going to love it.'

There was a sigh at the other end of the line. 'My dear, I'm afraid I've bad news for you. I can't come tomorrow. The doctor's not so happy about my progress, and wants me to stay off my feet for at least another week.'

'But . . . but that means you'll miss the opening, and Bayeux, and . . . oh, Alan!'

'I'm just as upset about it as you are, love. I had looked forward to seeing Bayeux again, but the doctor says it would be most unwise for me to travel just now.'

'And what about Mont-Saint-Michel? I've been reading guide books, and it sounds as if it's *all* hills and steps.'

Another sigh. He tried to hide it, but it came through. 'If my memory serves me, you're quite right. Shall we, as they say, cross that bridge when we come to it?'

Cross it in a wheelchair, I thought but did not say. 'I think I may just come home. Gilly's opening is tomorrow, and I can't leave her in the lurch for that, but then . . . oh, Alan, it's no *fun* without you!'

'You're just tired, darling. And hungry, probably. Have you eaten?'

I bit back a retort. Alan thinks all my problems can be solved by food. 'No. I just got settled in. Gilly has a few loose ends to tie up at the gallery, and then we're going to have dinner somewhere. Probably here in the hotel; it's easiest.'

'Don't do that. Ask the concierge about the best place to eat. And promise me you'll make it a thumping good meal.'

'It'll cost a fortune.'

'Probably. Remember all the French meals I haven't had these past few days, and all the money that's saved us, and blow it all, if you can. Include some excellent wine and drink a toast to me. Promise?'

I promised, reluctantly, and ended the call. Catching a glimpse of my face in the mirror over the dresser, I decided I'd better rearrange it. Gilly would be here soon, and I didn't want to show her how depressed I was.

As I washed my face and applied a little fresh makeup, I thought about when Alan and I had first met Gillian Roberts, a graduate teaching assistant at Sherebury University, embarking on her very first job, intimidated and unsure of herself. We had become embroiled in a series of nasty incidents at the art college, including the death of the department chairman, and had become almost surrogate parents, or grandparents, of young Gilly, who rapidly blossomed into a major talent in the

art world. She'd had a solo show in London, but this was her
first outside England. She was riding the crest of a wave, and
I couldn't pull her down.

When she knocked at the door, I was ready for her.

'Wow! You're looking splendid! That's a stunning hat!'

I thought so, too. The little black-and-gold fantasy was
ridiculous, but fun. It always lifted my spirits, which needed
it just then. 'I talked to Alan, and he gave me firm orders to
take you out to a posh restaurant for a thumping good meal.
His very words. I had a little talk with the concierge, and he's
booked us in to a place down the street that he assures me is
"*magnifique!*".'

'But I thought we were going to eat here. I'm not dressed
for—'

'Put on that gorgeous brocade jacket you bought last month,
and change your shoes, and you'll outshine everyone in the
place. Hurry. We've fifteen minutes.'

When we were seated at the restaurant, I got Gilly started
talking about the show, where the pieces were displayed, how
pleasant and considerate the gallery owners were, how she
was feeling. 'A little jittery, I guess, but I think it's going to
be all right. Yves and Hélène keep telling me the work is
"*merveilleux*", and unless they're just trying to make me feel
good . . .'

'No. It *is* marvellous stuff, Gilly. You know it is, and I'll
tolerate no false modesty. Now here we are, and we're going
to concentrate on the serious business of enjoying superb
French cuisine.'

I had had the concierge teach me how to tell the waiter that
we had only a little French, and knew only a little about haute
cuisine, and wanted him to compose a meal for us. '*Et du vin,
bien sûr!*' I hoped I got the request for wine right.

'*Entendu, madame, mademoiselle. Un repas pour les anges,
je vous le promets!*' And seeing the blank look on my face,
he added, 'Antoine will bring for you a meal fit for the angels
in heaven!'

I thanked him and then cast about for another subject to
keep Gilly from asking about Alan. 'Have you had time
to see the tapestry yet?'

'No, I thought we'd wait and do that when—'

'After your opening, of course. You've been much too busy for sightseeing. You know, I have actually been here once before. Maybe I told you. I was just out of college, I mean university.'

'I do speak some American, you know,' she said, grinning.

That took me off on a tangent. 'I remember once when a woman at passport control in Gatwick asked me if I was visiting England for a vacation – not "on holiday". I must have looked surprised, because she said, "Oh, I'm bilingual." With that perfectly straight face that used to make it impossible for me to tell if an English person meant to be funny. Ah, here's our wine.'

The wine steward explained that this was a little something to go with our first course. At least I think that's what he said; unlike Antoine, he either couldn't speak English or didn't care to. It was only a half-bottle, so I didn't think it was meant for the main course. Nor do I know what it was, except that it was white, and fruity without being sweet, and a perfect match for the seafood dish that was set before us a moment later. I don't know what that was, either, though I recognized scallops and tiny shrimps. Whatever it was, it was divine.

The main course was beef. I could tell that much. It was served in a sauce that was obviously devised by a magician. With it there were little balls of potato, cooked in some ingenious way, and tiny thin French beans, and another vegetable I didn't recognize. The wine steward brought a lordly bottle of something red, tasted it himself (obviously, and correctly, not trusting our palates), decanted it in front of a candle, and finally poured it for us with gestures that turned the simple act into a religious rite. Ginny and I were perilously close to giggling by the time he left us to our enjoyment.

We hardly talked at all during our meal. Course succeeded course. A crisp, tart salad followed the beef, and then a selection of gorgeous fruits and a platter of assorted cheeses, along with the dessert course which was something creamy and frothy and sweet. A different wine had accompanied each course, the dessert one something that tasted of apricots and summer sunshine. I looked with real regret at the cheese which was waiting forlornly on the table; it looked wonderful, but there was no way I could eat another bite of anything.

'I may never eat again,' said Gilly, with a sigh, 'but oh, it was worth it. I should warn you I may run off with Alan, if he makes a habit of providing meals like this. When is he getting here tomorrow?'

I was mellow enough with the wine to keep my composure. 'My dear, he can't come. I didn't want to tell you, but I knew you'd ask eventually. The ankle isn't healing as fast as we'd hoped, and the doctor wants him off his feet for at least another week. He's so terribly sorry. This lovely dinner was his way of cheering me up, and of course of congratulating you on a fine show.'

'How does he know it's a fine show? He hasn't seen it.'

There was just a little petulance in her voice.

'He's seen your work. And he knows you're a perfectionist.'

The waiter had caught the change of mood and approached, appearing distressed. 'Do the ladies require something else? Something is not right?'

'Everything is perfect, Antoine.' After all that wine, I'd given up any attempt to speak French, and anyway Antoine's English was fine. 'It was an incredible meal, and we are grateful. Could we have, perhaps, some coffee?'

'*Ah, oui, l'espresso, peut-être?*'

'Please.'

'I'm sorry, Dorothy,' said Gilly when he had left. 'I didn't mean to sound like a spoilt child. It's only that I'm really disappointed. And I know you are, too. But once the opening is over, we'll have a wonderful time seeing Bayeux together. You probably know lots of out-of-the-way places. You were saying you've been here before?'

'Only once, almost fifty years ago. I told you I was just out of college. My parents took me on a package tour, and I honestly don't remember a thing about it except the tapestry, and not much about that. And didn't you say they've built a new museum for it?'

'No, I don't think so. Just a new display at the old museum.'

'Well, anyway, we'll see that, and of course the cathedral, and anything else Yves and Hélène say we mustn't miss. When Alan first called, I was so upset I'd thought about going home after tomorrow, but . . .'

'But you're feeling better after that amazing meal.'

'And a gallon or two of wine didn't hurt. Gilly, do you know anything about etiquette in French restaurants? Would they allow us to take some of that cheese back to the hotel? I can't possibly eat it now, but wouldn't it make a great lunch tomorrow?'

Antoine had brought our espresso, and was hovering nearby. I think he had taken us under his wing, two ladies all alone – and one of them young and beautiful. *Mais oui*, of course the two lovely ladies could take home some of the cheese, he would package it up for us, and was there anything else he could do for us?

'Only *l'addition, s'il vous plaît*.' I was proud of remembering that high-school French phrase for requesting the bill, and Antoine tactfully pretended that my accent was understandable.

It was late when we got back to the hotel, but I knew Alan would be waiting for a report. 'Okay, you win,' I said when his sleepy voice answered. 'You were right as usual.'

'Good food and good wine did the trick?'

'Superlative food and wine, served by a delightful and most attentive waiter. I rather fell in love with Antoine. You don't even want to know how much it cost; you may as well start the bankruptcy proceedings first thing in the morning. I imagine Gilly will visit us in the poorhouse. But yes, I'm feeling a lot better, and we have plans to see everything there is to see in Bayeux as soon as the opening is over. But you needn't think I don't miss you. I hate sleeping alone.'

'There's always Antoine.'

He hung up before I stopped sputtering.

THREE

The opening went as openings always do, with additional flair provided by the French influence. The wine was probably as cheap as it always is on such occasions, but in France even a cheap wine can be special. Hélène, we discovered, had made the hors d'oeuvres herself; she was obviously a talented cook. Gilly was, of course, the star of the hour, and with Yves or Hélène at her side to translate when necessary, she graciously accepted the compliments showered upon her. More to the point, she sold a number of the smaller pieces, and there was a great deal of interest in the new line of Biblical figures. All in all, the evening was a great success which left both of us too exhausted to do anything afterwards but fall into bed.

The next day was Sunday, so Gilly and I went to the beautiful cathedral for a service neither of us could understand very well, and then for the next couple of days we played tourist. Bayeux is an interesting town, part medieval, part modern, though there isn't nearly as much new construction as in many old towns in Europe. Bayeux was spared much of the devastation during World War Two because neighbouring Caen took most of the heat in the Battle of Normandy. Much of Caen was destroyed, mostly by the Allies; most of Bayeux remains. I read about all that in a guidebook, and felt guilty, as I always do when thinking about the damage 'our side' inflicted on the great treasures of Europe, not to mention the hundreds of thousands of civilians we killed. Okay, yes, I understand that war is hell and 'collateral damage' (horrid term!) is inevitable. That doesn't make me feel one bit better when I look at pictures of Dresden. Or Caen.

So we saw the museums, including, of course, the Tapestry Museum, housed in a medieval palace but an entirely modern display, dimly lit, climate-controlled, the lot.

The Bayeux Tapestry is not a tapestry at all, really, since

it's embroidered rather than woven. It shows, in remarkable detail, the events leading up to the Norman Conquest and the Battle of Hastings. 1066 and all that, as a popular spoof history book has it. I learned a great deal about it when Alan and I spent a holiday in Alderney, in the Channel Islands. The people of Alderney recently finished a project, with the help of notables like the Prince of Wales and his wife, 'completing' the tapestry; the original ends in a ragged edge and is presumed to have had extra panels leading up to William's coronation at Westminster Abbey. The *Alderney Finale*, as it's called, had hung in the Tapestry Museum for a time until its return to Alderney, where Alan and I saw it.

Looking at the original, all 230 feet of it, I was struck by how little the colours had faded in the past 900-plus years, and how well the *Alderney Finale* had copied the original. 'Not so shabby, those eleventh-century needle workers,' I whispered to Gilly. Something about the place seemed to demand a church-like demeanour.

We saw everything we could fit into the short time at our disposal, and on the last day visited the gallery one more time to thank Yves and Hélène.

'Hello, Dorothy,' said a voice from a corner, and when its owner turned around I had to look twice to make sure I believed my eyes.

'Penny Brannigan! What on earth are you doing here?'

'I do paint,' she said, trying to hide a smile. 'I do occasionally visit galleries.'

'But isn't this a little off your beat?'

'I'm having a little holiday, resting up before the wedding season goes into high gear. I've never seen the tapestry before, and when I saw Gillian's name on a poster, I had to pop in and see her recent work.'

I met Penny some years ago on a brief trip to Wales. Penny's an expat like me, and a talented amateur watercolourist, though by profession a cosmetologist. She's from Canada originally, but has lived for years in a small town in north Wales. Alan and I have run into her from time to time, most recently at a retirement party for a friend of Penny's. And not long before that, Penny helped us solve a rather nasty problem at Sherebury's art college.

'You remember Penny, Gillian?'

'Of course. Without you, Penny, that frightful man might still be wreaking havoc at the college.'

'Well, he couldn't be allowed to stand in your way, at least. Gilly, your work was always good, but now – I'm stunned! I hope you're going to let me treat you both to coffee, or lunch, or something.'

'Oh, drat, Penny. We both have to catch trains in a little while. Gilly has to get to Paris for a plane back to England, and I'm taking a train to Mont-Saint-Michel.'

'Oh, dear.'

We looked at her, puzzled at her response.

'Oh. You hadn't heard.'

'Heard what, for heaven's sake, Penny?' I frowned.

'It was on the news this morning. A woman was caught on the sands yesterday as the tide was coming in. She nearly drowned, and as it is she took in enough water that they're not sure she'll survive.'

Oh, dear, indeed. I sat down on the nearest chair. 'That's terrible news. I had no idea – I mean, I knew about the incredible tides, and the quicksand, but somehow I didn't think people still tempted fate that way. What was she doing out there, anyway?'

'Look, Dorothy,' said Gilly, 'you want to hear all about this, and I simply must get to the railway station. Yves is driving me, and he's standing outside looking at his watch. It doesn't matter what train you get, does it?'

'Not really, I suppose.'

'Then you stay and let Penny take you for coffee, and I'll hear the details later. Penny, so nice to see you again, and Dorothy, darling, bless you for being my moral support!' She air-kissed both of us and sprinted out the door.

It was early for lunch, so Penny and I went back to my hotel. I'd checked out, but we could get coffee in the bar, and Penny bought us each a pastry. 'Because talking about disasters requires some fortification.'

'So,' I said when we had settled. 'Tell me all you know about this.'

'It's only what I heard on the news. The woman is German;

I forget her name, if I ever heard it. She was apparently travel-ling alone; nobody seemed to know much about her. Including why she was out on the sands at a dangerous time.'

'Why would anyone go out on them at any time? The quicksand of Mont-Saint-Michel is legendary.'

'But there are always people who think they know better than the authorities. I've never been to the Mont, but friends have told me there are warnings about walking on the sands posted all over the place, and yet people still do it. And I suppose if you venture out at low tide and get stuck, there's time for help to reach you. But this woman must have ignored the tide tables.'

'And you say you got all this from the news? In French? I'm impressed. I can barely catch one word in ten. I've been relying on the Internet in English, but they don't feature a lot of world news.'

Penny laughed. 'My French is pretty rusty, but I was watching in the lounge of my hotel, and a kind soul sitting next to me translated.'

'Well, then, I don't feel quite so stupid. But really, no one knows why she was there?'

'*Pardon, madame.*' Our waiter, who spoke excellent English, had overheard our conversation. 'There has been further news. The lady was digging, it is said. Perhaps for *les moules –* comment dit-on—?'

'Oh, I know that one! From a menu somewhere. Mussels, isn't it?'

'*Ah, oui, merci.* The mussels of Mont-Saint-Michel, they are famous, *n'est-ce pas?*'

'But – a visitor, a foreigner – why would she be digging for mussels?' I objected.

The waiter replied only with an eloquent Gallic shrug, as if to imply that the actions of foreigners were always inexplicable.

'I don't believe it for a moment,' I said in a low tone, when the waiter was out of earshot. 'It makes no sense at all.'

'I agree, but we may never know unless the woman recovers. And even then . . .'

'Post-traumatic amnesia. Is that a real term, or did I just

make it up? Anyway, the condition is real enough. Oh, well. I just hope Alan doesn't happen to see that item on the news. He worries about me quite enough without fear of something like that.'

'Where is Alan, by the way?'

I explained. 'And I'm hoping he'll be able to join me at the Mont. Although what he's going to do there with a bum ankle I can't imagine, if it's as steep and crowded as it looks in pictures.'

'He'll manage. I have great faith in Alan's ability to do anything he wants to.'

I laughed. 'There's that. The polite term is perseverance. Back in Indiana they'd have called him stubborn as a mule.'

'Just keep him off the sands, in case he takes it into his head to investigate the place where the accident happened. And you stay away, too.'

'Don't worry. There wouldn't be anything to see, anyway, several high tides later. Did you read about the one a while back that covered even the new bridge?' And we chatted about the tides there and in Canada's Bay of Fundy, which is near Penny's former home and has the highest tides in the world. That led us into a discussion of our human preoccupation with the biggest/highest/most of anything.

'I can't believe the prices people are paying for art these days,' I said, absent-mindedly taking a bite of a second pastry. 'That Picasso that went for almost $180 million? It's insane.'

'And when one thinks of painters like Van Gogh, who sold almost nothing and died bitter and mad . . .'

'And now people pay small fortunes for his work. It's almost criminal.'

'Mmm. And speaking of criminal, there's been an odd little trickle of art crime lately. At least it's thought to be crime. A few medieval manuscripts have been coming on the market, and no one knows – or will admit to knowing – where they've come from.'

'Stolen? But surely there aren't all that many just lying around for someone to steal.'

'Stolen, or possibly forged. I don't know all the details, but there's been a little buzz about the whole thing in the art world.'

'But what are they? Illuminated pages of something? I'd have thought that forging such a thing would take far too long to make it profitable.'

'Oh, some manuscripts can go for huge sums; you wouldn't believe. I read about a book of fifteenth-century poetry being auctioned at Christie's the other day for a couple of million pounds.'

I gasped.

'Of course that was a complete book, with lots of illuminations. The works I've been told about are single sheets, I believe sheets of music, but as I said, I haven't heard many details. If they're real, they could still be worth quite a lot to a collector.'

'Or even if a buyer can be convinced that they're real.'

And that led us to the old controversy about why a beautiful forgery wasn't worth just as much as an original work of art, and I got so wrapped up in it I had forgotten the time until Penny said, 'This has been delightful, but shouldn't you be thinking about that train you need to catch?'

'Oh, good grief, yes!' I looked around for our waiter, but Penny smiled and put her hand on mine.

'This is my treat, remember? You need to collect your luggage and find a taxi. I'll take care of the bill here. It was lovely to see you, and I hope you have a terrific time at the Mont.'

Seeing her again had made me miss Alan all the more. The three of us had shared good times together, and now I was leaving her behind, and no telling when I'd see her again, or, for that matter, Alan. However, I summoned up all the intrepid spirit I possessed and got myself and my luggage onto a train that was, I certainly hoped, heading in the right direction. Alan would have known for sure, and would have handled all the hassles. Ah, well. He'd surely be with me in a few days, so I'd just have to soldier on in the meantime. What, after all, could go wrong?

That's a thought one should never think while travelling. I had been told to get off the train at Pontorson, the station nearest to the Mont. That was easy. The train was modern, and equipped with lighted signs that showed the next stop. It also spoke them aloud, though without the words in front of me I might not have recognized some of the stops. However, I duly got out at Pontorson and looked confidently around for a taxi to take me to my hotel.

There were no taxis. Furthermore, there was no one I could ask. The station was in the middle of a badly-needed renovation, and was closed, with no personnel on duty. There was a little trailer-office off to one side, but it was closed. The posted office hours ended at '17.00', 5:00 to my American mind. It was now 6:15.

Now what?

I panicked for a moment. Stranded in a strange town, in a country where I spoke very little of the language . . . and night was coming on . . . and there might be lions and tigers and bears, oh my!

That bit of silliness brought me to my senses. France had been a civilized country long, long before some of said wildlife ceased roaming my native land. There might be the odd mugger, but somehow I doubted it. This didn't feel like that sort of place. I could phone Alan, but what could he do from so far away? Well, it really wasn't that far as the crow flies, only about a hundred miles, but psychologically it felt like from here to the moon.

I straightened my hat (a sensible one for travel), assembled my luggage, attached everything I could to the handle of my rolling bag, picked up the rest, and staggered across the station yard. There were lights across the street, and some of them came from a hotel!

The woman at the front desk was very pleasant, and spoke good English. I explained my predicament. I was booked in to a hotel very near the Mont, but there were no taxis, and I didn't know what to do.

'But it is not a problem, madame! There is a bus, but it is not easy with your luggage, and you are tired, yes?'

I admitted that I was tired. I would not admit that I was also depressed and near tears.

'We have a room for you for tonight if you wish, madame.

And we can phone your other hotel and explain. Do you wish to keep your booking there for the rest of your time here?'

'I suppose I'd better, because I'm expecting my husband to join me there in a few days. I'm sorry to give you all that work for just one night . . .'

'*Ça ne fait rien, madame.* It does not matter. If you will show me your passport, *s'il vous plait* . . . ah, but you are English?'

Even the French think I'm American, I thought with a sigh as I handed over the English passport. 'American-born, but I've lived in England a long time.'

'*Ah, oui.* Now, if you will please sign here . . . *merci.* Here is your key, and I will get someone to help you with your luggage. *Non, non, non, non, non*, it is no trouble.'

The porter was obliging. The room was small, but clean and comfortable. I sank down on the bed, pulled out my phone, and called Alan.

I didn't mean to let my voice wobble, but Alan knows me very well. 'Buck up, old girl. You're not lost in the wilds of a jungle somewhere. I've heard good things about the hotels in Pontorson.'

'This one seems very nice. It was just—'

'I know. You don't like the feeling that events have slipped out of your control.'

'Well, good grief, nobody does!'

'*Au contraire,* my love. There are lots of helpless types who would have just stood there at the railway station and looked forlorn until someone came to rescue them. You took the initiative.'

'Well, I certainly wished you were there to help me take it!'

'And I wish I had been. Soon, the doctor says. I'm to see him tomorrow, and if he gives me a clean bill, I can join you on Monday.'

'Oh, that's the best news I've had since I got here! But what about the walking and climbing and all that on the Mont? No, I know, a bridge to be crossed, et cetera.'

'Right.'

I hung up feeling much less tired than five minutes before.

The next morning I woke early, having had a fine dinner the night before at a restaurant recommended by the friendly concierge at my hotel. Yes, I knew he probably got a cut. I didn't care. He was kind, and I had dined well. The porter helped me get my luggage back across the street and into the bus, and I headed for Mont-Saint-Michel feeling pleased with the world. I was coping very well, with a little help from my new friends. I looked out the window at a not-very-inspiring view – fields and meadows – and then the bus rounded a corner, and I wasn't the only passenger who gasped.

It was one of those experiences I call 'Grand Canyon' moments: oh, yes, of course I've seen pictures, but I didn't know it was like *that*!

It had been over fifty years since I'd caught a glimpse of the Mont, and that was from quite a distance, so this was my first real experience, and it blew me away.

There's no way to describe it adequately. You've seen pictures, or you haven't, and anyway, no pictures can match the reality. An island that is an almost perfect pyramid rises out of the sea – or the sand, when the tide is out – rises to a peak that is, astonishingly, crowned with a tall, slender spire. Sounds interesting and a bit odd. The word 'magnificent' doesn't occur to you until a second or third glance. 'Miraculous' comes only when you see the real thing, looming before you, huge, impossible, ethereal.

Nobody on the bus said much until the road took another turn and the vision was lost to us. I let out the breath I hadn't known I was holding, and the woman sitting next to me shook her head as if to clear it and said, in an American accent, 'Was that real?'

'I don't know. It's not hot enough for it to be a mirage. Maybe a mass hallucination?'

The next glimpse wasn't quite so startling, and by the time we were dropped off in the middle of the group of hotels and restaurants and shops that had sprung up to serve tourists, we had grown, not blasé, no, but almost comfortable with the phenomenon that is Mont-Saint-Michel. In an odd sort of way we had taken up ownership. The world was now divided for us into two groups of people: those who had seen the Mont,

and those who hadn't. We were a trifle smug about belonging
to the A group.

One of the passengers, a nice man whose language I couldn't
follow – Italian, maybe? – helped me get my luggage to my
hotel, and I checked in. It was a slack time in the tourist season,
so for a miracle I could go to my room at ten in the morning.
I didn't like the hotel quite as well as the one in Pontorson,
but it was perfectly adequate, and the room was pleasant enough.
It had no particular view, just a bit of meadow and another
hotel. That was all right with me. I had the feeling that looking
at the Mont too much might dull my sense of awe.

When I had unpacked and got myself organized, I went
back downstairs to find that a light rain had begun. Not much
more than a drizzle, but the sort that can get a person awfully
wet in a very short time. I thought about the long walk once
I got to the Mont. The street, I had seen from pictures, was
steep and cobbled, and cobbles can be awfully slippery in the
rain. Hmm.

I trudged back upstairs to take off my hat and change into
sturdy walking boots and my hooded raincoat. I could shop a
little right here to kill some time and see if the rain didn't
let up.

The shops were about what you'd expect at one of Europe's
premier tourist destinations. There were souvenirs, some tacky,
some very nice, all vastly overpriced. There was a selection
of cheeses and biscuits and the like, again very expensive. The
racks full of rain gear led me to understand that inclement
weather was not unknown here, and most of the stuff was of
good quality and reasonably priced, but my raincoat was almost
new and I didn't want to try to carry an umbrella. For one
thing, they restrict one's vision and poke other people when
there's a crowd. And no matter what the weather or the season,
I expected a crowd on the Mont.

I couldn't find a thing I needed, and I was getting antsy. I
wanted to see that island, wanted to get there, wanted to
understand how – and why – anyone built a huge church in
such an unlikely place. I grabbed a quick sandwich in one of
the little cafés and went out in the rain to wait for the shuttle
to the Mont.

The only private vehicles allowed on the causeway out to the island are delivery vans and the like. Everyone else takes the shuttles. They're free and run frequently, almost non-stop in high season, I'm told. This one wasn't full, so I could sit, though I slid around some on the wet plastic seat. It was a short drive, and the driver told us (in several languages) to wait to get out until our tram got to the head of the line. He also told us that we must be back to catch the return shuttle in no less than three hours. Something about the tide. I didn't pay a lot of attention. Here I was, finally, about to set foot on the legendary Mont-Saint-Michel.

This isn't going to be a travelogue. Every writer who's ever visited the Mont has waxed eloquent about it, and truly, it's hard not to. From the moment I set foot inside the walls (and I had not even known it was a walled city), I knew why people from the four corners of the globe had made this a place of pilgrimage for centuries.

Yes, it's crowded. Even on a drizzly day before high tourist season began, I was hard put to walk without banging into someone. Yes, it's touristy and ridiculously expensive. I took one look at the menu outside Mère Poulard's establishment, famous for omelettes, and shuddered at the idea of paying thirty-five euros for an omelette, famous or not. The shops that lined the streets sold all sorts of interesting wares, but I balked at the prices.

Nevertheless. I found it possible, as I climbed the narrow street that spirals up toward the Abbey, to ignore the tourists and the merchants and even the rain. This was a place of true antiquity. Here the twelfth century was somehow still alive and flourishing.

So, however, was the twenty-first. A child with bright red hair, in a raging tantrum to match, pushed a stroller with a younger child in it over my foot. There was no real damage done; my walking boots are sturdy. But I was annoyed, the more so because the younger child was also screaming, and the mother who should have been looking after the little monsters was engaged in an argument with her companion, none the less furious for being conducted in an undertone.

'. . . dragged me all the way out here in the pouring rain, and then you're too cheap to buy a ticket to the church.'

'If I wanted to go to church, which I don't, it wouldn't be one where I had to pay admission! They would have thrown us out anyway, since you had to bring along those screaming kids of yours. Shut up, you two!'

The last was delivered in a roar that had no effect whatever on the children.

'You talk about *them* screaming!' Her face, which ought to have been attractive, was mottled with rage. Her bright blond hair hung down in dripping tails, making her look almost witch-like.

'If you can't control them, you shouldn't have brought them.'

'And just what was I supposed to do with them, leave them back home with their father? I never wanted to come here anyway . . .'

'Then why did you? Why don't you go home, if you hate it so much!'

'I might just do that! Not only have you upset the children, I've ruined my shoes climbing those damn stairs! I'm going back to the hotel!'

She caught the older child by his hand and dragged him out of the shop, leaving the man (second husband, maybe?) to cope with the baby, who by now was red-faced and wriggling frantically, trying to get out of the stroller.

I hadn't really intended to climb all the way to the Abbey. The wet cobbles made for treacherous walking, and anyway, I'd decided to wait until Alan could join me. Sightseeing isn't only more fun with a companion, it's also more interesting, because your companion can point out things you might have missed, and vice-versa. But I remembered sorrowfully that Alan might not be able to go all the way up to the top on a still-fragile ankle. And after that little scene in the shop, I badly wanted some tranquillity. I found an opening in the crowd, stepped back out on the street, and soldiered on.

Once I left the confines of the busiest tourist area, the going was easier. Apparently not many people wanted to see the Abbey badly enough to negotiate the slippery footing. I found myself at the end of the street, with no place to go except up into the Abbey precincts, or back the way I had come. I'd got this far. I'd go up.

Steps. More steps. I stopped counting at 200, and that was before I made it into the Abbey itself. I wasn't moving fast, but I had to stop frequently to catch my breath. I really was going to have to get serious about losing weight.

Right. In France, home of *haute cuisine*.

The Abbey wasn't crowded. I bought my ticket and a guide book in English. I didn't need the rack full of the books in languages from Arabic to Welsh (including a good many I didn't even recognize) to know that people from all over the world visited here. Even on a slow day I could spot Asians of several different ethnicities, Indians, and Africans, along with Europeans of every stripe and the ubiquitous Americans.

The personally-guided tours, as opposed to the audio ones, were meant for organized groups only, but the one that was just getting started seemed quite *dis*organized. The young guide who was leading it was trying, without too much success, to get them to calm down and listen to him. They were speaking English, but they were all babbling at once, and I had a hard time catching remarks. I hung around, since eavesdropping is one of my favourite amusements. Besides, I had some hope that I might, in all the confusion, be able to attach myself inconspicuously to their party.

'You are certain, madam, that he was with you when you entered the Abbey precincts?'

'He was certainly on the tram from the village,' said the buxom, commanding woman. Head of the WI in her community, I speculated. 'I sat next to him. He was most eager to see the Abbey.'

'Perhaps he stopped in one of the shops on the way up—'

A chorus of voices vigorously discounted that suggestion. 'I have never,' said the self-appointed spokeswoman, 'known a man to let shopping deter him from a goal. Bruce was interested only in the Abbey. Far from stopping along the way, he forged ahead of the rest of us and said he would wait for us here. I did *try* to make him understand we should stay together.' Her tone clearly indicated that the mishap was in no way her fault.

'The fact remains, madam, that he is not here, and we can wait no longer. When he does make his appearance, I fear he will have lost his place in the tour, unless it's within the next few moments.'

'I wash my hands of him,' said the woman in severe tones. No, not the WI, I decided, or not exclusively. Schoolmistress, and a rigid disciplinarian. They started off. I trailed in their wake. I had my audio gizmo, in case I was questioned, or couldn't hear what the guide was saying, but I much preferred a live human voice to a recorded one. You can't ask questions of a piece of plastic. Of course I couldn't question the young man, either, since I didn't belong with the group, but I could listen to the questions of the others, and I might be able to corner the guide later.

I've never been in any place quite like l'Abbaye du Mont-Saint-Michel. Frankly, I doubt there is another place quite like it. It was built over a period of many centuries, and bits of the very oldest structures still remain. Because it stands on a steep hill, its floor plan is irregular and lies on many different levels. Up more stairs. Down again. Up again. It was all fascinating, and worth the effort, but I'm not a young woman. We did get a chance, here and there, to sit for a moment and admire whatever was in front of us – the pillars of the Salle des Chevaliers, the austere beauty of the refectory, the gorgeous flamboyant pinnacles – well, we had to stand outside to see those.

I made it through the tour, though, and managed to avoid undue notice, or at any rate the guide ignored my unauthorized presence. I felt, in fact, rather proud of myself. I had blended in, and negotiated a million or so stairs. It's all that walking, I thought smugly. I may be overweight, but I'm pretty fit for an old bat. Walking four miles a day – well, most days – well, whenever I have the time – anyway, I'm in good shape!

Pride, they say, goeth before a fall. It was when we were leaving, going down some of those interminable interior stairways that we had climbed, that I had my downfall. Literally. My boots were wet from the little excursion outside to see the pinnacles. The stone stairs were worn in the middle by the passage of thousands of feet over the centuries. I don't know exactly how it happened, but somehow I slipped, grabbed for the railing and missed, and went bumping down seven or eight steps to land on the hardest floor I've ever encountered.

FOUR

Everyone was very nice. They checked me over for serious injuries before they would let me try to get up, and then three of the men in the group more or less lifted me off the floor and deposited me in a chair. The leader, whom I had mentally christened Margaret after a notable English prime minister, was somewhat sniffy about my tagging along with them, but she was distracted by thinking about how she was going to reprimand the missing group member when he was found. She also clucked about any delay that my accident might cause; some of the members were inclined to want to stay and help.

Peter, the guide, who spoke with an impeccable English accent, calmly took over. 'It is very kind of you, ladies and gentlemen, but we have rules about dealing with such incidents. In such an ancient structure, of course visitors have difficulties from time to time. It will take you some little time to get back to your bus, which is undoubtedly waiting for you. We will deal with this lady. Thank you for visiting l'Abbaye du Mont-Saint-Michel; I hope you enjoyed your tour. Thank you, no—' to the man about to give him a tip – 'but if you wish to make a donation to the Abbey it would be most welcome. There is a box near the exit.'

He waited until they were out of sight before turning to me.

'You knew all the time I wasn't with the group,' I said, trying to stand up. 'Oh, ouch.'

'Of course, madam. We are always given a count at the start of a tour, so we don't lose anyone. You had paid for admission and your audio guide, and the group was small; I saw no reason why you shouldn't tag along. In any case, your accent isn't quite . . . are you Canadian, perchance? No, don't try to stand up just yet. You're quite pale, you know.'

'I feel pale. No, I'm American, not Canadian, but I've lived in England for a long time. When I go home for a visit they all think I sound as English as can be, but here, no one is fooled. I think I could stand up if I could lean on you for a little while.'

'Better not, not just yet.' He leaned over and looked closely into my eyes, but so impersonally that I couldn't take offense. 'Probably no concussion; though one pupil is a bit smaller than the other.'

'They're always that way. Don't know why.'

'Ah. Do you have a headache at all?'

'No. Nearly everything else hurts, but not my head. And these slacks will never be the same again.' I looked ruefully at the growing blood stain on one knee. 'I haven't had a skinned knee since I was ten. I don't suppose there'd be a Band-Aid anywhere – I mean a plaster, or whatever they call them in France.'

'In whatever language, yes, we do have them. We've rather a complete first-aid kit, in fact. We sometimes have to deal with rather serious injuries, since it can take quite some time for proper medical help to arrive. Your colour's coming back a bit. Take my arm, and we'll go and tidy up your scrapes.'

I wasn't terribly surprised to be handed a small glass of brandy when I had sat down in the spartan but well-equipped first-aid room. After all, this was for centuries a Benedictine monastery, though it was now occupied by a new group of monks and nuns, the Jerusalem Community. And religious communities through the centuries have offered hospitality, including medical care, to strangers. I drank the restorative while the guide competently patched me up.

'There. Feeling better?'

'Much, thank you. I'm confused, though. Plainly you're an Englishman, and not a monk. How did you come to be guiding tourists in this place?'

He stood and brushed off the knees of his pants. 'Have you ever heard of Peter Abelard?'

I had to think a minute. 'As in Abelard and Héloïse? Of course I've heard of them, but I'm afraid my knowledge is pretty sketchy. He was a medieval monk, and she was a nun, and they had a love affair, and he got excommunicated or something.'

Peter grimaced. 'The usual misinformation. About the only thing that's accurate about the popular story is the time frame, although "medieval" is a fairly broad range.'

'All right, then, set me straight. I would just as soon sit a while before I have to negotiate all those stairs. Unless you have to be somewhere.'

'My duties are done for the day. I do a little guide work because I enjoy it, and the community here has been very kind to me. I like to return the favour. My real work is in Avranches, at the Scriptorial.'

I looked blank.

'You don't know the area?'

'I arrived last night. I've seen the Mont once, fifty years ago or so, but from the mainland. I've never actually been here before in my life.'

'All right, then. We'll begin at the beginning. Which was somewhere in the early eighth century, at least according to legend.'

'Right. You told us about that on the tour. The archangel Michael poked the bishop in the head and told him to build a church here. I have to say I doubt the archangel's understanding of construction problems. I never saw a less likely place to build anything more massive than a good-sized dog kennel.'

Peter smiled. 'Well, perhaps Michael had more pressing matters on his mind, like fighting the devil and all the armies of Hell. At any rate, Bishop Aubert, as ordered, built the church, or technically an oratory, a small chapel for prayer.'

'Yes, well, I know that bit. Can we accelerate the narrative a bit? The church was built, it was added onto and torn down and rebuilt, and so on and so forth, and became the home of a Benedictine abbey.'

'And that's really important. The Benedictines, as you may know, were great collectors of books and manuscripts. In their heyday the abbeys were centres of learning, with large libraries and large scriptoria where the books were copied. Even after the invention of the printing press made the work of the copyists less and less important, the abbeys still collected books, because reading was a vital part of the Benedictine Rule.'

'Have we left Abelard in the dust somewhere, moving so rapidly through the centuries?'

'Not at all. We've passed him by only about three hundred years, and we're coming back. Abelard, who was a fascinating character, was many things. Yes, a monk, after his enemies had him castrated.'

I made some little sound.

'Yes, that bit doesn't always make its way into the pretty love stories. You should read a book about him sometime; you might be surprised by the real story. Not, of course, that we know all of the real story. The man died in 1142, and accounts from that long ago are spotty and unreliable. However – yes, we're getting there at last – we do know that among his other talents, Abelard was a writer of considerable ability, and also a composer.'

I smacked my knee, and ignored the smart. 'Of course! *O Quanta Qualia!*'

Peter gave me a quizzical look. 'Madam, I have misjudged you.'

'No, you haven't. I mean, I really am ignorant about Abelard. I just happen to know he wrote a hymn called *O Quanta Qualia*, and I don't even know what the Latin means, because I've only ever sung it in English, and I don't think it's a very exact translation, but I'm a great fan of Dorothy L. Sayers, and that was her favourite hymn, only of course she sang it in Latin, she learned Latin when she was three or something like that . . .' I ran down.

'Yes. Well, you may not know that he wrote a great many other songs, and not only hymns. His love songs, presumably written for Héloïse, were said to have been the toast of Paris in the twelfth century.'

'Well, now, I love music, and the tune of *O Quanta Qualia* is very singable; it doesn't sound ancient at all. I wonder if I could buy a collection of those love songs anywhere.'

'No.' It was a flat, unequivocal reply. 'You can't buy a collection of them because they no longer exist. Nearly all his music, save that one hymn, has been lost.'

'Oh, what a pity!'

Peter was silent. I looked up at his face.

'There's more to the story, isn't there? You started all this by saying something about a scriptorium?'

'Scriptorial. It's a museum in Avranches – that's the nearest town of any size – which houses all the Mont-Saint-Michel manuscripts, all that are left, anyway. The Abbey was closed during the French Revolution and the manuscripts, fortunately, were sent away instead of being destroyed. Among those manuscripts are three copies of works by Peter Abelard.'

'Music?'

'No. Theological works. The amazing thing is that they're there at all.'

'You mean because the revolutionaries . . . no, that's not it, is it? I'm getting there. I may not have his life story right, but I'm certain he had run-ins with church authorities. So why would his writings be preserved in an abbey?'

He looked at me with approval. 'Spot on. They must have been unusually liberal in their outlook to have not only acquired his works, but copied them.'

His eyes were alight with the zeal that's common to a lot of people in diverse situations. The collector looks that way when a rare prize seems within his grasp, the gambler when the long shot is about to pull it off. And the scholar . . .

'You think the abbey might have collected his songs, as well. But you said the Scrip . . . what is it?'

'The Scriptorial.'

'Yes. That they have only three of his manuscripts, and they're theological treatises.'

'Yes, and that's why I think it's possible that . . .'

He trailed off as though afraid to finish his thought aloud. So I finished it for him.

'You think they might still be here, and you intend to look for them.'

FIVE

P eter looked around and put a finger to his lips.
'Oh, c'mon. There's nobody around. Anyway, you don't propose to go around tearing down walls or digging up the stones of the floor. Do you?'

'No, of course not, but do please keep your voice down. The acoustics in here are very odd; voices project in some places.'

'Not here. Peter, I've heard concerts in a lot of places. I know what a live space sounds like. This room is dead. Why are you so worried?'

'You are too perceptive, madam.'

'You can't keep calling me that. My name is Dorothy. And the question stands.' All right, I'm a curious person. Or nosy, if that word seems more appropriate.

'I'm not sure why you want to know, but the answer is simple. The Jerusalem Community has been very kind to me, but there are rules about what I do here. I show people around and answer questions. Nothing more. I am, of course, not allowed into the monks' and nuns' private quarters, unless by invitation. And I am very specifically not allowed into the parts of the Abbey that are closed to the public. Some of them are dangerous, you see.'

'Hmm. Because they are so old. Old enough to be interesting. What sort of time period are you thinking about?'

He held up his hands in the classic gesture of frustration. 'Madam, this is a ridiculous conversation. The idea that there might be any hidden manuscripts is a foolish notion, born of a deranged mind.'

'My name is Dorothy. Mrs Martin, if you simply cannot bring yourself to use a first name. And your mind is obviously not deranged, so what put the idea into your head?'

I could see him debating about whether or not to continue the struggle. Something about my expression must have told him I wasn't going to stop asking awkward questions, so he gave in. 'Very well, madam – Mrs Martin. I'll tell you the whole story, but not here. Are you staying on the Mont, or in the village?'

'Where the hotels are, and you catch the shuttle? If that's a village, I'm a French peasant, but yes, that's where I'm staying.'

'Good. We ought to be able to find a private place to talk there. Can you walk to the shuttle, do you think?'

'Probably. If I sit any longer I'll be too stiff to move at all. Onward and – er – downward.'

I'll never know how I made it. Without Peter's strong arm I couldn't have done it. How I hate the limitations imposed by advancing age! When I was a kid I lived on roller skates in the summer, and skinned my knees almost daily. I had scabs on top of my scabs. And I picked myself up from the sidewalk and skated off with never a thought to the pain. Muscles never ached, joints never refused to work.

Sayers's Lord Peter once remarked that he envied the young not for their hearts, but for their heads and stomachs. I envy them their joints.

Somehow I hobbled to the shuttle, where my obvious disability landed me a good seat, even though the tram was now crowded. The rain had stopped, a watery sun was trying to poke through the clouds, and the tourists had proliferated like ladybugs on the first warm day of spring.

'It's lunch time,' said Peter when we disembarked, looking not at his watch but at the crowds seated at the outdoor cafés. 'Is your car here?'

'I don't have one until my husband gets here, later this week. I've been travelling by train.'

'Oh. Then we can't drive into Avranches for lunch.'

'No. But we could buy ourselves some sandwiches somewhere and eat in my room. If it's privacy you want, we couldn't do better. If it's gourmet food, I'm afraid you're out of luck.'

'I'll eat anything.'

'Let me treat.' I handed him a wad of Euros. 'But you'll have to do the foraging. I can make it to my room, but not a step farther. I'm here' – I pointed to my hotel – 'room 104. And I'll eat anything, too, so long as it's filling. I'm starved.'

The shops looked crowded. I reckoned I'd have enough time to wash up and change into clean clothes before he came back, though not time for a lovely relaxing bath. I doubted I could get out of a bathtub, in any case. That would have to wait until Alan came along, with his assisting arms. With a sigh, I climbed the stairs to my room, feeling about a hundred years old.

When Peter returned and came in the door that I had left ajar, he found me on the bed, propped up with pillows. He looked a little embarrassed.

'I'm far too old, and you're far too young, to create a compromising situation. Sit down and let's see what you've got.'

He had found some lovely baguettes stuffed with ham, and some with cheese. There was a little tin of pâté and some biscuits. There was a bottle of white wine, nicely chilled, and plastic wine glasses, and finally an assortment of pastries of the sort only the French seem able to produce.

I dug in, and after a moment, swallowing a mouthful of sandwich, said, 'Okay. We're private. I've been thinking, and I've come up with some conclusions. First, you're a student of either music or theology.'

He took a swig of wine. 'Both, actually. Liturgical music and hymnody.'

'At Oxbridge?'

'Exeter. Do you know Exeter?'

'I've been there. Years ago. Lovely cathedral, though I don't like it as well as my own, at Sherebury.'

'Yes, you have a fine cathedral, and not a bad university.'

I rolled my eyes. Academic snobbery is universal. 'It's a good one, and you know it. Especially the art college. But never mind. You learned something at Exeter that made you hare off to France in the middle of term time, infuriating your professors and probably costing you quite a lot of progress towards your degree. A doctorate, I assume?'

'Yes. And the research here counts in as part of my work. I'm working principally at the Scriptorial, of course.'

'Ostensibly.'

'No, I am, truly. They have a few books of chants and the

like, music that was used in their daily offices. But I take your
point. There are far richer sources of medieval music elsewhere
in Europe.'

'And online. Don't look so astonished. I have managed to
limp into the twenty-first century, and I do know how to use
a computer. I was looking up something else in the British
Library, hit the wrong icon, and found myself looking at a
page from an old missal, illuminated capitals and all. So you
came here specifically to look for Abelard's music. Not at the
Scriptorial, but at the Abbey.'

'All right, yes! Dorothy, how do you do it? I haven't admitted
that to a living soul.'

'People talk to me. I don't know why.'

'You knew most of it already. I don't know how.'

'I taught school for over forty years. I learned a few things
about reading faces. Children are sometimes more open than
adults, but not always.'

'Your own face is open, you know. I could see the moment
you started to work out what I was doing.'

'Yes, I've been told I must never, never play poker.' I finished
my neglected sandwich and spread some pâté on a cream
cracker. 'So we've established what you hope to do. How are
you going to go about it?'

'There's the rub. I'd planned to have the help of a friend,
an archaeologist.'

'Ah. Who would have had ideas about where such things
might be buried.'

'Or just hidden. He's quite a clever chap, really. But he
can't come, after all. Some silly excuse about his girlfriend.'

I hid a smile. 'It's plain you're not in a serious
relationship.'

'Can't be bothered. Far too constraining. And this chap's
defection leaves me in an awkward position. I had counted on
him to have some ideas about where to look. I admit I hadn't
fully grasped how huge the Abbey was, or how complex. I've
no idea even where to begin. I've been trying for days to phone
him, to see if I couldn't get him to come for at least a day or
two, to point me in the right direction, but he isn't answering
his phone.'

The girlfriend again, I thought with a private smile. I wondered if they had eloped. 'And I suppose you can't ask anyone at the Abbey, anyone in the Community, I mean.'

'I don't think they'd be much help, to tell the truth. The Jerusalem Community has been in residence for only a few years, and the history of the Mont would hardly be their chief concern.'

'No, I imagine not. But isn't there an archivist or someone?'

Peter studied the pastry he was holding. 'The fact is,' he said finally, 'I'm not keen on telling the Community what I'm looking for.'

'Peter!' Penny's story came roaring back into my ears. 'You're not planning to steal whatever you find! If you find it!'

He put the pastry down with enough force to shatter its fragile layers. 'Of course not! What do you take me for? Steal from a monastery? Those people are doing a great deal of good! They work in the village, you know, earning their daily bread and spreading their concepts of charity and love. I wouldn't think of defrauding them of anything!'

Well, that might be true, or it might not. He sounded sincere, but the best crooks have that art. And *somebody* had been stealing manuscripts. Or manufacturing them. I wasn't yet ready to introduce the subject. I finished my pâté and looked at him over the top of my glasses. 'Then what *are* your plans?'

He gave me an exasperated look. 'I haven't had time to form any. Laurence, my friend, only told me last week that he wasn't coming. He didn't even have the courtesy to phone me; sent an email, the – er – miserable bloke. I had thought, perhaps, of making some enquiries in Caen.'

'Why Caen?'

'Well, the university.' When I looked blank, he went on. 'One of the world's great universities is at Caen. Didn't you know? Not as venerable as Oxford, of course, some three hundred years younger, but very well respected. I could probably find an archaeologist there to help me, but . . .'

'But you want this to be your own splendid discovery. If in fact there is anything to be discovered. Hmm.' I sipped some wine, stared at my glass, and pondered. 'I don't think I know anyone in that field at Sherebury. My friends tend to be either scientists – my first husband was a biologist – or artists. Alan might know someone, but he's still at home with a broken ankle.'

It was Peter's turn to look confused. 'At home? In America?'

'No, in Sherebury. Alan is English, and we've lived there since we married several years ago. He was to have come with me, but the ankle intervened. It's healing nicely, and he hopes to join me in a few days. I could call and see if he has any ideas. He knows almost everybody in town, and the ones he doesn't know, our neighbour Jane Langland does.'

'Is he an academic, then?'

I smiled. The wine was making me mellow. 'No. But he's had a good deal of experience with – I suppose you could call it research. Investigation might be a better word.' Peter was looking baffled. 'He's a policeman, Peter. Or he was; he's retired now. He was chief constable of Belleshire for many years.'

'I wish he were here, then. He might have some ideas about searching for the lost.'

Well, that added another point to his honesty score. 'Actually . . .' I thought better of what I'd been about to say, and closed my mouth firmly.

'What? You've had an idea. I can tell. That mobile face of yours.'

'Only a passing notion. Not worth passing on. If you're not going to eat that pastry, could you pass it over? I don't know what it is, but it looks wonderful.'

I finally managed to get rid of Peter, once he realized that he wasn't going to pry anything more out of me, and then, instead of indulging in my overdue nap, I went down to the lobby and sought out a computer.

I was back in my room and thinking about some supper when the phone rang. I answered it eagerly.

SIX

'Hello, love. How are you getting along in the wilds of Normandy?'

'Quite well, now that the sun's out. I went up to the Mont this morning, and managed not to make a fool of myself on the wet cobblestones.' I had decided not to tell him about my fall in the Abbey, not until he was here with me, anyway. He'd worry, and I wasn't really hurt. Bruises and general aches and pains don't count. 'More to the point, how are *you* doing? When can you get here?'

'Almost certainly by Monday. I've been behaving myself; the doctor was pleased when he saw me today. He has restricted me about stairs, though.'

'That's bad news. The Abbey is *all* stairs. Though you wouldn't absolutely have to go to the Abbey. There are a lot of interesting shops in the village, and other things to do in the area, but of course you know that, don't you?'

'Not the details. Helen and I visited before the children were born, but after that it got too complicated. And after she was gone, I buried myself in work. So I don't remember as much as you think. And if I can't manage the stairs to the Abbey, there's always another time.'

I felt my usual twinge of disorientation. I'm still not used to living in a place where the great European destinations were so close as to make 'another time' easily doable.

'There's that,' I acknowledged. 'And until you get here I can check out interesting places we can reach by car, where you won't have to do too much walking. Oh! I just thought! Can you drive?'

'The doctor suggests I hire a car with automatic transmission. It's my left ankle, don't forget, and there's really nothing to do with one's left foot in one of those. In fact, I'd thought you might venture to do some of the driving. What with no gears to shift, and keeping to the right – what do you think?'

'Hmm. And you could read the maps, and the signs in French – you know, it might work at that. But I sure wish you could get here sooner. I'm getting really antsy about a museum in Avranches. At least I think that's the name of the place. A town near here?'

'Avranches, yes. Pleasant little place, as I recall, but I don't remember it having a museum worth visiting.'

'It's new. Built this century, I think, though a lot of the online information about it is in French, and you know how great my French is! The thing is, it's where the Mont-Saint-Michel manuscripts ended up. I just heard of it today and I want to see it. Did you know about the Abbey library being taken away when the French Revolution closed all the churches?'

'Vaguely, and I can hear that you're panting to tell me all about it.'

Apparently it's not only my face that betrays my thoughts. 'We-ell, I met a *very* nice young man today who told me the story.'

'And you're planning to run off with him, are you? You'd better hurry. Monday isn't all that far away.'

'Yes, but you don't run all that fast, do you?'

He snorted.

'Actually, it's a great story.' I dropped the silliness and told him the story Peter had told me, about the manuscripts and the Scriptorial and Abelard, and Peter's quest for the missing songs. 'He has a friend who was going to help him, an archaeologist, but he bailed out at the last minute.'

I could just see Alan's face. 'And you don't have to describe your reaction. I can guess.'

'I didn't say a word to him!' I said indignantly, and realized too late that I'd given myself away.

'Aha! But you were thinking.'

'Well, okay, yes, but it's ridiculous. Can you see me, with two titanium knees and a bad case of claustrophobia, crawling around in the crypts of the Abbey or wherever, looking for lost sheets of vellum?'

'I can see you thinking about it. Knees and phobia notwithstanding, you love the idea of adventure.'

'I love it more when you're around to share it with me.' I

was suddenly a little teary, which was ridiculous in a woman my age who was going to see her husband in a few days.

'I will be soon.' He'd heard the almost-tears. 'Meanwhile, I've an idea. Why don't you get this young Lothario to drive you to the Scriptorial? Avranches is only a few minutes away from the Mont, and you could see the town and the manuscripts, and ask the museum people all the questions you want.'

'Not unless they speak English. I can order a meal and ask about a train timetable – sort of – and even then I don't always understand the answers.'

'Somebody will speak at least some English, and they'll certainly have guidebooks in several languages. Tourists come to the Mont from all over the world, and I'm sure the museum wants to cash in on that trade. And your boyfriend can always help you out.'

'I suppose . . . yes, Alan, it's a good idea. Unless Peter has to work at the Abbey tomorrow. But I can phone and find out. That is, I suppose there's a phone number in the guidebook I bought.'

'Bound to be. Now, About Monday . . .' And we made plans about when and where to meet, and I rang off.

I went down to dinner wondering why I hadn't told him Penny's story about manuscripts. Probably because I would have had to mention my vague suspicions of Peter, and I wasn't ready to do that. Well, there was no evidence, I insisted to myself. It wasn't that I was beginning to take this young man under my wing. Alan said that I always did that at some point in an investigation, and that once having settled where my sympathies lay, I refused then to consider any signs that pointed to the protégés guilt.

That certainly was not happening here. Certainly not. I defiantly had another glass of wine to quiet my sceptical half.

The next morning tested my patience to the limit. The minute I was dressed, I looked in the Mont-Saint-Michel guidebook and found several phone numbers that might prove useful. As I began to punch in the first one, the community at the Abbey itself, I remembered I had never bothered to learn Peter's last name.

Great. I was about to call a monastic community, probably disturbing them in their work or prayer or whatever they spent their days doing, to ask for a person whose full name I didn't know.

In French.

The pen of my aunt is on the bureau of my uncle. That was not likely to be of very great help, and all the rest of my French had deserted me.

I wiped out what I'd punched in and started over with the number of the Tourist Information Centre. I had started to speak before I realized that I was listening to a recorded message. Presumably it was telling me the office was closed. At least I was spared hearing that my call was very important to them, since I couldn't understand a word.

Well, okay, there was still the number for the Abbey, different from the one for the community. The gift shop, maybe?

'L'Abbaye du Mont-Saint-Michel,' said the voice.

Well, that didn't tell me much. I gulped and took a deep breath. 'Um . . . *parlez-vous anglais, s'il vous plaît?*'

'Yes, madame. May I help you?'

I let out the breath I'd been holding. 'Oh, thank goodness. My French is awful. But I don't know if you *can* help me. I need to speak to one of your guides, a volunteer named Peter. He's English, and I'm sorry, but I don't know his last name.'

'I do not know who that might be, madame.' The voice clearly indicated that she didn't much care, either.

'Is there anyone else who might help me? The person who schedules the volunteers, maybe? It's really important that I speak to this gentleman.'

'I regret, madame.'

'Wait! Don't hang up! If I come up to the Abbey, who could I ask?'

'The Abbey is closed to visitors today. Thank you, madame.'

One doesn't bang phones down anymore, but the click in my ear had a very final sound.

I went down to breakfast in no sweet mood. When I'm out of sorts, I want food, real, solid food. Alan is right about that, as he so often is. Croissants and brioches and café au lait are

all very well in their way, but they're no substitute for the
English breakfast I was craving. Carbohydrates don't take
the place of fat and protein.

When I'm at home, I'm quite happy with cereal and fruit.
Which just goes to show how contrary and perverse I can be.

I ate what was set before me. The fact that it was delicious
didn't improve my mood one bit, and when my phone rang,
and I didn't recognize the number, I snapped a 'Yes?' that
sounded furious even to me.

'Oh, dear. Is this Mrs Martin? Dorothy Martin?'

'Yes. Who's calling?'

'This is Peter, Peter Cummings. We met yesterday at the
Abbey?' He sounded ready to hang up any minute.

'Oh, Peter. I've been trying to reach you all morning! I'm
sorry I sounded like a witch, but I was annoyed. Mostly with
myself, for failing to get your number, or even your last name.
How did you find *my* number, though?'

'I remembered you said you lived in Sherebury. It's not all
that big a town, and you looked like someone who would go
to church, so I phoned the Cathedral. They knew right away
who I was talking about, so someone rang up your husband,
and he said they could give me your number.'

'Well, I'm glad they did. Now look, before we go any
further, I want to write down your number. I do know it'll be
on my phone, but I don't trust electronic gadgets. They fail
just when you need them most. Peter . . . Cummins, was it?'

'Cummings.' He recited the number, and I wrote it in the
tiny notebook I always carry with me.

'All, right, good. Now, you called me, so you go first.'

'I called with bad news, I'm afraid. I thought you might be
planning to go up to the Abbey again today, and I wanted to
tell you that you can't.'

'I know. I called them this morning when I was trying to
find you. They were very snippy, I must say, and didn't even
explain why they're closed. I thought they were open every
day.'

'They are, usually. The fact is . . . well, you know that man
who was missing from the tour yesterday?'

'Yes,' I said, suddenly full of foreboding.

'He's been found.'

'Oh, dear.'

'You already knew about it?'

'No. Your voice tells me this story is not going to have a happy ending.'

'No. He was down in one of the crypts. His head was . . . rather badly damaged. They don't know if he's going to recover.'

'Accident?' Another terrible 'accident' at the Mont, I was thinking.

There was a silence. I thought I could hear Peter swallow.

'They think not. Mrs Martin, when did you say your husband would be here?'

SEVEN

'Peter, where are you? We need to talk.'

'At home. My home here, I mean. I'm staying with a family in Ardevon, friends of my parents.'

'Where's Ardevon?'

'Not far. It's a very small village, a hamlet really, a few kilometres from your hotel.'

'So you have a car.'

'No. A bicycle.'

I thought for a moment. 'All right. I had been trying to call you because I wanted to suggest you show me the Scriptorial. Here's what I'd like to do. I think I can rent a car in Avranches for delivery to me here, but it may take a while. Since the weather is fine today, could you cycle over here to my hotel to meet me? Then, when the car comes, we can deliver the driver back to Avranches and then go to the Scriptorial. If you're willing, that is. I do want to talk to you about this latest development, because . . . well, I'll tell you when I see you. Is it a deal?'

'What do you—?'

'Not on the phone, if you please, Peter. How long will it take you to get here?'

'Twenty minutes.'

'Right. I'll see you then.'

'But I want to know—'

'I need to phone for that car, Peter. And after that I'm calling Alan. See you in a bit.'

I took a deep breath when I'd ended the call, and then went downstairs to try to find someone who could help me with car rental.

I got lucky. An American man who was checking out was just about to return his rented car to Avranches, and offered to give me a lift.

'That's very kind of you, but I can't leave for a little while. A friend is coming with me, and he's getting here by bicycle, so—'

'I'm in no hurry,' he said in a Midwestern accent that made me instantly homesick. 'Just getting a train to Paris, and it doesn't leave till late this afternoon. Maybe we could see the town together. If you want, I mean,' he added, and I could have kicked myself. A companion for the day didn't suit me at all, but the old adage about beggars and choosers came to mind.

'I'm not sure what Peter's plans are, so can we leave it open?' I said weakly.

My benefactor looked at me more closely, started to say something, and then changed his mind. 'Fine. I'll have some coffee while we wait. Want to join me?' Before I could reply, he said, 'Ma'am, I've got a wife and kids and four grandchildren back home.'

I accepted that as his intended reassurance of his honourable intentions, and grinned. 'Well, in that case . . . but I need to make a phone call first.'

I repaired to a far corner of the lobby and called Alan. He answered on the first ring. 'Listen, love,' I said in a low tone, 'I can't say much, but there's a good reason why I'd like you to come as soon as you can get here. I'm fine – no emergency – but my friend from the Mont and I need your advice and expertise ASAP.'

'A police matter?'

'Yes.' I saw Peter walk in the door. 'I have to hang up. If

you can fly into Avranches, I can pick you up. I'm hiring a car today. I'll tell you everything later.'

'I don't think Avranches has an airport, but I'll get there somehow. I'll ring you with a time and place. Don't go and do something that would get you hurt!'

I clicked off with a lighter heart. Alan was coming! All would soon be well with my world.

I went over to Peter and said, 'Slight change of plans. Follow my lead.' I led him to the table where the American man was sitting waiting for coffee and said, 'This is my friend Peter Cummings. Peter, this nice man has offered to drive both of us into Avranches, where he can return his rental car and we can get one. I'm sorry—' to the man – 'but I don't know your name. I'm Dorothy Martin.'

'Krider. A.T.' He shook hands with Peter, gestured both of us to sit down, and looked from one of us to the other, quite obviously trying to size up our relationship. Peter, in jeans and a T-shirt and sweating slightly from his bike ride, wasn't an obvious boy-toy, nor did I seem the type – years older, generations older than he . . .

I took pity on Mr Krider and put him out of his misery. 'I met Peter yesterday when he was guiding a tour of the Abbey and I took a stupid fall. We discovered a mutual interest in music and old manuscripts, which is why we wanted to visit the Scriptorial today. My husband wasn't able to come with me – an ankle injury that wasn't quite healed – but he'll be here in a day or two, and I thought I'd like to see what's in Avranches so we can revisit the best places together. Peter, Mr Krider has no obligations until late this afternoon, and would rather like to see Avranches with us, if you have no objection.'

I looked hard at Peter, my head turned away from Mr Krider, and made a face that I hoped he would interpret.

He wasn't sure what I wanted him to say. 'Well . . . that's certainly an idea . . .'

'If you have other plans, I sure don't want to interfere,' said Mr Krider in a subdued voice, and I suddenly felt sorry for him. He was probably missing his family and his home in . . . I was guessing Ohio. He had a sort of Ohio feeling about him, somehow.

I gave Peter the tiniest of shrugs and said, 'Good, that's settled, then. Peter, you know Avranches and we don't. Could you maybe show us around this morning? Then after lunch we can decide whether to stick together or go off on our own.'

Peter looked puzzled, as well he might, and I didn't want to explain in front of the kind American. 'I thought you wanted to talk,' he whispered as we trailed the man across the crowded, noisy lobby.

'Don't whisper,' I said. 'It carries. Wait.'

Mr Krider left us at the door while he brought the car around, and the minute he was out of earshot, I began. 'Don't interrupt, because this has to be quick. I called Alan and he's coming as soon as he can. He'll help, I know, but it can't be official because he's not only retired but off his turf. Meanwhile I'll do what I can. I've discovered a talent, late in my life, for untangling messes. We won't talk about it in front of Mr Krider, because nice as he seems, we don't know a thing about him except that he's American. I like him and he's probably okay, but we don't know for sure.'

Peter latched onto only one phrase. 'You're a . . . some sort of detective?'

'Not officially. But remember, we don't talk about anything important while Mr Krider's with us.'

He pulled up just then and I nudged Peter as we got into the back seat. He was looking like Inspector Clouseau, full of intrigue and mystery. 'Smile!' I hissed. 'Or at least try not to look so conspiratorial!'

His smile looked rather more like what an infant produces when its tummy hurts, but fortunately Mr Krider wasn't looking in the rear-view mirror.

'Do you know the way, sir?' asked Peter as we set off down the narrow road.

'Well, son, I got the car there. I reckon I can get it back. D'you think I should turn in the car right away, or keep it for driving us around?'

I looked at Peter. 'Parking can be a bit difficult,' he said, 'but it's a fair walk from the car hire to the Scriptorial.'

'Would there be a taxi?' I asked, bearing in mind my bruises and general stiffness.

'I'd think so. Or perhaps a shuttle to the railway station.'

'There's a shuttle,' said Mr Krider. 'I rode it when I picked up the car.'

'They might be persuaded to drop us off, then. The Scriptorial isn't far from the station.'

'And what is this Scriptorial place? Never heard of it.'

Peter's explanation, encompassing a history of Mont-Saint-Michel, the Benedictine order, medieval manuscripts in general, the French revolution, and the town of Avranches, was still going on when we pulled into the rental lot. Mr Krider looked as though he was drowning in the flood of information. 'Hmm,' was all he said as we got out of the car.

'You know,' I said as we walked to the rental office, 'if this isn't your cup of tea, I'm sure there are other points of interest in the town.'

He turned to me. 'Ma'am, I came all the way from Cleveland to Mont-Saint-Michel to see one of the oldest abbeys in the world, and I could only spend one day there because they went and closed it today for some reason. If some of its treasures are here in Avranches, lead me to 'em.'

Oh, my. And I had taken him for a well-to-do businessman intent on checking off one more 'sight' in the list of a hundred must-sees. At least I got the Ohio part right. 'What's your interest in old abbeys? If you don't mind my asking.'

'Don't mind at all. My son is thinking of joining the Benedictines, and I want to know as much about them as I can. Figured one good way was to trace their history.'

'Oh.' Honestly, I couldn't think of anything more to say, since I thought it would be rude to ask the questions that sprang to mind: is this son the father of some of those grandchildren you mentioned? How do you feel about this? What makes you think ancient Benedictine history will make you better informed about the order today?

He turned in his car and tipped someone to take his bags to the train station. I went about the business of reserving my car for later pickup. We found a taxi to take us to the museum, and I still hadn't said a word.

'You're wondering about my family,' he said when we were

settled in the back seat and making our slow way through city traffic.

'Among other things. Children, you said, and grand-children?'

He sighed. 'Two children, a son and a daughter. My daughter, Kathy, married young and produced four children in short order, including one set of twins. They're all in school now, and my wife and I were beginning to long for babies again. Grandchildren are so much more fun! Well, you'd know that, wouldn't you?'

'No, actually. I was never able to have children, and I didn't marry my second husband until his grandchildren were well past the baby stage. But I do understand. You have to care for and worry about your children, but grandchildren are for spoiling – and sending back to their parents when you get tired of them.'

'You got it. So when Roger was getting close to thirty, and didn't seem interested in marriage . . .'

'You thought he might be gay.'

'It doesn't necessarily follow, you know,' put in Peter. 'It could simply be that he's too interested in his career to think about settling down yet.'

'My wife and I tried to believe that, but he doesn't really have a career. He's had a series of jobs, none of them very interesting. But this religious stuff just came out of the clear blue sky.'

'That,' I said with a grin, 'is where inspiration is reputed to come from.'

'I suppose. But he'd never – I mean, we're Methodists!'

'Ah. Hardly a monastic sort of denomination.' Peter sounded a little condescending.

'Boy, you said a mouthful!' Either Mr Krider didn't catch the attitude, or he didn't care. 'I've worked in research all my life. Trying to figure out stuff is what I do. So when Roger blindsided us with this, I set out to understand it.'

Talk to him, I thought. Sit down with him and have a heart-to-heart. Have you ever tried to understand your son?

That was unfair, I scolded myself. You know nothing about this man. Maybe he's the best possible parent. He did, after all, travel several thousand miles to learn more about the Benedictines.

And then we arrived at the Scriptorial, and I got out of the cab with relief, lest my thoughts show on my face.

At first glance I thought we had been taken to the wrong place. 'But this is a castle. I read somewhere that the museum is new. Maybe I read the French wrong.'

'No, you're quite right,' said Peter. 'The Scriptorial was built in 2006, but within the old town walls. That's what you're seeing here. Not a castle, but fortifications, all the same. The museum inside is entirely modern. Shall we?'

EIGHT

The museum struck me as user-friendly, and with Peter as escort, everything went very smoothly indeed. He was able to translate for us, which might not have been necessary (there were some English-speaking staff), but was pleasant.

The museum was far more interesting than I had expected. There was a temporary display of Egyptian artefacts which I found a bit out of place, but attractive. Then, more in keeping with the main mission of the place, there were well-designed rooms showing just how medieval manuscripts were produced – making the ink and brushes, preparing the vellum, and so on. That part of the display went on to show very early printing techniques, long before Gutenberg and movable type. We lingered over these displays, even though I was itching to get to the main attraction.

When Peter finally led us there, I was a bit disappointed. Only a few of the treasures held by the museum were on display, and those in a carefully controlled environment. The lighting in the room was dim, and turned itself on only when we entered. The manuscripts were in glass cases, and were not easy to read, even if I had known more than a few words of Latin. The writing on several of them was very small, and slightly faded, and what with the low lighting and the darkening of the vellum with time, I couldn't make out more than a word here and there.

'The rest of them are in vaults. It's not good for them to be displayed for very long,' said Peter in a near-whisper.

'But then what good are they?' asked Mr Krider in a normal voice that seemed somehow out of place.

'Scholars and researchers can study them, under restrictions, of course. There's a balance between the need to use the works and the need to preserve them. Eventually they're all going to be copied digitally, and then anyone, anywhere in the world, can look at them without the slightest risk of damage. Until that project is finished, though, one has to come here.'

'I don't suppose,' I began. 'No, probably not, though.'

'You want to see one of the Abelard manuscripts.' It wasn't a question.

'Would I be allowed?'

'Yes, for a few moments, with me, of course. Mr Krider, I could take you in, but it would have to be separately. Too many people raise the humidity level beyond acceptable limits, I'm afraid.'

'Doesn't matter. I don't read medieval Latin, and I don't suppose I could make head or tail of anything I saw. You two go right ahead and enjoy yourselves.' His tone clearly indicated what he thought of our choice of amusements. 'I'm going to poke around here and see what I can learn about the Abbey and its history. There must be someone who speaks enough English to help me out.'

I wasn't sure what I hoped to gain from looking at something by Abelard. It wouldn't be in his own hand, but a monkish copy. I wouldn't be able to read the Latin. If I wanted to learn something about the man, it would make much more sense to find a modern translation of his work, and/or a biography.

But it wasn't so much Abelard I wanted to learn about, I realized. It was Peter's reaction to Abelard. And for that, watching him as he showed me the manuscript might be very instructive indeed.

Do you remember when you were a really little kid, three or four, and the whole world was new and interesting? You'd stop and crouch over a patch of dirt, intent on some tiny thing the grown-ups couldn't even see, and you couldn't understand why they wanted to hurry you along.

I felt exactly like one of those grown-ups, when we had put on our white gloves and sat down in front of the manuscript Peter had chosen to show me. It was, he told me, Abelard's most famous work, *Sic et Non* (Yes and No), one of the works that got him into so much trouble with the church authorities. To me it was just a book. Yes, extremely old, and worthy of respect for that reason. The leather binding was crumbling; the pages were chipped. There was nothing unusually beautiful about it, though some of the capital letters were 'illuminated', or at least drawn with extra flourishes, and the almost-perfect regularity of the writing was admirable.

To Peter, this was even better than a patch of dirt to a three-year-old – more like a Holy Grail. He almost genuflected before it. He pointed out the structure of Abelard's arguments, posing a question and then supplying several answers, often conflicting ones, and arguing the reasons for the apparent contradictions. Then, having done his duty by his guest, he started reading and was immediately lost in the twelfth century.

He never even noticed when I left.

Okay, so Peter's interest in Abelard was genuine. But there was still something a little odd about the whole situation. He was looking for music, or so he said. So why was he poring intently over a theological treatise? It couldn't be for the content. He could get that much more easily in a modern translation, or a transcription, if for some reason the Latin held some arcane detail not obvious in English.

I gave it up and went to see what Mr Krider was up to.

The layout of the Scriptorial is interesting, but somewhat confusing. It's intended to remind one of the configuration of Mont-Saint-Michel itself, an upward spiral leading to the pinnacle. But the continuous ramp made it hard to remember where I was. I wandered for quite a while before I spotted Mr Krider, and when I did, I stopped in my tracks.

He was deep in conversation with one of the museum staff, and they were both speaking in rapid-fire French.

I moved behind a display case. It was a glass cube, not a

great hiding place, but it was the first obstacle I could find. Had the man actually said he didn't speak French, or was I making assumptions? No, darn it, he'd gone off looking, he said, for someone who spoke enough English to help him.

Maybe that wasn't a direct lie, but it sure was intended to deceive. And I couldn't imagine why.

The two men were quite close, and were speaking in normal tones, but I could learn nothing from their conversation. Not for the first time, I wished I'd kept up my French. But good grief, how was I to know, over fifty years ago, that I was going to move to a place closer to France than Hillsburg, Indiana, was to Cincinnati?

Now I was in a predicament. Should I come out from my place of minimal concealment and say something of the order of 'Hah! Caught in the act!'

Well, no. My style is more 'Oops! So sorry,' while I sneak away pretending I didn't see or hear anything out of the ordinary.

But something was going on and I was pining to find out what, if I could figure out a good way to do it.

Think. I needed time to think. Which meant I needed to get out of there fast, before Krider turned around and saw me there.

I started to back away, trying not to let my sneakers squeak on the shiny floor.

'Dorothy, whatever are you doing?'

The conversation nearby came to an abrupt halt. Krider and the staff member turned. I turned around and clutched Peter while making an urgent 'Shut Up!' signal. 'Oh, goodness, you startled me! I was just – just trying to get a different angle on this display. And then I thought I saw – oh, there you are, Mr Krider! I was looking for you, actually. Did you find someone who could help you find your history? Or at least, whatever you're looking for?'

I shouldn't have said that. It slipped out. I had pasted a broad smile on my face, but his wore an expression I couldn't quite read, except that 'cordial' was not among the words that came to mind.

The next moment 'cordial' was the exact word. He smiled

and nodded. 'Why, yes, thank you, Mrs Martin. Everyone has been helpful, though most of the staff speak only French. It's amazing how fast it came back to me when I really wanted to understand. At least I got part of what they were trying to tell me, eh, *monsieur*?'

He made the mistake of pronouncing that word very well indeed. That wasn't Cleveland French. It was the real thing.

The staff member, who had enough English to understand that something odd was going on, smiled meaninglessly and melted away. Peter, who had remained obediently silent, took a breath.

I stepped on his foot and broke into rapid chatter. 'Well, I don't know about the rest of you, but I'm hungry. Breakfast was a long time ago, and I'm burnt out with looking at books I can't read. Peter, you know the town. Where can we get a decent meal?'

'Um. If simple food will do, there's a café not far from here where they do good *galettes*, for not a lot of money. Or there are four-star restaurants, of course, but—'

'But none of us is made of money,' I concluded for him. I wasn't sure what a *galette* was, and I waited for Krider (he of little French, supposedly) to ask, but he said, 'As long as I can have some of Normandy's famous cider with it, I'm your man.'

And how did he know Normandy was famous for cider? I was growing more and more interested in our simple American research worker.

Lunch was excellent. A *galette* turned out to be a savoury crêpe, filled with cheese and ham and onions and other bits I didn't recognize, folded in from the sides to make a square, and with a poached egg on top. A little odd looking, but delicious. I washed it down with a little cider, but only a little. Cider back in Indiana was just apple juice. On this side of the pond they ferment it, and it can range in alcoholic content from mild to nuclear. One taste told me this variety was well up on the scale, and I wanted to keep my wits about me. Waiting until Krider was well into his second glass, I put on my most innocent face and said, 'Mr Krider, you told us you're a researcher. Did you work for a university?'

'No, for corporations.' He hiccupped. 'Sorry. I was freelance. When a firm wanted to find out about how well the competition was doing, say, or how well their sales were doing in terms of demographics, or almost anything of that sort, they came to me.'

'Not scientific research, then.'

'Depends what you mean by scientific. Lab work, no. Didn't have the equipment for that. Or, I confess, the brains.' He finished his cider and burped gently. 'Pardon. No, I dealt with stas–saticks – with numbers.'

'You must have had a huge staff, then, to collect the data.' I tried to sound extremely impressed.

'Nah. Pay lots of money for people to sit at computers? I could do the sitting myself.' He laughed and hiccupped again. 'Pardon. I can find anything on the Net. All over the world, companies hired me to give 'em info. Nothin' I couldn't find. You gonna finish that cider?'

'No, it's a bit strong for me. Would you like to have it?'

We managed, Peter and I, to get him out of the café before he actually passed out, and into a cab headed for the train station. Peter asked the driver if he knew when the next train left for Paris, and learned that it wasn't for another hour or so. I hoped the man would wake up by then and remember to collect his bags before boarding. But it was, after all, no business of mine. Except . . .

Peter said it first as we stood in front of the café watching the cab disappear. 'There's something not quite right about that chap.'

'Yes. He's not what he appears to be. Look, I need some coffee to offset that cider. Let's find someplace cheap where we can sit and talk.'

The day was warmer, now that the rain had gone, and there were lots of sidewalk cafés nearby. We chose one that looked inexpensive, ordered coffee, and gave each other speculative looks.

'You wanted to talk to me earlier,' said Peter. He sounded accusing. 'It sounded important.'

'Yes, but I didn't want to say much in front of Krider. I'm really glad now that I didn't, because he's up to something. I don't know what, but did you hear him speaking fluent French just before you came into the room, back at the Scriptorial?'

'No. So that's why you pretended you'd just got there.'

'Right. I didn't want him to know that I knew. He suspected though. That's why he made that stupid remark about picking it up fast.'

'So what were they talking about?'

'I haven't the slightest idea. I can sometimes understand a little, if it's spoken really slowly, but these two sounded like a couple of Parisian cabbies.'

'But I don't understand. Why would he want us to think he couldn't speak French?'

'Again, I have no idea. But that isn't the only thing he lied about. I never heard such an unlikely tale as that tarradiddle about his "research". Nobody would pay anyone to look up stuff on the Internet that they could perfectly well find themselves. So that got me wondering about the rest of his story, his son the would-be monk and all that. I'll join a convent myself if any of that is true. I just wish I had any idea what sort of game he's playing.'

Peter gave me a long, thoughtful look and finally said, 'Mrs Martin, who are you? Or what are you?'

'That was the other thing I wanted to tell you. And the name is Dorothy, remember? But it's true I'm not exactly what I seem. Or I am, but . . . I'll start over. I'm a perfectly ordinary retired schoolteacher, originally from Indiana. But when I first moved to Sherebury, I became involved quite by accident in the investigation of a murder actually in the Cathedral. That was how I met Alan, who was still chief constable of Belleshire at the time. And then there was another murder, and . . . well, I discovered I was rather good at talking to people and putting two and two together. So I've become a sort of unofficial consultant to the community when something odd happens.'

'Sherlock Holmes.'

'Oh, no, not at all! He was brilliant, and besides, he was a professional.' I thought about mentioning some of the famous fictional amateur detectives and decided this child was far too young to have read Christie or Sayers or the rest of the splendid crew from the Golden Age of detective fiction. And it was time to change a subject which always embarrassed me. 'So what I'd like to do is sit down with you and make some lists about what's been happening. Things we know, questions we need to ask, that sort of thing.'

Peter didn't look impressed. 'I suppose we could, but why? I can't see that it will accomplish anything.'

'It will help to organize our thoughts, so when Alan comes we can present him with a clear picture of events. And I don't know about you, but I don't like muddles, in my house or in my mind. If you've finished that coffee, let's find a cab and pick up my car, and then you can drive me back to my hotel.'

NINE

'I can't do this legally, you know,' said Peter as he slid behind the wheel of my rental car. 'My name isn't listed as a driver. And I'm not brilliant at driving on the wrong side of the road. You'd be a safer bet.'

'But I'm not brilliant at driving in France. And it's been quite a while since I've driven on the right, myself. It's only a few miles. Just drive as if you had a fragile old lady in the car, which isn't far from the truth, and you'll be fine.'

'Fragile – hah!' But he started the car, backed it out of its space, and set off. His white knuckles and set face reminded me of myself, the first few times I'd tried to drive in England. I smiled and closed my eyes. If he thought I was relaxed about his driving, it might help.

Somewhat to my surprise, we got back to the village, or whatever it was called, where my hotel was, without incident. I hadn't thought to book a parking place in the hotel's small guests-only lot, but Peter stayed with the car while I went in and took care of that detail, and then we settled in the bar over glasses of mineral water. Neither of us was ready yet for anything stronger after that cider!

I took my small notebook out of my purse. 'Now. What was the first odd thing that happened?'

'Eve ate the apple,' he responded promptly.

I grinned. 'Yes, well, that was the beginning of it all, but I was thinking of more recent events. And more local.'

'For me, it was Laurence letting me down.'

'Laurence?'

'My archaeologist friend.'

'Oh, yes. When exactly did you find out he wasn't coming?'

'What does it matter? It nearly put paid to my whole project.'

'I'm trying to put things in chronological order. You were already here at the Mont, right?'

'Yes. That would have been at the very beginning of May. I expected him to join me shortly, but instead there was a note saying he'd be delayed. And then he sent me that email crying off. And then I tried to phone him, several times, but he never answers. Well, I told you.'

'Yes, you did, and I didn't think much of it at the time, but now . . . hmm. Peter, has he ever been hard to reach before?'

'No. That's why I'm so annoyed. It's a slap in the face, not answering when he knows it's me . . . oh.'

I watched as it sank in. 'Exactly. Not like him, is it? That note. Was it handwritten?'

'Typed. Looked like a print-out. I did wonder at the time, if he was going to go to the bother of writing something, why he didn't just email it to me. Mrs . . . Dorothy, you don't think something has happened to him?'

'I don't know, but I do know Alan will want his full name and address and phone number – all that.' I'd been busily writing down everything Peter had said, and now turned a page. 'All right, we'll come back to that. Now the next thing, I believe, is the lady who got caught in the quicksand. Have you heard anything about how she's doing, by the way?'

'No. Why are you including her on the list? She's nothing to do with Laurence, or me, or the chap from the tour. I think he should be next.'

'How do you know she has nothing to do with the rest? I don't know that, and it's another peculiar thing. No one seems to know why she was out there on the sands digging. They've said it was for mussels, which I think is nonsense. She's German. I refuse to believe that a foreigner came here with not only the desire, but the equipment, to dig for mussels that she probably had no place to cook, anyway.'

'Aha! Now who's jumping to conclusions? She could have been visiting friends or family in the area who told her about the famous Mont-Saint-Michel *moules*, and so she went out to dig some for them.'

'Aha yourself. In that case, why have your purported friends/ family not told the authorities that's what she was doing?'

'Maybe they have. Have you been watching the news, or reading the papers?'

'No, and it wouldn't have made me any wiser if I had. My French is virtually confined to please and thank you and where's the loo. We could ask the concierge, though. Well, *you* could ask the concierge. He speaks quite a lot of English, but I think you'd get more information.'

He got up and went to the desk, and came back shaking his head. 'The woman is making progress, medically, but she's still unconscious, and no one has come to identify her or even inquire about her. So you're probably right. Not here with someone she knows.'

He looked so disconsolate I hastened to cheer him up. 'Never mind. It was a good idea, and asking the question put us a little further forward. At least we know now what theory we can discard. And speaking of identifying her, surely the hotel or wherever she was staying has reported her missing, right?'

'So far, the police haven't been able to trace where she was staying, at least not that I've heard.'

'Then how do they even know she's German? No ID, no passport . . .'

'Actually, they don't, I suppose, but when she was screaming for help, it was in German, according to the bystanders.'

'Curiouser and curiouser. It's almost as if she was deliberately flying under the radar. So do we know anything more about this woman?'

'Can we posit an unfamiliarity with the sea and tides? She apparently didn't consult the tide tables.'

'Yes. Full points for that. Neither, apparently, did she read the warning signs. Or are they written only in French?'

'No, English and German as well, and something else –
maybe Italian or Spanish.'

'Then the woman is either stupid or arrogant. They often go
together. She thought she knew better than the authorities.'

'Or whatever she was hunting was so important to her that
she thought she could risk it,' said Peter soberly.

'Yes. What *was* she hunting?'

'Nobody knows.'

'But we can make some guesses. We've ruled out shellfish.
What else could one expect to find in quicksand?'

'It's said that the sands will sometimes thrust to the surface
things that have been buried for a long time.'

'I've heard that too,' I said, 'but never, come to think of it,
from a reliable source. Mostly in novels, come to think of
it. I have no idea whether it's true. If it is, whatever comes to
the surface would have to be pretty sturdy stuff. Sand and
saltwater would be pretty hard on most things.'

Peter was silent.

'What?' I said after a moment. 'You're thinking of
something.'

'No. It's too stupid.'

I waited.

He cleared his throat. 'It's only that I was thinking . . . um
. . . do you know anything about the history of Normandy?'

'Precious little. I know about William, of course, who
conquered England. Actually, I didn't know a whole lot even
about him until I saw the Bayeux Tapestry. Americans aren't
taught much European history, or at least they weren't when
I was a child.'

'You know about the Vikings?'

'Oh, please! I'm not *that* ignorant. Besides, I've spent a bit
of time in Scotland over the years, most recently in Orkney.
Reminders of the Vikings are all over the place there, from
runes carved in one of the tombs to the language, which still
has strong Norwegian roots. Norway is only a few miles . . .
oh. Wait. Norway. Norsemen. Norman. Good grief!' I smacked
my forehead. 'Talk about stupid! It never occurred to me.
You're telling me the Vikings came here, too, and that's how
the place got its name.'

'Roughly speaking, yes. It was a long time ago, of course, and I don't remember all the details, but what comes to mind when you think of Vikings?'

'Rape, loot, pillage. Those three words are always included in any Viking story.'

'Yes. Loot.'

'But what . . . oh, no. You're not suggesting that hoary old legend about Viking gold? C'mon. After . . . what? A thousand years of the fastest and highest tides in Europe? Even supposing there had once been Viking gold buried in these sands, which I for one don't believe for a moment, it couldn't possibly still be here.'

'I told you it was stupid.' He sounded sulky.

'So you did. And I insisted you tell me your idea, anyway. Sorry.' I sighed. 'We're not accomplishing much, are we? I think I need some coffee.'

So we had some strong coffee and a pastry or two, which I certainly didn't need, and went back rather half-heartedly to my list.

'So we have your colleague deserting you for unknown reasons and then a German woman digging on the sands for some unknown reason and nearly drowning. Then what?'

Peter gave me an odd look. 'You turn up.'

'Peter! There's nothing odd about that. I'm a tourist, remember? The Mont does attract a certain number of them.'

'You're also by way of being an investigator, and you ask a lot of questions.'

I sat silent for a moment. 'And you don't know a thing about me except what I've told you,' I said slowly. 'All right, that's fair enough, if you'll let me include you on my list of oddities. Your presence here is a lot more questionable than mine.'

'But I've told you—'

'You've told me a story. You seem like a pleasant young man, and I would be inclined to believe you, if it were not for the stolen manuscripts.'

'I– what do you mean, stolen manuscripts?'

'You either know perfectly well what I mean, or you're not such an expert in the field as you claim.'

'I never claimed to be an authority on manuscripts! My interest is in Abelard, and especially his music.'

'Which you could not reasonably have expected to find here.'

I let the comment lie there.

Peter moved his coffee cup around on the table. Tore the paper off a packet of sugar cubes.

'Oh, all right, so I didn't tell you everything.'

'You're not a student.'

'No.'

I waited.

He sighed. 'I *was* a student, but now I work for an art dealer in London, a small shop in Chelsea. He was brought one of the manuscript pages that you seem to know about. Their circulation isn't general knowledge.' He quirked an eyebrow.

'An artist friend told me. Go on.'

'My boss wasn't mad keen to buy it. The seller wasn't very prepossessing and the provenance looked iffy. William – the boss – knew about my interest in Abelard and the twelfth century in general. He thought I might be able to learn something about the business, and I've been wanting to come back to the Mont, so . . .' He spread his hands.

'Your friend who was going to come and help? Is he real, or just another fairy tale?'

'He's real, only he's a medievalist, not an archaeologist. And I am truly worried about him. Art thieves aren't any less prone to violence than any other criminals. I do wish he'd answer his phone calls.'

'Mmm. And now we have two more odd things, the man who was injured at the Abbey, and Mr Krider, who has told us a story with as many holes in it as a sieve.' I ran a hand through my hair. 'What *do* you suppose he's up to?'

'I don't know. I can't think anymore. I'm going to phone the Abbey and see if they're open tomorrow. The least I can do is work another day or two before I tell them I'm leaving. They really have been good to me, you know.'

'So why would you want to leave?'

'I'm not learning anything about the stolen manuscripts. Or forged, or whatever they are. I can't stay away from my job

forever when I'm not making any progress with what William
wanted me to do.'

'I hope you'll stick around for another few days. Alan's
coming, remember. Maybe he can help us make sense of all
this. But while you're on the phone to the Abbey – if you can
get through – why don't you ask them about the guy who got
hurt? They might give you details they wouldn't tell just
anybody.'

'I suppose.'

'And then we'll have a good meal, and talk about what's
been happening.'

Meanwhile I was going to call Alan and pick his brains. I
couldn't imagine what he might know about an American
named A.T. Krider, but he would have some ideas about ways
to find information. And all right, so I just wanted to hear his
voice. It had been a frustrating day.

It continued to be. Alan wasn't picking up. I tried both our
landline and his mobile. Voicemail on the landline, 'Not in
service' on the mobile.

Unlike me, Alan was very good about remembering to charge
his mobile, and he almost never turned it off.

I immediately went into panic mode. Something's happened
to him. He's fallen again and reinjured his ankle. He's had a
heart attack! He's in the hospital dying, and I'm not there!

'There's some news, but you may not– what's the matter?'
Peter had reappeared.

'I can't reach Alan! I can't think what's happened!'

Peter might be young, but he was observant. He went to
the bar and brought me back a glass with something amber
in it. 'Drink this.'

'What is it? I don't want—'

'Brandy. Drink it.'

I took a swig. It was raw stuff, not fine cognac, but it did
the trick. I shuddered and sat down. 'Thank you. I guess I
needed that. I just . . . it's foolish of me, I suppose, but Alan
is very good about staying in touch, so I worry when I can't
reach him.'

'He's a reliable sort?'

'Very.'

'Then he'd make sure someone let you know if something had happened to him.'

'Oh. You're probably right.'

'Of course I'm right. Now stop worrying, finish the rest of your medicine while I get myself a glass of wine, and let me tell you my news.'

I wasn't very interested in his news, and I couldn't stop worrying. But I settled back and made myself look like I was listening.

'I don't know for certain if it's good or bad news,' he began.

I tried to look interested.

'I phoned the Abbey, you know, and I got through to the volunteer coordinator, who was very pleasant. I said I might be leaving soon, and he pleaded with me not to go, so I said I'd think about it. And then I asked about the wounded tourist, how he'd happened to be in that part of the Abbey and so on. It is closed off to everyone, by the way, even the community, because it's unsafe.'

'Uh-huh.' I looked at my phone, willing it to ring.

'Dorothy, do listen to me,' he pleaded. 'This may be important.'

'Not as important as Alan. Not to me.'

'Yes, but you want to hear this. My friend at the Abbey said they had no idea how the chap got into the area, that they didn't know what had happened, only that someone in the Community heard a noise that sounded like something falling and went to investigate. Carefully, you understand, because the place is unstable. The monk was afraid something had subsided, or something else had happened that might threaten the Abbey. So when he went in with a torch, he found this chap lying on the ground with a whacking great dint in his head. They all rallied round, then got him up and out and into an ambulance.'

'So they took him to the hospital.' Where my husband might be at this very moment.

'Yes, and today one of the Community went to see how he was getting on. And – wait for it – he wasn't there.'

That jolted me out of my preoccupation. 'What do you mean, he wasn't there? Had he been moved to an intensive care facility or something?'

'The hospital staff know nothing. A nurse went in to give him some medication and he was gone, clothes and all. He's done a runner.'

'But – with a head injury – surely that's not a good idea! He could have concussion, bleeding in the brain—'

My mobile rang.

TEN

'Hello, love, sorry I couldn't give you advance notice, but I was able to get a plane at the last minute. I'm at the airport in Rennes, about to get a train to Pontorson. Can you meet me there in about an hour? I'll phone you when I'm almost there, shall I?'

I did manage not to burst into tears, but only just. 'I'll be there.' I clicked off the phone before my voice started to waver. 'Alan's on his way,' I said to Peter. 'He'll be at the station in Pontorson in an hour or so.' I looked at my watch. 'How long will it take us to get there?'

'Five minutes, if there's no delay getting out of the Mont traffic. Ten at the most.'

'Oh.' Now that he was so near, I was wild with impatience to see him.

'You aren't still worried about him, are you? I'm sure you've worked out that he didn't answer his mobile because he was on the plane.'

Oh. Well, no. I hadn't got beyond my enormous relief that he was all right, and near, and I was going to see him soon. 'Umm,' I said, and Peter grinned.

'You're going to have to drive, you know,' I said sternly. 'You insisted on giving me that brandy. I don't know the French laws about drinking and driving, but I'm not taking any chances.'

'Besides, I know the way to the station.'

'That, too.'

I would have liked something to eat, to soak up the brandy,

and to fill the time. But I wasn't in the mood for a snack, and a proper meal would have taken too long. An hour, less five or ten minutes, is too short a time to do much of anything, and far too long to do nothing. The only reading material at hand was in French, and I couldn't concentrate, anyway.

Time does pass, no matter how slowly. The earth does continue to turn on its axis at its accustomed pace. After I had picked up *Le Monde* for the twentieth time and put it down again, Peter took pity on me. 'I suppose we could go. It's early, but you're going to wear out that newspaper you can't read.'

'You're a gem, Peter. I'm sorry I'm being so silly. It's just that we've not been separated very often in our married life, and with all the peculiar things going on . . .'

'And you're in a strange place where you can't speak the language. I do understand. The keys, please?'

Alan called while we were on the way, and after all we weren't terribly early, and the train got in, and Alan stepped off, and I discovered that my titanium knees would actually let me run to his arms.

'Now there's a greeting for you! Not that I'm not pleased, love, but is something wrong?' He held me away from him and searched my face.

'Not now. I'm just really, really glad to see you.' I looked down at his feet. 'What's with the boot?'

'In place of a cast. It allows me to walk on the foot. More or less.' He was also carrying a cane, which he waved with a grimace.

'Oh, well, this, too, shall pass. Anyway, Alan, meet Peter Cummings, who's been my navigator. Peter, my husband, Alan Nesbitt.'

We straightened out the usual confusion about our different surnames, and then Alan said, 'I don't know about you two, but I'm famished. I've been travelling since early this morning, and my last meal is but a distant memory. Peter, you've been staying around here for a bit, I gather. What restaurant would you recommend?'

'Sorry, sir, but my budget runs to take-away sandwiches. I believe there's some fine food to be had in Pontorson, and of course in Avranches, but that's a bit further afield.'

'Dorothy, have you a choice, then?'

'The place where I ate the first night, here in Pontorson, was quite good. And it's nearby. And as it's early yet, we might be able to get in without a booking.'

'Lead me to it. Oh, thanks, Peter, but I can manage the bags.' He gave me a sideways grin, and I knew he was amused at being considered an old duffer incapable of carrying his own suitcase.

'Yes, sir, but with your cane and all, I thought I'd help.'

Alan shrugged. I made a face at him and handed him the car keys. He held the door open for me, and then the back door for Peter.

'Oh, no, sir, I can catch the bus here for the village. My bike's there; I'll get home easily.'

'Nonsense. You're having dinner with us. It's the least we can do, if you've been keeping my wife from getting lost. Now, love, where's this restaurant?'

I had walked there, of course, and I was no longer sure where it was, but Alan didn't mind driving in circles, and we found it eventually and had a wonderful meal. I don't know if it was really better than the first time I'd eaten there, or if it was just that my world was now complete again.

We talked of nothing in particular. The weather back home, the animals. 'They're all missing you, in their different ways. The cats follow me about and want a good deal of lap time. Watson won't let me out of his sight and keeps whining, poor chap. He can't understand why you've deserted him, and of course he doesn't know you're coming back.'

'Oh, dear. And now you've left, too. But Jane will spoil him rotten. Watson's our sort-of spaniel, Peter. A mutt, but a lovable mutt.'

Peter said all the right things, but I could see that he was getting edgy. He wanted to talk about our constellation of disturbing events, and this public place wasn't a good spot for that.

'Right, then,' said Alan, who reads people even better than I can. 'I gather there are a few things we need to discuss. Suppose we have our coffee back at our hotel – yes, and a sweet, my dear, if you can still find room for one – and we can talk. That suit you, Peter?'

'That, sir, is what I've been wanting to do ever since I met your wife – talk to you about what's been happening!'

'Then off we go. Would you like to drive, Peter, since you know where we're going?'

Alan waited until we had cups of strong espresso in front of us, along with something sinfully chocolate for me. The lounge at the hotel was busy and noisy enough that quiet conversation was reasonably private.

'Naow then,' said Alan in a pretty good Cockney accent, 'wot's all this?'

I'd heard him do that before, and only smiled, but Peter choked on his coffee. Clever Alan!

'Constable Plod, I presume?' said Peter when he had recovered.

'In person, sir. I understand you have a story to tell me.'

So we told him, both of us, interrupting each other, correcting each other. We tried to be thorough, so it took us through another round of coffee and then some cognac.

'So.' Alan tented his fingers, a gesture that always reminded me of the late, much lamented Alistair Cooke, whom Alan resembled in other ways as well: height, girth, all-around niceness. 'Let me see if I have this right. Item: you, Peter, have been delegated by an art dealer to look into some perhaps stolen, perhaps forged, medieval manuscripts, possibly of considerable value. In order to do this you came to Mont-Saint-Michel and spun a tale to the Community at the Abbey, and incidentally to my wife.'

Peter flushed. 'Well, sir—'

Alan held up a hand. 'My wife finds parts of your story somewhat puzzling, as do I, but as we know about the suspect manuscripts from another source, we'll let it go for now. Next item: a woman, presumably German, though there is no identification to determine her nationality, or anything else about her, goes out on the notoriously dangerous sands of the Mont and starts digging for something. We have no idea what. The tide comes in and she nearly drowns. She has not yet recovered sufficiently to be questioned.'

Here was Alan the chief constable with a vengeance. His

Constable Plod identity had been discarded. I thought momen-
tarily of reminding him about our Viking gold speculation,
and then thought better of it.

'Along the way your friend, Peter, be he archaeologist or
medievalist, fails to show up as promised. On the strength of
one typed note you accept the fact that his domestic problems
are keeping him away. You do try to phone him, but with no
luck.

'Then, my dear, you appear on the scene, and with your
usual good fortune find yourself embroiled in a puzzle. How
did you manage it this time?'

I had deliberately not told him how I'd met Peter. Now I
had to confess. 'I fell at the Abbey and scraped my knee.
Peter, who was guiding the party I'd joined, patched me up,
and we got to talking, and . . .' I spread my hands. Alan gave
me the kind of look that told me he'd press for details later.
Well, when we undressed for bed, he'd see the bruises and
guess most of it. For now I gave him my most innocent smile,
which deceived him for not a moment.

'Finally, an American man just happens to be around the
hotel when my wife needs a lift to Avranches, just happens
to offer to take her and her new friend, just happens to decide
to accompany them to the museum housing the Mont-Saint-
Michel manuscripts. He tells them a story that is peculiar, to
put the best possible face on it, lies about his knowledge of
French, and becomes, at lunchtime, incapably drunk on
Normandy's famous cider. That last, I may add, is perhaps the
most believable part of this entire saga. I've tasted the stuff
myself, and I'm reasonably sure it could fuel a jet, if not a
moon rocket.

'Now, is that a fair summation of the story thus far?'

Hmm. It hit all the high points, but I thought he'd been a
bit hard on Peter. He, however, seemed only somewhat embarrassed, rather than offended. He put down the glass he'd been
nursing, which was still half full. 'I'm not much cop as an
investigator, am I, sir? I did tell the truth about the gallery I
work for, but they didn't exactly send me here to look into
the manuscript problem. I was due for a bit of a holiday, and
I love this part of the world, so I said I'd come here, talk to

the people at the Scriptorial, ask a few discreet questions, and see what I could find out. They agreed to help with my expenses. I *was* a student at Exeter, Dorothy, but since I took my degree I've been working at this and that, hoping to find a real job in my field.'

'Music and theology,' I said with, I hoped, no inflection whatever.

'And medieval studies. I left that out of what I told you, but the rest is true.'

'Small wonder you haven't been able to find a proper job,' said Alan. 'Even taken together, those fields are hardly burgeoning with openings, I shouldn't think.'

'No. I was not very practical, I'm afraid. My father tried to persuade me into a course of study that would lead to a lucrative position, but I've never taken a whole lot of interest in money.'

'Which means you've always had enough.' Again, I thought my tone was neutral.

'Yes, I'm a spoilt brat. I admit it. Until the past year or so, I'd never even thought about where my food or clothing or shelter was coming from. I'm from the West Country, a village near Dartmoor. That's why I chose Exeter. My father isn't wealthy, not the landed gentry or anything like that, but he does quite well in business, and he's always been generous with me.'

'Too generous, perhaps?' Alan's tone was carefully neutral.

Peter considered that. 'Not foolishly, I don't think. When I was at university, he made sure I had the necessities, because he wanted me to concentrate on my studies. He's like that. He didn't approve of what I was studying, but he made sure I was able to do it without distractions over paying my rent or that sort of thing.'

'But once you had graduated – sorry, had taken your degree – then you were on your own, right?'

'I wanted it that way,' Peter assured me. 'I thought it was high time I stood on my own feet. I hadn't quite understood how much everything costs in London. I share a grotty bedsitter with two other chaps, and it's as much as I can do to meet the rent every month.'

'So you need money,' said Alan, conversationally.

'I do. But not enough to steal manuscripts, nor yet to forge them. Not that I could do that, anyway. I'm a good musician, but hopeless at visual art. I had honestly hoped to find some of Abelard's music in these parts, because finding such a treasure would get me a post at almost any museum or university.'

'And you would not, of course, be tempted to sell it to the highest bidder.' Alan again.

'Tempted? You can bet I'd be tempted! But I wouldn't do it. You forget, one of my areas of study was theology.'

'That,' said Alan drily, 'probably means you know the difference between right and wrong. It does not necessarily mean that you put those theories into practice.'

Peter raised his hands, helplessly, and I decided it was time to intervene. 'Look, I think we're all tired. Suppose we call it a day and reconvene tomorrow. Peter, will you be all right cycling home in the dark?'

'Yeah, sure, but I don't know about coming back tomorrow. I told you they want me back at the Abbey, and I think I owe them that. Goodnight, Dorothy. Goodnight, sir. Thank you for the meal.'

I shook my head at Alan and followed Peter out of the lobby. 'Peter, you mustn't mind Alan. He's thinking like a policeman. Which, after all, was why you wanted him here.'

'He doesn't believe a word I say.'

'That isn't true. He's reserving judgment, and I must say, in view of the number of lies you've told, he's justified. And if you'll take my advice, you'll come back tomorrow and tell him nothing but the strict truth from now on. He's very good at detecting lies. And incidentally, after more than forty years as a schoolteacher, so am I. Good night.'

ELEVEN

Several interesting things happened the next day. I was feeling so bouncy and refreshed in the morning, after a very satisfactory night spent with my long-lost husband, that I actually got up early and went for a little walk before breakfast. I didn't walk far, but it doesn't take long to get into real country from the 'village' that acts as the service area for Mont-Saint-Michel's tourists. I was enchanted to see a flock of sheep being driven to pasture by a man in a truck and two energetic and self-important dogs. Okay, the truck was twenty-first century, but the rest of the scene had probably been happening for the past two or three hundred years, at least. I assumed these were destined to be the famous Normandy 'pré-salé' lamb, seasoned on the hoof by grazing on the salt meadows washed at high tide by the sea.

The sheep were charmingly silly, and I rather hoped they were all too old to be slaughtered for the dinner table. Of course that meant their babies . . .

I decided, like Scarlett, to think about that tomorrow, and turned back toward the hotel.

I found Alan and Peter sitting in the lounge over coffee and pastries, chatting amicably.

'Join us, my dear. I've just ordered extra coffee and croissants; I was sure you'd be back soon. Did you enjoy your walk?'

I told them about the sheep, in between bites of exquisite pastry and sips of incomparable coffee. Croissants have become a staple all over the Western world, and for all I know the Eastern world too, but the French are still better at them than anyone else.

Had I cavilled yesterday at the lack of an English breakfast? Well, I wasn't myself yesterday. Now Alan was here.

I smiled at him and Peter and said, 'You two seem to be getting along fine this morning.'

Alan grinned. 'You didn't say anything last night, but I know you thought I was a bit hard on him. No ill feelings, eh, old chap?'

'I deserved it,' said Peter, also grinning. 'I should have known better than to try to pull any wool over your eyes – or Dorothy's. She's as good at spotting flim-flam as you are, sir.'

'You're not a terribly good liar, you know,' I said, holding out my cup for more coffee. 'But why did you bother to lie to me? You didn't know me from Adam, and I surely don't look like a threat to anyone.' I smoothed down my short grey hair, tossed into disorder by the morning breeze. 'I'm the sort authorities automatically dismiss as harmless, and most people simply don't notice. Women of a certain age are invisible.'

'Anyone who dismisses you, my love, is making a huge mistake. I only regret that I met you too late to draft you into the constabulary. However, we've only delayed the news long enough for you to get some caffeine and calories into your system.'

'What news? What's happened?'

'Our friend Mr Krider has returned, singing an entirely different tune this time!'

'No! Tell!'

Alan poured me more coffee, offered milk and sugar with careful deliberation, held out the plate of brioches, shoved the little basket of assorted jams my way. I cracked, as he knew I would. 'Alan Nesbitt, I swear if you don't tell me this minute I'm going to pour this over your head!'

He grinned. 'I wondered how long you'd hold out. Peter, you begin.'

Peter was grinning, too. 'I spotted him when he walked into the lobby about an hour ago. I cycled over early, because I didn't know when you'd be up and about, and I wanted to apologize. I'd thought about our conversation last night, and I was kicking myself for acting like a lout. I saw you out walking, Dorothy, but you were too far away to hear me shout, and you looked like you were having a good time, so I went on.'

I held up the cafetière in threatening fashion.

'Yes, right, to the point. So I walked in the lobby, and there was Krider, just getting up from his *petit déjeuner*, cup and saucer and crumby plate left behind. Well, I may not be the world's most observant soul, but I know this hotel serves breakfast only to residents – well, and their guests. So it looked very much as though Krider had spent the night here.

'So I simply walked up to him and asked him if he'd missed his train yesterday.'

'Ooh! And what did he say?'

'Well, he had the grace to look embarrassed, and then he said—'

'I said I'd been spinning you a yarn.' Krider walked up to the table. 'If I may, I'd like to tell you all about it.'

'Mr Cummings has told me a bit,' said Alan, 'but we've not had a chance to tell Dorothy the story.'

'And it would be refreshing to hear a true one,' I said tartly. 'I've been hearing far too much fiction of late.'

Krider bowed his head. 'Yes, I deserve that, and I'm sorry. When you've heard my explanation, I hope you'll forgive me.

'I really do have a wife and family back home, Mrs Martin.' His accent had become much less Midwestern, I noticed, and his manner more cosmopolitan. 'Both my children are daughters, however, and both are married with children. And my trip here has nothing to do with either of them. Nor am I a research worker.'

'I did manage to figure that out,' I said. 'Really, Mr Krider, I'll give you points for thinking on your feet and making up a glib story as you go along, but essentially you're almost as bad a liar as Peter.'

'And that makes my real reason for being here all the more embarrassing. Someone once wrote a book called *Telling Lies for Fun and Profit*, about writing fiction.'

'Lawrence Block,' I murmured. 'Great book.'

'And you see, I'm here because – well, to tell the truth, I'm trying to write a novel. Set at Mont-Saint-Michel.'

It was a good thing I'd swallowed my last sip of coffee. 'So you came here to gather material. That makes you a researcher, after all.'

'Oh! I suppose it does.'

'One thing you didn't tell me, sir,' said Peter, polite but still dubious about trusting this man, 'is why you felt you had to lie to us about knowing French.'

'Sheer stupidity! I thought if I claimed not to know much of the language, no one could possibly suspect me of . . . er . . . casing the joint, so to speak. And I didn't want anyone to know what I was doing, in case I write a terrible book and make a damned fool of myself.'

'And why choose Mont-Saint-Michel, of all places?' I wasn't going to let him off easy. I don't like being lied to. 'Do you know the place well?' Perhaps he'd lied about that, too, at least by implication.

'Never been here before in my life. But I read a book, oh, years ago, when I was in school, called *Mont-Saint-Michel and Chartres*. Written by a guy named Henry Adams. You probably never heard of it—'

'I read it, too. Years ago, as you say. A remarkable book.' Alan cleared his throat. 'Regarded as a classic, Mr Krider. I take it you enjoyed it?'

'I fell in love,' the man said simply. 'I had to come and see for myself, but things kept happening to keep me away. Then last winter I had a heart attack. A mild one, and my own fault; my wife told me the snow was too deep and heavy to shovel, but I had to prove I could do it. Well, I couldn't, and it was a wake-up call for me. I decided if I was ever going to see those two places with my own eyes, I'd better do it quick.'

'Your wife didn't mind?' I had another of those stabs of memory, Frank in the ambulance, lights flashing, siren wailing . . .

'She wanted to come with me, to make sure I didn't go and do something stupid, but Amy, our youngest, is expecting twins in a couple of weeks, and Madge just didn't think she could leave her. So I came, and the first thing they do is close the place!'

I was beginning to believe him. That last bit of frustration sounded genuine. 'I believe they're re-opening the Abbey today, isn't that right, Peter?'

'Yes, and I'd better get over there, if you'll all excuse me. You could come with me, sir, if you like. I can leave my bike here and take the shuttle. I'm a guide, and I could slip you into a group to make sure you see everything.'

'That would be very kind, young man. Thank you for your generosity, and again, I apologize for my stupid charade yesterday.'

'Well!' I said when we had watched them out the door. 'What did you think of that?'

'I think,' said Alan with a grimace, 'that it will be a dreadful book, if it ever gets written. I also think I need a little exercise. I've been sitting far too much these past couple of days, but I still can't walk very far. Would there by chance be a swimming pool in the vicinity? And no, I don't propose to swim in the bay.'

'I'm certainly glad to hear it. And I agree with your prediction about Krider's book. If the man can't even tell a convincing lie, how on earth can he string together enough to make a novel? Maybe it'll be one of those stream-of-consciousness things.'

'Those went out of fashion decades ago, surely. It's certain to be autobiographical. All first novels are. But you're ignoring my plea for a swimming pool.'

'You were the one who booked this hotel, and I'm sure you looked up every single one in the area. But I very much doubt there's a public pool closer than Avranches, if there. If we go to the Mont, you'll get all the exercise you could possibly want, and more.'

'Ah, well. I'll go back to the room and do the sitting calisthenics the physio taught me. Boring, but they get things moving. And after that . . . my love, I think you've been fretting about all this too long. This was to be a holiday, after all. Now that we have a car, why don't we do a bit of exploring? You've seen only Bayeux and the Mont, and there's a great deal more to Basse-Normandie.'

'Hmm. I admit I've wanted to see some of the D-Day landing beaches. Are they nearby?'

'Not far. I'm guessing you want to see Omaha Beach, since it was the one where Americans were most involved.'

I shuddered. 'No. I've read too much about that bloodbath. I don't want to see the place where so many young Americans died. Maybe I don't want to see the beaches at all, come to think of it. It was a horrible war.'

'Think of it this way, love.' He took my hand. 'All war is horrible, but in that one we were fighting a madman. Hitler had to be stopped, and it was the courage and sacrifice of your young men, and ours, and the Canadians and the Australians and the Poles and all the rest, who stopped him. We owe them all an unpayable debt, but we can keep their memory alive.'

'And burying my head in the sand isn't the way to do that, is it? All right, then. But not Omaha Beach.'

'What I had in mind was Gold Beach. That's at Arromanches, which is just outside Bayeux. I understand they have a fine museum about the landings. I thought we could take that in, then have ourselves some lunch, and perhaps visit Gilly's exhibit, if it wouldn't bore you to tears.'

'Idiot! You know I can look at her work forever. All right, then, it's a plan. As soon as you've finished tying yourself into knots.'

TWELVE

The sun was shining. The air was fresh, with a gentle breeze that brought with it scents of the sea. I was with my beloved husband again, and he was coping quite well with driving, since his left foot wasn't involved. I resolved firmly to forget all about medieval monasteries and missing manuscripts and enjoy myself.

Somewhat to my surprise, I succeeded. The little town of Arromanches was charming, although very touristy, as one might expect. The Landing Museum (*Musée du Débarquement*, French even I could decipher) was unexpectedly fascinating. There was a short movie about the landing, screened at intervals with the soundtrack in various languages so I didn't have to struggle with French, and I learned a lot. I had read at some point about the artificial harbours constructed for the war effort, but I remembered few details. They were Churchill's idea, I learned, the solution to a basic problem involved in a military operation.

The thing was, the big equipment needed by the Allies – trucks, tanks, big guns, tons of supplies – required big ships, and they in turn required deep harbours. The only ports with such facilities were, as one might expect, heavily defended by the Germans. The problem was that the only way to capture these ports was with the equipment that couldn't be landed until the German defences were disabled.

So they built artificial harbours – called, for some reason, Mulberries – at the landing beaches. First, old ships were sunk to create breakwaters and enclose the harbours. Then sections of pier were shipped across the Channel and assembled on the spot, stretching far out into the Channel to deep water. Of course it was more complicated than that, but that was the gist of it. There were to be two, one at Omaha Beach and one at Gold Beach. They were both almost finished when a terrible storm struck Normandy, the worst in over forty years. The gale-force winds and high seas destroyed the Mulberry at Omaha Beach, but the one at Gold Beach, though damaged, was repaired and used for the next ten months, and greatly aided the liberation of Normandy.

Alan and I went back into the sunshine, blinking, and walked (slowly, because of his ankle) to a vantage point where we could see out into the peaceful Channel. After more than seventy years, bits of the Mulberry were still visible. Several of the caissons that had supported the pier were there, and far out, nearly on the horizon, I imagined I could see part of one of the scuttled ships.

And down below us on the sandy beach, children played, running and shouting, oblivious to the reminders of war, fear and death and destruction.

'That's the way it should be, isn't it, Alan? They're – what – four or five generations removed from the war?'

'About that. I was only a few weeks' old on D-Day.'

'And I wasn't born yet. Your parents – was your father in the war?'

'Not in this stage of it. He was injured in the evacuation from Dunkirk in 1940.' Alan settled himself on a bench to rest his ankle in its awkward boot, and felt for the pipe his doctor had forbidden some years before. 'Drat. I keep forgetting. One needs a pipe to tell a story.'

'Yes, but go on without it. Your father was in the Navy?'

'No. He planned to enlist, but my brother was a tiny baby and he wanted to give my mother a little time to recover from the birth before he signed up. He was a fisherman, you remember.'

'Yes, out of Newlyn.'

'Yes. How much do you know about the Dunkirk operation?'

'Not much, except that thousands of British troops had to turn tail and run back to England when the Germans got too close.'

'Actually, it wasn't quite like that. The evacuation had been planned for some time, when it became evident that Hitler was going to take the Low Countries and France. We hadn't the military strength to prevent that, so we had begun to gather ships and boats to take our men back to England.'

'"He who fights and runs away may live to fight another day",' I quoted flippantly.

'Exactly. It's often said sneeringly, and fighting against overwhelming odds seems heroic, but in this case the decision was the right one. Germany had been building up its military strength for years; we had not, and we were ill-prepared to defend our interests. Our forces would have been slaughtered had we not evacuated, and Germany might well have won the war!'

Alan is rarely combative, but his voice had risen and his 'Chief Constable' manner was in evidence. I put my hand on his. 'You're preaching to the choir, my dear. You don't have to convince me; I agree.'

'Yes. Well.' He cleared his throat. 'In the event, Hitler moved faster than we anticipated, and we were nearly cut off. The powers asked every craft that could carry even a few men to come to Dunkirk, and my father took his fishing boat.

'It was an amazing sight, he used to tell me. Thousands of "Little Ships", as they came to be called, converged on the beaches of France. Literally on the beaches; in most cases there were no landing facilities at all. The RAF provided air cover, and though there was still great danger, it worked out remarkably well. In the end over 330,000 troops were saved, not only British, but French and Belgian as well.

'But in the mass confusion, accidents were bound to happen. In the pitch dark, my father caught his foot in a coiled hawser and went sprawling. He didn't notice the pain, he said, until they were about halfway home. Then it began to be so bad he could hardly steer the boat. He had a boatload of foot-soldiers, no sailors, but one chap knew his way around a boat, so he took over, and another bloke gave Dad a flask of whisky for the pain. He said he didn't know another thing until he woke up in hospital with a raging headache and a cast on his leg. He'd broken most of the bones in his right foot, and they told him they could patch him up, after a fashion, but he'd never be fit for active duty.'

'And he was a fisherman. Not exactly a sedentary occupation.'

'He managed. Managed very well, in fact. We weren't rich, but we never went hungry. My brother helped him as soon as he was old enough, and they wanted me to work with them, but my heart was set on a police career. I've felt a bit guilty about that from time to time.'

I squeezed his hand, and we sat in silence, watching the waves come in, listening to the cries of the children and the gulls, sounding much the same.

'Your father would have loved this, Alan. This is what everyone fought for. Peace, in the real meaning of the word. Sunshine and families picnicking on a beach. We're so lucky, all of us, to have had those brave men – yes, including your father – who made it possible.'

I don't know how long we would have sat there, wrapped in peace and memories, if my insides had not rumbled irritably. 'Alan, I'm hungry. I didn't know it until this minute. And this bench is getting awfully hard.'

'And I'm getting stiff. I was back in the past, and forgot how old and creaky I am. Did I lose my cane somewhere?'

'No, here it is. Where shall we go for lunch?'

'Bayeux, I think. It's quite near, and I suspect the food here would be somewhat overpriced.'

I looked at the tour buses lined up along the street and agreed.

We were lucky enough to find a pleasant-looking restaurant in Bayeux, with parking almost in front of it, and ordered a substantial meal. While I was digging into a wonderful plate of *foie gras*, my unruly thoughts returned to my nagging questions about all the peculiar things that had been happening, and even came up with a new one.

'Alan, it just occurred to me. Was Mont-Saint-Michel involved in the war at all? Maybe part of the "Atlantic Wall"?'

'I confess I don't know, specifically. I would assume that it was occupied by the Germans. All of France was occupied territory, and Mont-Saint-Michel, as a fortified island, might have seemed especially attractive to the Germans. Why?'

'That German woman. Assuming she is German, which I guess we still don't know for sure. Suppose she was out there digging on the sands for something lost during the war, or buried, or . . .' I ran down at the sight of Alan's face. He was trying not to laugh at me

'My dearest love, you told me about Peter's Viking gold speculation, and your response. The same objection about the tides applies.'

'Well, but it's only been seventy-some years since the Germans left, if you're right and they were there at all. It's not quite the same as a thousand or so.'

'Two high tides, two low tides every day for seventy years. You do the math.'

'Yes, but consider.' I wasn't going to give up my idea without a fight. 'It's a well-known fact that the Nazis looted art treasures all over Europe, and nobody knows for sure where a lot of it went. Now just suppose for a moment that some of it was hidden in the catacombs, or whatever you want to call them – the nether regions of the Abbey.'

'Not impossible,' said Alan, who likes to indulge me when he can.

'And suppose further that some of those ancient storerooms collapsed over the years. In fact, parts of the Abbey have done just that from time to time.'

'Go ahead.' This time his doubt was clearly evident.

'All right, but just listen before you decide I've lost my marbles. The point is, I don't know how far down the earliest bits of the Abbey go, nor how high the water table is. It seems to me just within the bounds of possibility that the sea could occasionally, over the years, have made its way into the lowest cellars, or catacombs, or whatever they are. And if it did, it could have carried off who knows what when it receded. Wait!' His expression was growing more and more doubtful. 'I'm not asking you to accept that such a thing ever happened. Nor am I saying that I think it's true. But a person from outside the area, a person with a compelling reason to recover something she believed had been in the Abbey, might well have accepted a story like that. It's amazing what you can believe if you want to. Don't you think?'

The waitress came just then to whisk away my empty plate – I'd eaten a huge serving of pâté without even noticing, which was a crime against the palate – and substitute a *galette* that looked and smelled heavenly. Alan waited until she had gone and then said, 'You know, you might just have something there.'

My mouth was full, but I raised my glass in silent salute.

'However.'

I swallowed. 'I knew there had to be a catch. Heaven forfend my theory would meet with unqualified approval.'

'Don't be sarcastic; it doesn't suit you. There's nothing wrong with your theory, per se. It's so far-fetched as to be absurd, but as you say, someone in the grip of a monomania might think it made perfect sense. No, the trouble is that it doesn't fit in anywhere with all the other incidents. Peter and the manuscripts. The disappearance of his friend. The chap in the undercroft. Krider and his proposed novel.'

I took another bite; the food was too good to let it sit getting cold. 'All right. I accept that. There's no neat pattern. But is there a reason why there has to be?'

I knew what he was going to say before he said it. 'You know my methods, Watson. Goldstein's Theorem of Interconnected Monkey Business.'

Abe Goldstein, the lovable old professor friend of Gideon Oliver in Aaron Elkins' marvellous mystery series, had become a favourite character of Alan's, as he had long been of mine. One of Abe's frequent sayings was that when a lot of funny things were happening together, they had a way of being related. 'Hey, I taught you that law,' I said. 'Not fair to invoke it against me. But you're right. Two strange things happening in the same place at more or less the same time could be coincidence. Five or six, no. There has to be a pattern. But I'll be switched if I can figure it out.'

'Finish your lunch, and we're going to have an apple tart to follow. Here in the land of Calvados, one must pay tribute to apples. Then – I'm sorry, but I don't think I have the stamina for Gilly's exhibit. Perhaps we could go sit in a quiet park somewhere and think it out.'

I actually wanted to do some more exploring in Bayeux. The taste I'd had with Gilly had whetted my appetite for more of the delightful little city. But I knew Alan couldn't walk very far, so I agreed that a park bench sounded delightful. He consulted the waitress in French I couldn't follow at all and got directions, and when we got to the car, he suggested that I drive. 'I can navigate, darling, so you won't have to read a single sign, and as you'll be driving on the right . . . what do you think?'

What I thought was that I'd be terrified. I'd lived in England long enough to become accustomed to driving on the left, and I was afraid I'd make some awful mistake. However, if Alan thought I could do it, I'd have to give it a try or ever afterward count myself a coward.

'Sure,' I said in what I hoped was a nonchalant tone, and climbed into the driver's seat. From the look of his grin, I don't think I fooled him for a moment.

The whole thing turned out to be so easy I was ashamed of my fears. Traffic wasn't too bad in the town. That is, it was no worse than in any medieval city built for foot- and horse-travel, and I'd become used to narrow streets and awkward corners in Sherebury. The park was actually out on the edge of town, and was pleasantly cool and green. The school term hadn't ended yet, so the only children in evidence were preschoolers – shrill and energetic, but closely watched by their mothers.

One little boy – I think (it's hard to tell when everybody wears shorts and shirts) – threw a ball with wildly erratic aim, and it hit my foot. He came running up to get it and, prompted by his mother, said '*Pardon, madame*' in a sweet, shy voice.

'*Ce n'est rien, mon petit*,' I said, a long-forgotten phrase swimming up from my memory when it was needed. The child giggled, either at my accent or my misuse of his language, and ran away with the ball.

His mother recognized me for an Anglophone, and apologized in English.

'Not at all. No harm done. He's a sweet little boy, and his manners are charming.'

'Thank you, *madame*. But he is a little girl!'

'Oh, dear! That's why he – she – laughed. Not "*mon petit*" at all, but "*ma petite*". It is I who should apologize, for being so unobservant.'

'She acts more like a boy. It is all right.'

She went back to her child, and Alan and I sat down on the nearest bench. 'What an adorable child,' I said. 'I always turn to jelly when a baby like that speaks perfect French. It sounds so precocious. And then his mother – her mother – has perfect English. I feel distinctly inadequate.'

'You did just fine, love. Your accent isn't bad, and you weren't to know the child was a girl. I couldn't tell, myself.'

'Quite a contrast to those brats on the Mont. Oh, I didn't tell you about them, did I? An American family with perfectly awful kids.' I related the incident. 'It's really why I went on up to the Abbey that day. I'd planned to wait till you got here, but I wanted some peace.'

'And then you met Peter, and your peace was shattered. Dorothy, do you have your notebook with you?'

'Do I ever go anywhere without it?' I pulled it out of my purse.

'What have you noted so far about our little problem?'

'Well, Peter and I made a list of sorts.' I turned to it. 'I don't know that we accomplished much. Certainly we didn't come to any startling conclusions.'

'Let me see, if you will.' He looked it over and then

handed it back. 'Hmm. Summary of events, a few stories with enough holes in them to make lace. Not a lot of detail, is there?'

'Almost none. I guess it was a pretty silly exercise.'

'It's a start.' He sat in thought for a moment. 'What we need, my love, is a great deal more information about these people. If this were a police case, I'd have a staff looking into their backgrounds.'

'But it isn't a police case. No crime has been committed.'

'You're forgetting probable art theft. And we don't yet know what's happened to Peter's friend Laurence, nor to the man injured at the Abbey.'

'Still, the French police have apparently not been called in. And anyway, we don't have a staff to do research on these people.'

'No. But we have Peter, and ourselves, and the Internet. And I still have friends back in the Sherebury constabulary who'd be willing to do a spot of checking for me. My dear, if we're barking up the right tree and there's some thread that ties all these incidents together, it will be found somewhere in everyone's past.'

'Do you have your laptop at the hotel?'

'Do I ever go anywhere without it? Now, why don't you make another list, just names this time, and we'll get to work when we get back to the hotel.'

On our vacation, I thought, but didn't say.

THIRTEEN

The trouble was, I didn't even know most of the names. Peter Cummings, A.T. Krider. I had no idea what the initials stood for. Peter's friend Laurence – no surname. The German woman and the man injured at the Abbey were nameless, as far as I was concerned.

Alan wasn't worried about little details like that. 'Phone Peter. He'll have the details for his friend, and can get a name and so on for the man in the cellar. Krider's here in the hotel; he won't be a problem. As for the woman, if she's still unconscious and they've not yet found her identification, I'll have to use a bit of persuasion on the local authorities, see if they've learned anything at all about her.'

'Will they cooperate?'

'If I put it to them the right way. You mustn't forget that Mont-Saint-Michel tourism is the major prop of the local economy, and a tourist nearly drowning on the sands is terrible publicity.'

'And your French is good enough that they'll listen to you.'

'Not up to Peter Wimsey's standard, but not all that bad. All right now, woman. You're officially deputized. Phone Peter and invite him over here for a grilled meal.'

'The grillee being Peter.'

'Right.'

'And I'll go down and ask the hotel staff where to find the nearest reasonably efficient police facility.'

Peter told me he couldn't get away until the Abbey closed for the day at seven, and it was now only mid-afternoon. I considered a nap, my usual afternoon preference. I was, after all, on vacation. But Alan came up to the room just as I was taking off my shoes. 'I'm off to Avranches, love. That seems to be where local incidents are investigated, at least in the early stages. I was going to invite you along, but Krider just walked into the bar. He seems settled there for a bit, and I thought you might be able to engage him in some useful conversation. One American to another sort of thing.' He looked at the shoe I had just removed. 'Unless of course you'd rather relax for a bit.'

I picked up the shoe and put it back on. 'I'd much rather nap, thank you very much. But since I'm the one who's been insisting we had to find out what's happening, I don't have much of an excuse for wimping out, do I? You're not going to have to walk much when you get there, are you?'

'I phoned. There's a car park close to the building. I'm doing very well, love. Don't fuss.'

'You know how talented I am at fretting. Go talk to the nice *gendarmes*, dear, and I'll tackle Mr Krider. Oh, and we're expecting Peter for dinner. He'll meet us here and then we can decide where to eat.'

'*Agents de police*, darling. At least I think so. The police system in France is rather convoluted, and has changed a bit since I was well-acquainted with it. A *gendarme* is more like a soldier. Armed and all. Or, come to think of it, like a Chicago policeman.' Alan gave me rather an offhand kiss and hurried away, while I decided how on earth I was to ask a man I barely knew to tell me his life story.

By the time I got to the lobby, though, I thought I had a plan. The first part was a little tricky; I wasn't sure I wanted to cosy up to a man at a bar like some lady of dubious reputation. Fortunately, he saw me and waved, which gave me my excuse. I walked over to him.

'And how was your day at the Mont?' I asked.

'Fine, fine! Can I buy you a drink? Or is your husband about to join you?'

'No, Alan's gone off to Avranches. He's trying to find a swimming pool.' Which was true, if misleading. 'And I'd love a drink. Plain tonic, please.'

The barman, with his array of fine wines and ciders, was disappointed at my request, but filled it graciously, with more ice than they'd have given me in England, and a nice slice of lime.

'So why a swimming pool? Is he some kind of fitness freak or something? Not,' Krider added quickly, 'that it's any of my business.'

'He does like to keep fit, but that's not what this is about. He broke an ankle rather badly a while ago, so his favourite exercise, walking, is out of the picture until the bone has healed a little better. Swimming, on the other hand . . .'

'Got it. And swimming in the bay is definitely not recommended. Well, here's to his full recovery. He's going to have a hard time seeing the Mont if he's a little rocky on his pins, though. Definitely not handicapped-accessible.'

'True, but he's been here before, so it isn't a great tragedy. We'll see what we can without causing him trouble, and I've already explored a little before he got here. But you never answered my question, really. Was your visit today successful?'

He looked moodily into his wine. 'Yes and no. I learned a lot more about the place. It's got a fascinating history, you know? Going way back before the Abbey was begun.'

I just nodded. I really didn't want him getting into fifteen hundred or so years of history of the island and the Abbey. Luckily he didn't seem disposed to lecture.

'The thing is, it's all neat and interesting and all that, but it sure didn't give me any ideas for my book.'

Aha! 'You know, I've been thinking about that. I read a lot, especially mysteries, and I've even read some books about writing. Not that I want to write, you understand, I'm just interested in the process. And a lot of really good writers say they begin by writing biographies of their characters.'

He frowned. 'How can you write a bio of somebody who doesn't exist?'

'Well, but that's the point. You, the author, have to make them exist, make them live, make them real. You can only do that if you know them really well, as well as you know your best friends, or even better.'

'You mean, I have to make up every detail of their life? But that would make the book way too long, thousands of pages. Bo-ring!'

'No, the details don't go in the book, these writers say. But knowing them, knowing what makes your characters tick, lets you know how they're going to talk and move and act, so you can make them come alive for the reader.'

'Yeah, I get it. I guess. But I wouldn't have the first idea how to go about doing that.'

'That's what I was thinking about. Suppose you were to start with yourself. Someone like you is probably going to be a character in the book, right?'

'Well, yeah, I guess. I mean, he's kinda different, but – yeah, I guess he's pretty much me.'

'Okay, so what do you know about him? Start when he's really young. No, I know what you're going to say, but the way a child lives has a lot to do with how the adult is going to turn out. "The child is father to the man," you know. So: childhood.'

It took forever. Mr A.T. Krider (he wouldn't tell me what

the initials stood for) was perhaps the least imaginative person I've ever met. My betting was that he couldn't write a novel to save his life, but after a long afternoon of extracting information bit by painful bit, I had the following:

He'd lived all his life in and around Cleveland, except for four years at Ohio State getting a degree in accounting (with, rather surprisingly, a minor in history). He'd never participated in college sports, having broken a good many bones in various childhood accidents. ('Clumsy was my middle name.') He'd thought about a fraternity, but never pledged, saying he thought all that partying and drinking was a waste of time. He'd met his wife at college, but hadn't seriously considered marriage until he'd begun graduate school. He'd been loath to marry in case he was drafted, but the draft ended, and he decided to marry his sweetheart. They waited till he'd finished his MBA and landed a good job before starting a family. Two daughters, four grandchildren and two more boys expected any minute.

He'd spread his hands when he got that far. 'That's it. Not terribly interesting, right?'

'No. Because you left out the interesting parts. What would you spend all your time doing if you could? What kind of music do you like, what kind of books? Did you like your job, or hate it? What were your parents like, and what did your father do for a living? Where do you fit on the wealth scale, from barely making ends meet to rolling in it? What are your views on politics and religion? What do you absolutely loathe? What scares you, or makes you laugh? Those are the things that make a person who he is. You've given me a cardboard cut-out.'

So we'd started over, and I'd finally wrung a few interesting details out of him. I related them to Alan when he came back from Avranches. 'The man is just about as vanilla as they come,' I said, holding out a glass. 'I'll have a nice little tot, thank you. Mining information is hard work. And where did you manage to find that?'

He held up the bottle of Jack Daniel's with a look of triumph. 'Found an off-licence specializing in imported spirits. You don't want to know how much it cost.'

'No, I don't. And thank you very much.' I took a satisfying sip. 'Aah.'

Alan poured some for himself. 'Here we are in France, the home of world-renowned wines. Specifically, we are in Normandy, where cider and Calvados reign supreme. And we're drinking American bourbon.'

'Sour-mash whiskey, dear. Bourbon is made in Kentucky. Jack comes from Tennessee. And very nice, too.'

'But you were saying that Krider is vanilla.'

'Mostly. There was a faint chocolate or at least cinnamon-flavoured nugget or two.'

'For example?' He leaned back in his chair and propped his injured ankle up on the bed.

'Hurting?' I nodded at the foot.

'Mild ache. Nothing serious.'

'Good. Well, let me do the vanilla part first. Upper middle-class all the way. Undergrad degree in accounting, then an MBA. Middle-management jobs at first, then CEO of a small company, then a larger one. Exemplary husband and father.'

'According to him.'

'He didn't actually put it in those terms, but one wife for almost forty years argues at least some respect for marriage vows. They took a couple of cruises together, that sort of thing.'

'But she didn't come with him on this little jaunt to France.'

'No, and that's one of the mildly interesting bits. He says it was because their daughter is about to give birth, and that may be the case. But I got the impression that wifey isn't as enthusiastic about the Mont as he is.'

'I've wondered about that enthusiasm. I find it hard to believe that a single book, read years ago, could prompt him to leave wife and home and imminent grandsons. Though it is a remarkable book.'

'That's another bit, you see. I told you he took his degree in accounting. That was exactly in character. But he minored – sorry, he had a secondary field of study – in history.'

'I do speak quite a little bit of American, you know,' said Alan with a grin. 'Marriage to you has sullied the purity of my English. No, don't throw that pillow; I'll spill my drink.

And I agree that the study of history is unexpected. Not the sort of field that would guarantee a lucrative income.'

'That was my reaction. But the real kicker came when I asked him about his hobbies. He hemmed and hawed a good deal, but finally admitted that he's been taking lessons in . . . guess.'

'Something wild and frivolous, I gather from your tone. Piano lessons. No, guitar.'

'Way off. He's been learning to paint. And – wait for it – what really fascinates him is illumination.'

'Not, I gather, as in Thomas Kinkade.'

'No, more as in medieval monks. He's been trying to learn how to do illuminated letters, like the ones in—'

'In recently-surfaced manuscripts, which were perhaps forged.'

He put down his glass and stared at me.

FOURTEEN

'**N**o. Surely not. Too much of a coincidence.' Alan picked up his glass again and took a healthy swig. 'If you're thinking he might have forged the blasted things, I can't believe it. He only started painting a few years ago, and in odd hours stolen from his other commitments. Unless he's extremely talented, he couldn't possibly have acquired the skills needed to pass his work off as genuine. No, but it's interesting, isn't it? And it could explain why he came to the Mont, which once had such a terrific collection of manuscripts.'

'Many of which still exist at the Scriptorial. Dorothy, he must have known about that museum. But you say he acted as if he'd never heard of it. Why did he tell such a pointless lie?'

I shrugged. 'He's been telling one lie after another since I met him. For that matter, so has Peter.' I held out my glass. 'Can you reach the bottle without getting up?'

He poured me another splash. 'Enough?'

'A gracious plenty, as a southern-born friend of mine used to say. Okay, it's your turn. What did you find out from the police in Avranches?'

'Not a great deal. The Survivor of the Bay, as they're calling the mysterious person – *le Survivant de la Baie* – is still unconscious.'

'Isn't that more than a little odd, Alan? I mean, she might have been unconscious for a little while, but it's been days now. I don't suppose she could be faking it?'

'Probably not, not for health professionals. The coma is very worrisome, because it might indicate brain damage. That's not uncommon in cases of near-drowning, you know. The hospital staff don't yet have a firm prognosis, but they would like to locate next of kin.'

'Not easy, unless they've found some identification.'

'Not yet. They have come to some provisional conclusions, however. There is, in the car park for the Mont, a car that has not been moved for several days, nor has anyone been seen approaching it.'

'Which car park? The one here, or down the road?'

'The big one, down the road – as you put it in your quaint American fashion.'

He knew he was safe from a pillow attack as long as he held his glass. I contented myself with sticking out my tongue at him.

'Of course, the police investigate any car that's been apparently abandoned. For one thing, in the present state of madness in the world, the thing might be rigged to blow up. When it's a hire car, with someone paying money for every day the car sits there empty, suspicions increase.'

'So they checked this one out,' I said, 'and discovered it was rented by some rich Swiss banker who – let's see – is staying at a hotel actually on the Mont and found it more convenient just to leave the car where it was.'

'No. Clever idea, but wrong, my dear. They investigated and found that the car was hired by a man named Carl Philipp Bachmann, with an address in Leipzig.'

'Oh, well, not our drowned woman, then. Or nearly drowned. Whatever.'

'As you told me, wait for it. Of course they tried to get in touch with anyone at that address.'

'Tried? No one else lives there?'

'No one lives there, full stop. There is no such address, and apparently no such person. Rather an ingenious alias, don't you think?'

'I don't – oh! Bach. Carl Philipp Emanuel Bach. And from Leipzig, yet. Did he – the real C.P.E. Bach, I mean – ever live there?'

'His father J.S. did, at least, for the last twenty-five or so years of his life. It's reasonable to suppose the son was there at some stage. But we're wandering from the point, which is that the car was hired under a false address.'

'Wouldn't the guy have had to show a passport?'

'Perhaps not, within the EU, only a driving licence, and if the chap at the agency was rushed, he might not have paid close attention. All they really care about is a valid credit card.'

'Well, I suppose that obvious intent to deceive made the police even more suspicious.'

'Indeed. They called in the help of other *judiciaires,* with bomb-sniffing dogs, the lot. They found nothing at all amiss with the car.'

'And anyway it has nothing to do with the . . . what did you call her, the survivor of something?'

Alan's face took on a remarkable resemblance to the way our cat Samantha looks when she's just finished lapping up the cream she's spilled on the table. '*Survivant,*' he said, watching me.

'Yes, okay, so your French is good and mine isn't. You don't have to rub it in.'

'Your French is coming along nicely, but you've forgotten some of the grammar. Nouns, you will remember, are either masculine or feminine in gender.'

'Right. I assume there's going to be a point to all this eventually.'

'You're getting testy, love. More bourbon?'

'More information! And no more French quizzes.'

'I was trying to give you a hint. The noun *survivant* is

masculine. The feminine would have an e on the end, *survivante.*'

'Oh. That's funny, isn't it? Are you sure you didn't just hear it wrong?'

'I saw it in writing. Also, I know I got it right, because they gave me one other piece of vital information.'

He paused. I gave him a look.

He grinned. 'The doctors and nurses learned very quickly that *le Survivant* is a man.'

I was still reeling from that shock when someone knocked on the door.

'That'll be Peter, I expect,' said Alan softly. 'We invited him for dinner, remember? Not a word of this to him, love.'

I just nodded.

We offered Peter a drink, which he refused, saying all he really wanted was a gallon or so of water. The day was hot, and he'd been up and down stairs at the Abbey all day. So we went downstairs and snagged a table, and asked for a large pitcher of water while we chose our meal and our wine.

'How were things up at the Abbey today? Back to normal?' Harmless question, just making conversation while I tried to get my mind working again. The survivor of the bay was a man. Why masquerading as a woman? Why had the police not released that information?

I missed Peter's reply, but caught Alan's follow-up question. 'And did Krider enjoy his visit?'

'I can't really say. He deserted me in the gift shop and I never found him again.'

'The gift shop! I wouldn't have thought he'd have much interest in souvenirs. He doesn't seem the type to take home "A present from Mont-Saint-Michel".'

'No.' Peter grinned. 'Might I have another glass of water, please? No, he was looking at the manuscripts.'

The waiter arrived just then. I ordered the first thing I saw on the menu, which turned out later to be some sort of seafood dish. The other two ordered, and Alan got the wine decision out of the way as quickly as he decently could, wine being a sacred matter in France. As soon as the *garçon* was out of the way, I swallowed and said, nonchalantly, 'Manuscripts?'

'What's the matter?' asked Peter. 'You sound upset.'

So much for nonchalance. 'Swallowed the wrong way. I didn't know there were manuscripts in the gift shop.'

'Modern copies, of course. I think some of the monks and nuns may make them. They're still rather expensive, but it turns out Krider's fascinated by them. Even fancies himself a copyist.'

I didn't quite groan, but I exchanged an eloquent look with Alan. All that work, all my patience extracting from Krider something Peter found out in a few minutes!

I'm not often at a loss for words. *Au* very much *contraire*, as anyone will tell you. But Alan saw that I was struggling for a conversational gambit, and said smoothly, 'Have they heard any more up at the Abbey about that poor chap who fell down in the crypt, or wherever it was, and then vanished?'

Peter looked sober. 'They're not talking a lot about him. At least, the members of the community aren't. They're all about silence and peace, you know. Even when the cares of the world invade their sanctuary, they pray about it rather than fretting about it. It's rather a serene, sensible way of dealing with troubles, actually.' He looked and sounded a little defensive about voicing this outrageously uncool sentiment.

I found my voice. 'You're quite right about that. I'm a confirmed fretter, myself, and it's so unproductive. I wish I could develop the habit of serenity. There are far worse ways of handling problems than wrapping them in prayer. But you implied that other people at the Abbey – the lay employees, I suppose – are in fact talking about that poor boy.'

'Quietly. They're rather expected to conform to the philosophy of the community, even though they're not officially part of it. But of course they talk among themselves, in the gift shop and when the guides get together. The gist of it is, the chap's been found. He didn't get very far from the hospital before he collapsed, and they brought him back, but he isn't doing well at all. In fact, the word is that his family has been asked to come.'

'They think he's dying?'

The waiter, who had reappeared with our wine, took a step back at the sound of the distress in my voice. '*Monsieur*?' he asked doubtfully.

Alan reassured him, and the wine ceremony proceeded, but when it had been poured and the waiter had retreated, I wanted to know more about the young victim. 'Where is his family?' I asked. 'The leader of the group he was with sounded English.'

'Yes, the group was from Hertfordshire, organized by St Albans Cathedral. It's a great pity their holiday ended so badly. Well, it was more of a pilgrimage, really. St Albans was once a Benedictine abbey, as you may know.'

I shook my head; Alan nodded his.

'The biggest and most important one in England, according to their records,' Peter went on. 'Among their claims to fame is the only English Pope, Adrian IV, who came from the town – his father was a monk at the abbey – and a notable scriptorium in the twelfth century.'

'Aha! Another tie to manuscripts!' I took a sip of my wine, discovered its excellence, and took another. 'This can't all be coincidence. It just isn't possible that at least three people concerned with manuscripts would come to the Abbey at the same time, and one of them would be grievously attacked. There's a rat i' the arras, or something rotten in the state of Denmark, or whatever cliché you prefer. And Peter, you still haven't heard anything about your missing friend? Because if something's happened to him, too . . .?'

'I know. I've tried every way I can think of to reach him. No luck.' Peter looked beseechingly at Alan. 'I know you've retired from the constabulary, sir, and I hate to ask, but is there a way . . . that is, do you know . . .?' He ran down.

'You want me to set in motion a search for your friend.' Alan's voice was neutral.

'Well . . . I do realize you can't officially . . . but I had hoped . . .'

'Oh, for the love of Mike!' I'd had enough. 'Just come out and say it. If Alan can't do it, he'll say so, but stop pussy-footing around! He doesn't bite, you know.'

'Yes, all right. Yes, sir, if there's a way you can look into his disappearance, I'd be grateful.' He took a sip of wine. I suspected his mouth was dry.

'There are people I can ask. Unofficially, as you point out. Dorothy, may I borrow your notebook?'

I felt under the chair for my purse, and then remembered. 'Oh, I don't have it, because I left my purse up in the room. I can run up—'

But Alan had summoned the waiter and addressed him in French too rapid for me to follow, and then turned back to Peter. 'He'll bring us some paper and a pencil. I want you to write down everything you can tell me about this chap. Full name and address, phone number or numbers, email address or addresses, place of business, contact information there, names of friends and family members – the lot. If you don't have it all at your fingertips here, find it at your lodging, or get it somehow. The more information you can provide to me, the less I'll have to ask my colleagues.' He took a healthy swig of his own wine, and then added, 'And if I find you have been lying to us, or concealing something vital, I'll call off the search and have my friends begin to investigate you! Ah, here's our dinner. We'll stop talking about problems and concentrate on this admirable food.'

Alan the Chief Constable had spoken.

FIFTEEN

Peter was understandably somewhat subdued for the meal, and made only brief replies to our attempts at conversation. When we got to the matter of dessert, he asked to be excused. 'That was a terrific meal. You've been feeding me so well, I'm going to need a new belt. But I truly don't want anything more, and I should go and get to work on that information you wanted, sir.'

'You do that, and leave it at the desk for me. And remember—'

'The truth, the whole truth, and nothing but the truth. I'll remember.'

'Good lad. Dorothy and I will . . . yes?'

The waiter had appeared at his side, handed him a piece of paper, and then asked a question. It appeared to be about dessert, because Alan said something that included the word *'pommes'* – I recognized that one as 'apples' – and *'Calvados'*. The waiter went away, and Alan unfolded the paper.

'I had a good deal of wine, Alan. If you're going to give me applejack as well – what is it?'

For his face had changed. He handed the piece of paper over to me, but it was in a handwriting I found nearly illegible, and in French. I raised my eyebrows.

'Oh, sorry. I forgot. It's from the police in Avranches. The *survivant* is awake and able to speak. They promised to let me know, and said I might visit if I wished.'

I stood. 'What are we waiting for?'

The waiter, who had obviously read the note he gave Alan, spoke to him as we headed for the door. I suppose he was saying he'd save our dessert and drinks for us. I didn't care at the moment. I wanted to talk to this woman – er, this man – who'd caused such consternation, in so many ways.

'I don't suppose she – he – will speak English, though, will he?'

'Most educated Europeans do. If in fact he is European. He gave a false German address; he could be from almost anywhere.'

'Oh. Of course.' Alan turned out of the hotel car park. 'Where are we going? I never asked where the hospital was.'

'Avranches. A *polyclinique*.'

I nodded to show I could figure out what that meant.

'French lessons, as soon as we get home,' he said, but his mind was on other things.

So was mine. 'Alan, does any of this make any sense to you? I keep trying to find a pattern, and every time I think I do, the kaleidoscope turns and I'm back where I started.'

'We don't know enough, love.'

'We don't know anything!'

'Perhaps we will, soon. No point in speculation now.'

I continued to speculate all the way into Avranches, but I did it silently. Alan was right, of course, but it was maddening to have a few pieces of a puzzle and not even get a start on the picture.

'But what if it isn't the same picture?' I said aloud.

'Mmm?' said Alan, who was getting into a bit of traffic. Avranches is not a big city, and the dinner hour was nearly over, but all the drivers on the road seemed intent on homicide, at high speed.

'Just an idle thought,' I said quickly, trying not to wince or scream as we passed a big black car, a limousine of some sort, with a red sports car coming at us. We had at least an inch to spare. I'd talk about my idea at a more propitious time.

It was a depressing idea, though. What if all these pieces belonged to different puzzles? What if it was not one set of peculiar events, but several, unrelated to each other? Then, even if we solved one, the others would remain, tantalizing us.

And it wasn't just a question of peculiar events, either. That guy at the Abbey had been attacked, and might die. That's murder! And what about Peter's friend, who might be anywhere, or – the thought came unbidden – or nowhere? There was no assurance that he was still alive, and quite a lot of suspicion that he might not be.

Did it all really revolve around medieval manuscripts? What an unlikely source of trouble, or so I would have thought. And yet that famous book, *The Name of the Rose*, dealt with just that idea. At least I thought it did. I'd read it when it first came out in English, and my memory of it was pretty vague. And then there was the Ellis Peters book, one of the Brother Cadfael series, with several important scenes in the scriptorium of the abbey at Shrewsbury. I remembered that one better than the Eco book, but the scriptorium there served merely as a quiet and relatively private setting for an angry scene to be played out. The work done there, the manuscripts themselves, played no part.

Could that be the case here? Maybe the manuscripts were simply some sort of background for . . . well, for something fairly nasty, if a young man lay near death because of it.

Unless it was all meaningless, all unconnected. The kaleidoscope gave another turn, and the pattern dislimned.

The hospital's visiting hours had ended, but a uniformed

gendarme, or *agent*, or whatever he was, was stationed by the front desk, waiting to escort us to the patient's side. He spoke to Alan in low tones as we walked through the rather complicated maze of corridors. As the language was French, I didn't even try to eavesdrop. They're all alike, I was thinking. All hospitals everywhere. They look clinical, despite their best efforts at sweetness and light. They smell of disinfectant fighting somewhat unsuccessfully against other, more menacing odours. And they've all grown, like Topsy, making a map the first thing one should acquire upon entering. Though I've never known a hospital that offered maps. Perhaps they don't want people wandering unsupervised through the maze.

I was thinking about hospitals to avoid getting back into the kaleidoscope, searching hopelessly for answers. When we arrived at the room, I was suddenly not sure I wanted to go in. 'Alan!' I whispered urgently. 'I don't even know his name!'

'Neither does anyone else at this stage,' he replied, patting my hand. 'All shall be well.'

It was part of one of my favourite quotes from Dame Julian of Norwich, the fourteenth-century English mystic, who is famous for her serene proclamation, 'All shall be well, and all shall be well, and all manner of thing shall be well.' It never fails to calm and refresh my troubled spirit. I smiled gratefully and went into the room.

The man lying in the bed looked very ill indeed. He had tubes in his nose and his arm, and wires hooked up here and there. In health I thought he might be a big, husky man, but now he looked shrivelled. His face was a pasty grey, but there was a dark, heavy growth of beard. I wondered how he could have maintained a disguise as a woman; he must have had to shave twice a day, at least.

And why had he wanted to do that?

The nurse in the room was the kindly sort, rather than the dragon I was half-expecting. She spoke quietly, and of course in French, but even I could tell that she was expressing concern about her patient's condition, and gently but firmly setting limits to our visit. A finger to her lips told us to speak quietly; and *'dix minutes'* was easy to translate.

The French police officer stepped forward and sat down

beside the bed. Alan told me later what he said, so I know that he introduced himself and then asked the man, in French of course, what his name was.

I needed no translation of his answer. 'I'm sorry – I don't speak French.'

The accent was pure Midwest. I couldn't help myself. I moved to the bed and said, 'You're American! And so am I. What on earth were you doing, letting yourself get caught in the quicksand of Mont-Saint-Michel?'

'Dorothy.' Alan quietly moved me aside. 'We do want to know that, sir, but first let me congratulate you on still being alive. It was a near thing, you know.'

'I do know.' He paused to cough, and the nurse moved forward, but Alan held up his hand. 'And what I want to know is,' the man continued when he could speak, 'who was the son-of-a-bitch who left me there to die?'

That flummoxed Alan for a moment, so I could say, 'We still don't know your name.'

'Sam Houston. Don't laugh, and don't make me laugh. I'll start coughing. My father was from Texas, but we moved to Chicago when I was fifteen, and I've lived there ever since, except for a few years in the Marines.'

Alan managed to get his home address, and his address in France, and then the nurse shooed us out.

'And after that little bombshell, I need a stiffener,' I said firmly when we all got ourselves back to the hospital lobby. 'You ask this nice policeman where we can get some decent whisky, Scotch or American, I don't care.'

'We've still that bottle of Jack back at the hotel.'

'And we have to drive back there eventually anyway. Done.'

I spent the short trip to our hotel trying to organize my chaotic thoughts. If I thought nothing made sense before, now I was completely at sea. Why was an American man masquerading as a German woman? Why had he been digging out on the sands of the bay?

He apparently remembered what had happened. Someone was with him. Someone he didn't know? That person – well, probably a man, given the term Sam had used for him – that man had abandoned him to the tide and the quicksand.

So who did we have now in the cast of characters in this bizarre story? Two Americans, one young, one middle-aged. (No one more than ten years younger than I counts as 'old'.) Both from the Midwest. I had learned a lot about Krider's background, but we knew nothing about Sam. The police would find out, though. Now that they had a name and a nationality, they could trace him. A European might not have needed a passport to come here; an American would.

Except – oh, dear. An American friend told me an interesting story a year or so ago. On a holiday from America, she had spent some time in the Channel Islands and had chosen to come to France in a small boat that made day-trip runs to Cherbourg. Her only travelling companion was a French girl who was returning home. When they landed, the girl helped her find the Tourist Information centre, where the staff helped her find a hotel. It wasn't until she was settled in that she realized no one had asked her – an American – to show a passport. No formalities at the docks – she just walked up into the town. And from there she travelled all over France, never once showing a passport. She hadn't intended to sneak into the country illegally, but that, in effect, was what she had done.

What if Sam had done the same thing, intentionally or otherwise? Then there wouldn't be a paper trail the police could easily follow.

Well, that was creating a problem where none might exist, and goodness knows I had enough without making one up!

Back to the cast of characters. Krider, Houston. Krider was more or less taped; Sam would be able to tell us more when he felt better. Then there were two young men about whom we still knew little or nothing. Peter was writing down information about his friend Laurence for Alan. Laurence was English, so Alan could invoke the power of the English constabulary in searching for him. The man in the crypt – well, Peter knew he was from Hertfordshire, and the Abbey had records of the group he came with. And of course his parents might be here soon, if the Abbey officials had been able to reach them. If the poor boy died, though, the true story of what he was doing in the crypt might die with him.

And that's a terrible thought, Dorothy Martin, I scolded

myself. You should be praying for his life because he's a suffering human being, not because he's involved in a very odd puzzle. But the fact remains that he could help solve that puzzle – if he lives.

I had reached that point in my unproductive musings when we got to the hotel. Alan parked the car while I went in. The desk clerk called to me. 'Madame, a note for you.'

That would be Peter's information about Laurence. I tucked it into my purse and went upstairs.

A knock at the door. Alan's forgotten his key, I thought. I opened the door to a young waiter, who rolled in a small cart carrying plates, glasses, a bottle, and something that smelled heavenly. '*Votre tarte tatin, madame,*' he said with a smile.

Well, given the aroma, even I could figure out that meant some sort of apple pie. I fumbled in my purse for a tip, but Alan showed up just then and gave the boy some money.

'I'd forgotten about dessert,' I said, sitting down at our minute table with a satisfied sigh. 'What exactly is it?'

'An upside-down apple pie, but very much unlike any apple pie you've ever tasted. It must be eaten warm, and here's some crème fraîche to have with it. And some Calvados.'

I dug in, and after the first bite forgot about everything that was bothering me. This was heaven on a plate. I had no idea what sort of apples had been used, but they were in a buttery caramel sauce that enhanced their bright tartness. The tanginess of the crème fraîche set it all off perfectly, and the Calvados – well, it's true that I'm overly devoted to the pleasures of the palate, but this was pure bliss and I refused even to feel guilty about it. I did manage to refrain from picking up my plate to lick it clean, but it was a near thing.

'Coffee?' Alan picked up the silver pot and raised his eyebrows.

'No, thanks. It might keep me awake.'

'I ordered decaf.'

I don't usually have anything to do with decaffeinated coffee. To me the phrase is an oxymoron. But in France it might even taste like the real thing. 'Well, then.' I accepted the cup he poured for me and put it down to look for my purse. 'Now I suppose we should look at what Peter came up with about his friend.'

'I suppose we should.' Alan sounded as enthusiastic about it as I.

I made a decision. 'No. I don't want to, and neither do you. We've had enough of this for the time being. Let's pretend we're an elderly couple entitled to our sleep.'

Alan put his cup down, too. 'My love, you do have brilliant ideas. Although I'm not sure how sleepy I am.'

Somewhat later, we slept very well indeed.

SIXTEEN

I slept late the next morning. It was a perfectly gorgeous morning, and I suddenly realized it was Sunday. At home peals of bells would have reminded us about going to church.

I'm usually groggy first thing, but for some reason I felt wideawake. I nudged Alan, who was still slumbering peacefully. 'Hey, sleepyhead. It's Sunday! What are we going to do about church?'

'Mmff,' said Alan. I called for coffee and croissants, and while I waited for their arrival, I went downstairs to work out a plan.

When I returned, and Alan had absorbed enough caffeine to re-join the world, we talked about our options. There weren't many.

'I doubt there's an Anglican church nearer than Paris.' I finished a croissant and licked my fingers.

'You're probably right. So we'd need to go to Mass somewhere.'

'And I'm sorry, dear heart, but the Abbey is out of the question. There are something like 350 steps. I climbed it once. I'm not sure I could do it again. And with that bum ankle, you couldn't do it at all.'

'No lift?'

'No lift. But while you were emerging from the fog, I went down to the lobby and checked some of the tourist guides. There's a small parish church, Saint Pierre, about halfway up the village street. The street is cobbled, but I think you can make it if we go slowly.'

'The service will be in French, you know.'

'Of course. I do rue the day when the Latin Mass was abandoned. Wherever Frank and I went in our travels, we could go to church and follow what was happening, because we'd heard things like the Lord Nelson Mass, and the B-Minor, and so on, and knew the words in Latin. But it'll follow the same basic pattern as our Eucharist back home, and French is based on Latin, after all. How hard can it be?'

Alan poured himself another cup of coffee and buttered a brioche. 'I'm not sure, Dorothy. I hate to sound like an old crock, but the doctor did drill into me that I was to stay off my feet as much as possible. As I recall, it's a fair walk from where the tram drops one to the Mont itself.'

'Aha! That's why I organized a wheelchair for you. Aren't you proud of me? I took my phrase book and found a picture of the handicap symbol – you know, that stylized wheelchair thing – and the concierge was most helpful. I also learned that the trams are fully wheelchair accessible.'

'You handled all that in French?'

'Well . . . the concierge speaks pretty good English, actually. And there's a leaflet about the trams – in several languages.'

Alan took a bite of his croissant and a swig of coffee. He looked grumpy.

'Look, love, I know you hate looking old and feeble. So did I, when I couldn't walk much right after they did my knees. But you're *not* old and feeble; we both know that. It's just that blasted ankle. What do you care what people think, people who don't know you and will never see you again?'

'You are a managing woman.' He tried to sound cross, but a twinkle was just under the surface.

'I am, when necessary. And you'd better finish your breakfast and get in the shower. Mass starts at eleven, and it'll take us a while to get there.'

When I was a girl back in Indiana, no Protestant would have dreamed of entering a Catholic church, or vice-versa. How things have changed – and for the better. For the most part, the various branches of Christianity are far more tolerant of one another, without discarding our deeply-held convictions. And the Anglican diocese of Sherebury isn't all that Protestant, anyway; we keep to High Church practices which some would consider popish.

All the same, it felt a little odd to be entering a beautiful little church with several statues of Mary and lots of banks of votive candles. We left the wheelchair at the door, and by unspoken consent headed for a pew at the back, in a corner, where we could watch what others did and not be too conspicuous.

'We probably can't take Communion,' I whispered. Alan gave a minute shrug, which I presumed meant he wasn't sure.

I didn't have too much trouble following the Mass, which was celebrated very simply. I could not, of course, follow the readings or the brief homily. The congregation was not large; there are only forty or fifty residents of the Mont, not all of whom, I presumed, are churchgoers. Visitors to the village on a Sunday morning would tend to be either tourists, interested in sightseeing, or pilgrims, who would attend church at the Abbey. When it came time for Communion, Alan held a whispered conversation with one of the attendees, who shook his head. We stayed in our seats. Alan made sure to put a fair-sized donation in the collection when it came around, and we stayed to chat with the priest when the service was over. At least Alan chatted; I nodded and smiled.

'Nice chap,' said Alan when we were out in the sunshine once more. 'Now. An omelette *chez la Mère Poulard*?'

'It can't be any better than the ones *chez* Dorothy, and I can think of a whole bunch of things I'd rather spend our money on, like a proper Sunday lunch. I don't suppose we could find roast beef and Yorkshire pudding anywhere?'

'Paris, probably. Some of the big hotels there cater to the English.'

'Forget it. Let's see if anything in the village appeals.'

We took our time wandering back down past the shops and

cafés, all very busy now that Sunday morning had passed. Alan had refused to use the wheelchair. 'It's too hard for you to wheel on the cobbles, and it's awkward in a crowd. I have my cane and the boot, and your elbow at need.'

I didn't insist. I'd got him to use it on the way up. I choose my battles. I dragged the thing, folded up and hard to control, behind me, and tried not to show my irritation with it.

There wasn't a single eatery that appealed to my mood. They were either very limited in menu or very expensive, or both. I did pause now and then to drop into a shop, especially when there was a bench inside where Alan might rest for a bit. One had an intriguing display of tapestries depicting, of all things, illuminated manuscripts, or at least illuminated capital letters. They were somewhat stylized, not as elaborate as the originals, and were, I was sure, machine-made, but they were beautiful. I paused near the doorway to inspect one and check the price, and while I was mentally translating the price into pounds sterling and deciding we still couldn't afford it, a man collided with the wheelchair, sending it bruisingly against my knee.

'Can't you control that thing?' he snarled. 'I might have damaged this, and it cost an arm and a leg.' He was gone, his bulky bundle under his arm, before I could recover and tell him *he* might have damaged *me*.

Alan was irate. 'That chap wants a kick where it would do the most good!'

The pain in my knee was subsiding. A sudden blow always makes them hurt like fury, but it doesn't last long. 'I agree. But then he's a New Yorker, and they're often like that. Comes of living in constant noise and bustle.'

'A New Yorker? You know him, then?'

'No, but the accent is unmistakable.'

'You caught that in just a few words? I just thought he sounded American.'

'Would you recognize a Welshman from just a few words? A New Yorker is just as distinctive, to any American. Besides, I've encountered him and his temper once before, my first day on the Mont. Once heard, never forgotten. Alan, for heaven's sake climb into this thing and let me wheel you the rest of the way. It's really easier that way. And let's try Avranches for lunch.'

We lingered over lunch, which was very good, but very French. I was beginning to long for English or American food, which just shows how old and set in my ways I've become.

'What now, light of my life?' asked Alan after we'd finished the last cup of espresso. 'Back to the hotel?'

'No, if we go back we'll just want to take a nap. There must be a place here in Avranches where we can just sit and talk. In some privacy. Is there a library?'

'Only the one in the Scriptorial, I believe.'

I shuddered. 'No, thank you. I've had quite enough of manuscripts for the time being.'

'Then what about a church? There's a beautiful one not far away, *Notre Dame des Champs*. Looks like a cathedral, though it isn't.'

'There wouldn't be a Mass going on?'

'I don't know, love, but at this time of day I'd doubt it. It's nearly three.'

'Then let's try it.'

The church was very beautiful. A long nave, full of light, led to an altar in a small apse. The gothic arches looked so much like those in the Cathedral at home that I was instantly homesick. 'It's very well preserved,' I whispered to Alan.

'Nineteenth century,' Alan whispered back, waving the leaflet he had picked up.

'Oh.' My nostalgic sentiment died a quick death. Alan grinned at me, but forbore to comment until we had found a small niche where normal conversation seemed less impolite.

'It's still beautiful, you know,' said Alan.

'I know. And I know I'm completely irrational. But I like things to be real, not copies. Our Cathedral is real.'

'And costs a fortune to maintain in its glorious ancient reality. You would prefer, here, a Victorian red-brick box?'

'No, of course not. I said I was irrational. It's just that . . . oh, it's the old, stale issue: why is a beautiful copy of a painting or whatever not as valuable as the original? Penny and I talked about it just the other day, and came to no conclusion. One never does. The copy may be beautiful. Well, this church is. If the original is very old, the copy may be in much better condition. As this church is. I suppose that the real problem is that the creative genius that sparked the original has been pirated. It's not so bad with a building, I guess. This is probably not an exact copy of some other church, and anyway it's not being passed off as an original Gothic edifice. A painting, now, a forgery of a Renoir, say – that's just plain theft, no matter how beautiful the forgery might be. It's the dishonesty of it that makes my blood boil!'

My voice had risen. Alan put a finger to his lips. 'Easy, love. We're in a sacred place, even if it is somewhat spurious, to your mind.'

'You're right. Sorry,' I said to Alan, to whatever people might be in the church, and to God. 'And anyway, that's not what we need to talk about.'

'Not directly. But there is a bearing. I'll get to that in a minute. First, do we believe that all the odd things happening on and around the Mont are connected?'

I took a deep breath. 'I do, for one. I've thought about it and thought about it till my brain is turning cartwheels, and I can't give any sensible reason for my belief, but yes, I do believe there's a connection somewhere. What it is, though . . .?' I held up my hands in the classic 'don't have a clue' gesture.

'I agree. And I further believe – without a shred of evidence – that the connection has something to do with manuscripts. Which is most unlike the policeman in me.'

'No, it's not. When you were a working policeman, you often knew more about a case than you had evidence to prove. Instinct counts.'

'Not in a court of law. Be that as it may, I can't bring myself to ignore my strong feeling that there's too much about manuscripts in all this mess for pure coincidence.'

'I don't actually believe in coincidence, anyway. The universe is an orderly place.'

Alan raised one eyebrow.

'Oh, I know, the world is a mess, everywhere you turn.

But there are patterns. Patterns always emerge, given enough distance from a situation – distance in space or time, or both.'

Alan uttered a dry, sceptical sound. 'The distance may sometimes be astronomical. Or geological, if we're talking about time.'

'I know that!' My voice was rising again. I tempered it. 'Yes, you're right. But I still say the reason we're not making sense of this case it that we're too close to it. We can't see the patterns. The trouble is, I can't work out a way to step back, so to speak.'

'Ah. That's where I was heading. We were talking about copies, forgeries, and their relative value. I think we need to go back to Penny's story about the possibly forged manuscripts coming into the art market.'

'Okay, but what—'

'Try to forget everything that's happened since you heard that story. What did Penny actually say?'

'Now you're acting like a policeman again. Question the witness. Alan, so much has happened since, and I always hate to admit it, but my memory . . .'

'Isn't what it was. Neither is mine. What's to prevent our talking to her, right now?'

'But . . . oh.' Years of living in England have not dispelled the American mindset that France is Very Far Away and a phone call to or from there is Almost Impossible and, if possible, Very Expensive. I looked at Alan, who almost always knows what I'm thinking, and pulled out my mobile.

'Not here, love, don't you think? You'll get a better signal outside.'

So we went back into the hot sunshine, moved into the shade of the north side of the church, which was also, fortunately, away from traffic noise, and I placed the call to Penny in Wales.

SEVENTEEN

Penny sounded far away. Her voice seemed to echo. 'Penny, it's Dorothy. Where are you? You sound like you're in a cave.'

'Almost. Let me call you back.'

The line went dead and we waited several minutes for the call-back.

'Is this better?' The voice was now clear.

'Much. Look, is this a bad time to call?'

'No, it's fine. I was just coming out of an old slate mine. It's a wonder there was a signal at all. What's up?'

'I won't ask what you were doing in a slate mine. The very thought makes my knees go wobbly.' It was true. My claustrophobia kicks in even when thinking or reading about dark, enclosed places.

'All right, I won't tell you. What can I do for you?'

'It's a long story, but Alan and I find ourselves embroiled in a series of odd events here at Mont-Saint-Michel, and he thinks the whole thing might have to do with medieval manuscripts. Yes, well, I said it was a long story. So he wants to know what you told me about the manuscripts that keep turning up. I can't remember exactly. I'll give him the phone.' I also handed him the notebook I always keep in my purse, and a pen.

His side of the conversation wasn't very informative, consisting mostly of affirmative noises, but then I perked up my ears. 'And is there any hint of just where these might be coming from?'

Darn. I should have asked that when Penny and I first talked. Of course I hadn't known then that the matter would come up rather urgently in a few days. Only hadn't she said something then about not knowing their origin?

Alan thanked Penny, said, 'Yes, I'll certainly tell her,' and ended the call.

'She sends her love, and says she'll tell you all about the slate mines one day.'

'I don't think I want to know. But what did she say about the manuscripts?'

'What you had told me. That they were showing up on the market, no provenance, no history. Of course dealers are wary, but they are of excellent quality, and appear to be genuine. The more reputable dealers won't touch them, but in the nature of things not everyone is so particular, so some of them are being sold for quite fabulous sums.'

He stopped there, but his face had that 'wait for it' look.

'And?' I demanded.

'And, just within the past few days, some of them have been traced back to . . .'

'Mont-Saint-Michel!'

'Aha! Thought I'd catch you. Not at all. They've been traced to America.'

It was a good thing we were no longer in the church, because I was seized by a minor fit of hysterics. 'It wanted only that!' I wheezed when I could speak. 'A German woman who turns out to be an American man, drowning in quicksand! An English archaeologist who turns out to be an art detective. An Englishman of unknown profession getting coshed in a French abbey, then disappearing and reappearing again. Another Englishman disappearing, apparently permanently. And now ancient works of ecclesiastical art coming from America. America! A country which, at the time these works were presumably produced, was still inhabited by aboriginal peoples who knew nothing of Christianity. Get me into a straitjacket and take me away!'

'You've forgotten the American man who claims to be here because he has a thing about the Mont, and who just happens to be an artist dabbling in manuscript techniques,' said Alan drily. 'Suppose we get out of here and give you a chance to recover, and then I have a plan.'

I didn't say a word on our way back to our hotel. My mind refused to work at all. The expression 'blank mind' took on a whole new meaning for me. Alan chivvied me into the hotel, sat me down at a table in the lobby/lounge, and ordered strong coffee and a large chocolate croissant.

'That coffee,' I said after one scalding, bitter sip, 'could trot a mouse, as some of the out-of-date English authors used to have their characters say.'

'Good. I told them that was what you needed. If that and the chocolate can't bring you back to rationality, I'll go ahead and send for that straitjacket. Drink up.'

It was awful stuff. I hadn't known the French could make bad coffee, but I found that if I stirred enough sugar and milk into it, I could get it down, and maybe it wasn't so bad after all. Just very, very strong. I polished off the croissant to take the taste away, and sat back. 'All right. Sanity restored. Of course I may never sleep again.'

'Good,' he said again. 'You were worried about wanting a nap. Perhaps we've averted that. Now.' He looked around the room. It was filling up. Low conversations provided a background buzz, and most of what I could hear was in French. 'Shall we go up to the room, or would you rather talk here?'

'Seems safe enough here. We'll need to keep an eye open for our friends, though.'

'Right. Now what I had in mind was this. I'd like to start from the supposition that all these people are lying to us, every single one of them, to one degree or another. Let's dig out what we really know about them – know of our own knowledge, not from what they've told us – and see where that leaves us.'

'Gosh.' I tried to think of what I knew about any of them. 'There sure isn't much.'

'No. But possibly more than we think. Where shall we start?'

'How about with the first thing that happened – the drowning?'

'The near-drowning. Fine. We know that it was first reported to the news media that a German woman had nearly drowned.'

'But it wasn't! It was an American man.'

'Now, now! It is a known fact that the *report* was about a German woman. We'll leave that for now, but it is suggestive, don't you think, that lies crop up at the very beginning? It will be very interesting to winkle out who lied to the press, and why.' He made an entry in the notebook. 'We do know that the nearly-drowned person is a man and that he is American. We have a name, which may or may not be true, and a story about his being left to die. Again, a possible lie.'

'I'm pretty sure the name is true. Do you know who Sam Houston was, in American history?'

'Haven't a clue.'

'Well, I'm a trifle foggy on the details, but I do know he was president of Texas after it had won its independence from Mexico, and then governor when Texas became part of the United States. He's *the* big hero in Texas; there's a huge military base in San Antonio named after him. The point is, the name is too well known to be used as an alias. It would be like you trying to call yourself – um – Henry Tudor. It wouldn't wash.'

'Almost blasphemy.' Alan agreed with a nod. 'And so attention-getting it would defeat your purpose, if you were trying to hide. I understand what you're saying. But suppose we went on a little jaunt to America, and I introduced myself as Henry Tudor. Would anyone notice?'

'Oh. I suppose it would depend on how well educated they were. But probably nine people out of a random assortment of ten wouldn't blink an eyelash. Americans aren't taught a lot of English history. I get your point. Sam wouldn't be running much risk with that name here in France. But honestly, I still think it's for real. His embarrassment when he told us seemed genuine. I don't suppose they've found his passport yet?'

'Not so far as I know. I'll ring the police in Avranches again tomorrow.'

'Well, that's that for now, then, but we can come back to him later. Excelsior! The next things come in a bunch. I met Peter, and he spun me a fine story about Abelard and his works, and then—'

'No. Stop there. What do we know for a fact about Peter?'

'Not much. He's English, or has an incredibly good ear.'

'Ear?'

'For an accent. Well, you've heard him. His is so Oxbridge it could cut glass. Even though he didn't go to either great university, or he says he didn't. He claims to hold a degree from Exeter. But we have only his word for that.'

'Easy enough to check, though.' He made another note.

'Assuming the name he gave us is genuine.'

'Again, easy to check, if we can get hold of his passport.'

'Alan, he might not be carrying his passport. Do you, travelling to France? I do, travelling or not, but it's because I always had to, as an American. I don't know what will happen when Britain officially leaves the EU, but for now . . .'

'Well thought out, but yes, I do always carry mine. In these uncertain days, one never knows when identification will be required. But even before the terrorists grew so bold, I carried mine routinely, as a matter of habit. Pack bag, pick up passport. A young man might not have formed that habit. We can but try, and if we can't find one, we'll try to have a look at his driving license.'

'He doesn't drive. Not here, anyway. Bicycle.'

Alan sighed. 'One might be tempted to think he was trying to conceal his identity. I'd think he would have had to show some form of identification to get the job at the Mont.'

'He's a volunteer. They might have wanted ID, even for that – but on the other hand, they might not.'

'Woman, there is such a thing as carrying caution too far! If the boy has some identification, we will find it, somehow. Passing on. What else, if anything, do we know about him?'

'He's educated, whether at Exeter or somewhere else. Everything about him gives that away. And he truly does know a lot about Abelard. Even if the story he told me was just an elaborate red herring dragged across my path, it was full of details that could easily be checked on the Internet.'

'Or obtained from that source in the first place.'

'Yes, but why would anyone bother? Just on the off chance that he might require an excuse to be at the Mont?'

'He could have mugged it up to tell the Abbey community.'

'Now who's being overly cautious? Anyway, he didn't want them to know what he was up to.'

'Or so he told you. In fact, he told you two different stories to explain his presence here, neither of which may hold a grain of truth.'

It was my turn to sigh. 'All right, don't rub it in. There are at least a few grains, though, unless we're wildly off base about everything. He's really on a quest having something to do with medieval manuscripts, or I'll eat my hat.'

'That's as fine a hash of mixed metaphors as I've heard in months. I'll have to be more careful in future about loading you with caffeine. It seems to have odd effects on your brain. Have we finished for the moment with Peter?'

'Not quite. Alan, he truly wanted you to investigate the disappearance of his friend, and the accident, or whatever it was, to the tourist at the Abbey. He wasn't running from the police; he was positively holding his breath till you could get here.'

'A point in his favour, I agree.' He made a note. 'Of course he knew that I'm retired, with no official standing.'

'And we're in France, where you'd have no standing anyway. Yes, but it's plain to me that he really does not know what happened to those two men, and he's genuinely worried about them.'

'I'll give you that. Very well.' He consulted his notebook. 'Peter Cummings, if that is his name, is English and well-educated. He is also, and you're not going to like this bit, a member of the upper classes.'

'Alan! What a thing to say! Why does that matter, and how do you know, when we're not even sure of his name?'

'As to how I know, how do you know he's an educated man? His whole demeanour proclaims his class. And it matters because, A, it means there are certain things we can predict that he will do, or not do, in certain circumstances. Not an infallible guide, certainly, but it might sometimes shorten the odds. And, B, it will make him easier to trace, once we're sure of his name. He certainly went to a public school, and the much-maligned Old Boys Network can be very useful.'

Thus spake the policeman. I simply bowed my head in acknowledgement and said, 'On to his vanishing friend?'

'We do know some things about him, or at least I have the information Peter gave us. I've not had a chance yet to check it.'

'Can we drop the caution for the moment and assume Peter's told you the truth about him? Let's have it.'

Alan pulled a piece of paper out of his breast pocket and began to read. '"Laurence Cavendish." There's surely another upper-class lad for you. "Age twenty-six. Addresses The Larches, Doddington, Kent and New College, Oxford." Whew! The air is getting thin up here. Then he lists several phone numbers, an e-mail address, and the names of several friends, with apologies that he doesn't have their addresses or other contact information.'

'That's too easily checked not to be true.'

'It would seem so. I'll phone Derek soon and put him on it. What did Peter tell you about him?'

'First he said he – Laurence – was an archaeologist, and then said that wasn't true, that he was a medievalist.'

'Hmm. It will be interesting to know whether New College offers degrees in either field.'

This time I was thinking along with him. 'Because there may very well be a man named Laurence Whatever-it-is living in Kent and studying at New College, but who isn't missing and never intended to join Peter here in the first place.'

'You, my dear, are beginning to develop the cynical mind of a detective. Pity. You used to be so open and trusting.'

'That was before I knew you. And I don't know about you, dear heart, but I need two things in quick succession, the loo and a glass of something tall and cold. Be right back.'

When I returned, there was a frosty glass of something with a wedge of lime floating in it, and lots of ice. 'Ah! I do love the French attitude toward ice.' I took a healthy swig. 'And they use English gin. Good for them. What's that, cider?' I pointed to Alan's glass.

'When in Rome, do as the Romanians do. Excellent cider. And it was I who told them you required as much ice as tonic. Have some snacks before I snaffle them all.'

'You'll need them to offset the cider. But they look good.' I took a handful of nuts and a couple of those delectable little pickles known as *cornichons*.

'Right. Where were we?'

'Talking about Peter's friend Laurence.'

'Ah, yes. And reaching a dead end, until I can get Derek on the blower and confirm some of what Peter's given us.'

'Couldn't you call him now?' Chief Inspector Derek Morrison, once Alan's right-hand man in the Sherebury constabulary, could easily have climbed the ladder all the way to the top on Alan's retirement, had he wanted to, but he had preferred to remain a detective. 'That's what I'm good at, and it's what I enjoy,' he had told Alan. 'Administration's not my cup of tea.' So he was now the best detective in the force, nearly ready for retirement himself, and a dear friend who was always ready to give us a helping hand with one of our unofficial investigations.

'Sunday afternoon? Surely we can give the man a little peace.'

'It's not official, and nothing that requires anything more than a phone call or two. You know he'd love to hear from you. He doesn't need to do anything about it today, but it would be nice to get things going first thing tomorrow.'

'Very well.' Alan picked up his phone, conceding the point with a speed that told me he was just as anxious as I to see some daylight.

Derek was at home. He had a booming voice; I could hear almost every word he said. He would be delighted to help. Of course, no trouble at all. If he could just have the particulars . . .

Alan read them to him. Derek asked him to repeat them and he did.

There was a long pause at the other end of the line. Then I heard a long sigh. Alan looked at me and held the phone a little away from his ear so I could hear more clearly.

'Chief, you may not like this, but I'm already searching high and low for one Laurence Cavendish. He was reported as a missing person three days ago, and as his father is an MP, every force in the country has been alerted, not excepting the Met. How do you come into it?'

EIGHTEEN

Alan told Derek he'd call him back. We went up to our room for greater privacy, and using the speaker on his mobile, Alan and I told Derek the whole story.

'But you see, Derek, we don't know how much of what Peter told us was the truth, because he certainly made up a lot of stuff when I first met him. Apparently he didn't make up the story about Laurence being missing, though.'

'No. He had told his parents he was going to France for a week or two.'

'He still lives at home?' Alan interrupted.

'He lives in college, though he spends some holidays with his parents. They live in rather a grand house not far from Canterbury, so it's a pleasant place to relax. They're a close family, and as he is their only child he's rather careful about respecting their parental concerns. One gathers his mother is rather delicate.'

Apron strings still firmly attached, eh? I rolled my eyes; Alan nodded.

'The holidays haven't begun yet, have they?'

'No, the long vac doesn't begin until mid-June. However, as Cavendish is a graduate student, and is not sitting for any examinations this term, he is more or less his own master. What he told his parents was that he was pursuing some research in the old French abbeys. He's by way of being a medievalist.'

The English have their own delightful euphemisms. I rolled my eyes again, and Alan mouthed 'dilettante'.

'So if he was supposed to be away in any case, why did his parents get the wind up?'

'He had told them he'd call when he arrived in Normandy. He was to fly to Paris, where he planned to take a train to Pontorson. Well, he arrived in Paris; the airline confirms that. After that – nothing. There is no record of his catching a train from Paris, and they're checking these things much more care-fully these days.'

'Indeed.' Alan and I both sighed.

'If he used any other form of transport – bus, taxi, hired car – we've not yet been able to trace it.'

'He could have hitched a ride,' I said tentatively.

'Dorothy, as far as we can tell, he could have caught a low-flying UFO to Mars or been teleported to the *Enterprise*. There is simply no trace of him after he left the gate area at Charles de Gaulle.'

There seemed to be nothing to say to that. Alan assured Derek that he'd tell him at once if we learned anything on this side of the Channel, and Derek promised the same cooperation.

After Alan ended the call, we looked at each other. 'We have to tell Peter,' I said.

'Yes. You'd better let me do that. His reaction might be instructive.'

I let that go. I'm pretty good at reading faces, and detecting lies after forty years of teaching school is second nature, but Alan is a trained detective with a healthy measure of intuition. And I'd failed to spot Peter's first round of lies immediately. Yes, Alan was the man for this job.

'Right away?' I asked, looking at my watch.

'No. It's nearly dinner time, and we've given that chap quite enough meals. I'll call him later and ask . . . No. I'd rather take him unawares. Do you know where he's staying?'

'Only that it's in Ardevon, not far from here.'

Alan poked at his phone, swiped fingers here and there, and performed other mystic rites. Me, I use my phone for phone calls, but I do realize it can do almost anything if you give it the right commands.

Alan looked up. 'There's only one reasonable way for a cyclist to get from Ardevon to the Mont. He'd have to go up this road.' He pointed to a line on the screen. I nodded with what I hoped was an intelligent look. 'He might branch off here, or here, but to start, he'd be here. I propose to drive there first thing tomorrow morning and intercept him as he's on his way to the Abbey. And, dear heart, I'd rather you didn't come with me.'

'You think I'd offer sympathy. You're right. I might. But on the other hand, I might not. I'm not feeling terribly sympathetic just now toward that young man. I don't know what he's up to, but I have this feeling it's nothing good. And I'm really worried about his friend.'

'Yes. It isn't easy for a living person to disappear for any length of time these days.'

I gulped at the word 'living' and changed the subject. 'How hungry are you? Shall we go down for some dinner?'

'Actually, I'm feeling rather like a stuffed sausage. Too much to eat in the past few days, and too little exercise. Perhaps we could go across the street to the shops and pick up some snacks, instead?'

'Can you walk that far?'

'Don't insult me, woman! The doctor said I could do anything I liked, so long as it didn't cause pain. I'm to stop the moment it begins to hurt.'

I knew my husband well enough to take that remark with about a tablespoonful of salt. He would define 'pain' in any way that suited him, up to debilitating agony. However. 'That sounds like a good idea. They have some wonderful pâté. At about three times what it ought to cost.'

Alan shrugged. 'Of course. Shall we?'

We made it to the shops just in time. It seemed they closed early on a Sunday. The selection was somewhat limited, but there was one little tin of pâté left, and a lovely chunk of Brie. There were of course apples – certainly from storage, in May, but still probably edible – and one small crusty roll. 'I still have some cream crackers, and we can get some ice and chill this, and it'll be a perfectly fine supper.' I held up a bottle of Sauvignon Blanc that looked okay, though I'd never heard of the vineyard.

There were still some plastic wine glasses left from my improvised picnic with Peter earlier in the week. Alan and I set out our food on the tiny table in our room, using paper napkins filched from the hotel lounge for plates. I cut the cheese in half using the Swiss Army knife I'm never without, while Alan filled our wastebasket with ice from a machine (an amenity I thought we probably owed to the many

American tourists who had passed through over the years).

While we waited for the wine to chill, Alan got out the notebook with his jottings about our various characters.

'Let's see. We can add a little to our profile of Peter. He was telling the truth about Laurence Cavendish, at least up to a point. He is in fact a graduate student and he did in fact plan to come to France.'

'And he has indeed disappeared.'

'We don't know why he came to France, only what Peter told us, and what Laurence told his parents. That could all be a network of lies.'

'Yes.' I dismissed the unproductive thought. 'Very well, who's next?'

'The nameless victim of the apparent attack in the bowels of the Abbey.'

'But he isn't nameless, really. The police know who he is, or they couldn't have sent for his parents. And the people leading the tour know. We just haven't taken the trouble to find out.'

I hadn't meant it to sound like an accusation, but it came out that way. Alan said, 'We've been a bit busy.'

'I know. I'm sorry. His name doesn't matter right now, anyway. Let's call him John Doe.'

'Isn't that name usually used for murder victims in the States?'

'So I gather from fiction, anyway. Don't you think it's appropriate? If he dies, he'll be a murder victim. Oh, Alan, we shouldn't be flippant about it. The poor man!'

He busied himself with an entry in the notebook. 'Facts: he was a member of a group tour from St Albans.'

'Perhaps a fact. Peter gave us that information, remember.'

'Too easily checked to be a lie, I'd have thought.'

'You're probably right. And he failed to assemble with the group when they were ready to begin the tour of the Abbey, though he had been on the tram from the village.'

'Peter again?'

'No, this time an impeccable source: me. I was there when the tour group assembled, and heard Madam being furious because one of her sheep had gone astray.'

Alan's attention sharpened. 'This was the group that Peter led through the Abbey?'

'Yes, the group I joined. I shouldn't have, really, but they were rather a large group, and in some disarray because of the missing man, so I thought I'd tag along. I'd paid my entrance fee!' I added defensively, and Alan smiled.

'No one's going to arrest you for defrauding the Abbey, love. But how did Peter react to the chap going missing? Anything interesting there?'

'You have to remember I didn't know Peter at all at that point, but as far as I remember he acted just as one would expect. Annoyed, but trying to remain patient and polite to the paying customers. If he was at all distracted or upset, I didn't notice. There was nothing at all to hint that he knew anything about the missing guy, or cared particularly.'

'Then that may be all we can set down about the poor chap, at least until I call the Avranches police tomorrow and see what they know about him.'

'I do hope he's going to be all right. I said a prayer for him in church this morning.'

Alan smiled. 'So did I. I assume that an Anglican's prayers will still ascend from a Catholic church. Now, before we tackle the two most confounding characters of all, why don't we see if that wine is chilled?'

NINETEEN

It was, and after a cool refreshing glass of it, and a sampling of our snacks, I felt ready to tackle our two knottiest problems. 'How about we do Krider first? We haven't touched him yet.'

'Your wish is my command, dear lady.'

'Oh, yeah? Since when? But I'll take it when I can get it. Okay, A.T. Krider. I have a fairly complete bio of him in that notebook somewhere.'

Alan flipped pages. 'My word,' he said when he had read

a little. 'How in the world did you get him to tell you all this?'

'I made like a teacher. He told us he was trying to write fiction. I told him I'd read somewhere that many writers of fiction begin by creating biographies of their characters, and when he said he wouldn't know how to begin, I suggested he start with a bio of himself and go from there. Then the leading questions seemed natural.'

'Hmm. Ohio born and bred. Degree in accounting. You told me those bits. Minor in history, interested in illuminated manuscripts, which is the only interesting nugget.'

'All of it, of course, as reported by Krider himself. I'm inclined to believe most of it, though, because I don't think he's bright enough to realize I was fishing for information. And it didn't come out like someone making up a story as he went along.'

'Hmm. Not jury evidence, but a reasonable conclusion. What don't you believe?'

'That nonsense about why he's here. First he was scouting out the Abbey because his son was thinking about being a monk. Then he didn't have a son, he was just here because he'd been fascinated by the Mont ever since he read the Adams book. Then he was going to write a book himself, a novel set here. That man couldn't write a novel if someone was going to pay him a million dollars a word. He simply hasn't the imagination.'

'So why is he here, really?'

'If we knew that, we'd know a lot about why they're all here, wouldn't we? Alan, it all ties together somehow, but it's beginning to look like those knots in illuminated letters, all convoluted, with no beginning or end.'

'I think an interview with him is in order. Soon. The stakes have been raised now that we know for certain that Laurence is officially missing. If he's still staying at the hotel—'

Alan's phone made its odd burbling sound.

'Hello? *Oui, c'est moi.*' He listened intently for a few moments, then uttered a little more French and ended the call. 'That was the police in Avranches. Mr Houston is awake and feeling much better, and is eager to talk to both of us.'

I picked up my purse and followed him out of the room.

The nurse on duty was not the pleasant one we'd seen before. It was obvious just from her body language that she disapproved of us and all our works, and her conversation with Alan, in whispered French, left no doubt. I couldn't understand a single word, but I knew exactly what she said, anyway.

Alan dealt firmly with her tirade, and closed the door after her so rapidly that he almost nipped the heels of her sensible shoes.

'What was that all about?' Sam asked from his bed. He was sitting up and looking much healthier – some colour in his cheeks and some strength to his voice.

'She isn't happy about our being here,' said Alan moderately. 'She thinks you'll overtire yourself. She wants us to stay only five minutes.'

'Damn five minutes! Sorry, ma'am. But I've got things to say, and I'm going to say them if it takes all night. You tell that witch I'll have a relapse for sure if I'm not allowed to get all this off my chest!'

'Do you mind if my wife takes notes? And I should make certain you understand that this interview is strictly unofficial. I am here only through the good offices of the Avranches police, who are allowing me to take a statement from you, because of the language barrier. I have, I repeat, no official standing.'

'I'm not worried about that. I want the police to know what happened, and I'm darned if I want some official translator taking down every word I say and maybe getting half of it wrong. But I'd like to know who I'm talking to.'

'My name is Alan Nesbitt, and this is my wife Dorothy Martin. I was a chief constable in England for some years.'

'And I was a schoolteacher in Indiana before I retired and moved to England and married Alan. So now you know where you are.' Alan handed me the notebook he had put in his pocket. I got out a pen and sat ready.

Sam ran a hand through his hair. 'Blamed if I know where to start. It's all pretty complicated.'

'How about telling us why you came to Mont-Saint-Michel?'

'I'll have to go back a ways first, I guess. I told you I live in Chicago. You know anything about Chicago?' He looked at me, and I nodded.

'I do, Mr Houston. My first husband and I used to visit the museums there often, take in the Chicago Symphony, that sort of thing.'

'Then you'd know Hyde Park.'

Alan looked a little startled, and I grinned. 'There's one in Chicago, too,' I explained. 'Only it's not a park, just a neighbourhood, near the University of Chicago. Incidentally, Barack Obama and his family lived there for years – when they weren't living at a somewhat more famous address.'

'Right,' said Sam. 'Well, that's where I live. I teach at the university. Medieval studies.'

Ah. I made a note, but didn't comment.

Sam saw my interest in my mobile face, though. 'Aha! That means somethin' to you, doesn't it? I've been readin' newspapers, as soon as they let me have 'em. I can read French, I just can't speak it worth a damn, or understand it at all. And I hear a lot of funny things have been going on around here.'

'You might say that.'

'And they all seem to have somethin' to do with the Mont. Me almost drownin' on the sands, some poor kid gettin' bonked on the head down in the sub-basement, another one fallin' off the face of the earth. Nobody seems to have a clue what it's all about.'

'We have one idea,' I said, glancing at Alan. He nodded. 'We think everything somehow has something to do with medieval manuscripts.'

'I don't know about everything, I only know about my part. I've been pretty cagey about it up till now, but I reckon it's time to come clean.' He shifted in his bed. 'Could you reach me that glass of water?'

The nurse came in. It's a pity nurses have forsaken their starched uniforms and caps, because her demeanour cried out for starch. She addressed Alan in furious tones and issued an obvious command.

Sam roared at her. I don't know how much English she

understood, but someone who spoke only Swahili could have followed the gist of his profane remarks. She retreated, very much on her dignity. Again, I lamented the lack of starch. Poor woman!

'She'll be back,' said Sam with a sigh. 'She's one of the old school.'

'You were saying,' I prompted.

'Right. Manuscripts. You've put your finger on it, ma'am. Have you ever heard of Peter Abelard?'

And there it was. The connection. But what about him? I nodded. So did Alan, We waited for Sam to continue.

'Good for you. Most people haven't, these days, and he was one of the most famous men of the twelfth century.'

'*Sic transit gloria mundi*,' murmured Alan, earning a look of surprise and respect from Sam.

'Wow. I guess English policemen are a speck better educated than the American breed. Anyway, yeah, you're right. Worldly glory passes away, all right. But I've made a specialty of him all my life; taught about him, read about him, got obsessed by him, you might say. I knew the Abbey here had once had some of his manuscripts, and I was mighty intrigued by that.'

His accent became thicker the longer he talked – and his vocabulary more colourful. You can take the boy out of Texas, I mused, but . . .

'See, Abelard was judged to be a heretic. Not by everybody, but he was tossed out on his . . . er . . . backside more than once. So it was kinda peculiar that a big, famous Abbey would set out to copy his stuff.'

He shifted again, and again I handed him the water.

'So okay, you know about the French revolution and all that. And the manuscripts all went to Avranches, and most of 'em crumbled away over the years.'

'We know most of this part of the story.' I couldn't help butting in. 'We've met a young man who volunteers up at the Abbey, who's also interested in Abelard and the manuscripts. You probably know that three of Abelard's survived. They're at the Scriptorial.'

'Yes, ma'am. But there were rumours that the Abbey

still had some, hidden away somewhere. You've been to the Abbey.'

It wasn't a question, really, but I replied, 'I have. Alan hasn't, at least not for years.'

Alan gestured with his despised cane.

'Okay, I get it. If the Abbey were in America, they would have put in an elevator years ago. ADA required.'

'Americans with Disabilities Act,' I murmured to Alan. 'Maybe not,' I went on, to Sam. 'It's a church. Churches are exempt. But we digress.'

'Okay. But anyway, you both know the place is built like a Dagwood sandwich. This stacked on top of that, stacked on top of t'other. There are layers on top of layers, built over somethin' like eleven- or twelve-hundred years. There's no tellin' what-all's under the parts tourists can see. Well, the rumours are that some manuscripts were gonna be burned hundreds of years ago when some churchman decided they weren't fit to be in an abbey. And some of the monks thought that wasn't right, so they stashed 'em away someplace safe. Wa'al, life bein' what it is, those old monks died and nobody remembered that those old books were hidden away, until just lately. Mebbe somebody found somethin' down there in the cellar. Mebbe somebody far away was cleanin' out his attic and found an old letter from one o' the monks tellin' about the whole business. Don't know. But when I started hearin' whispers about it, struck me that those lost books could likely 'a been by Abelard, cause his stuff woulda been a prime target for burnin'. So I got me a plane ticket and come to see fer m'self.'

I had something like a dozen questions I wanted to ask, but that nurse was going to come back any minute. I contented myself with making notes, hoping I could read my hurried scrawl later.

Alan said, 'And how did you come to be out on the sands that day, Mr Houston? Or is it Dr Houston?'

'Shucks, I ain't been nothin' but Sam since I was in knee pants. Yeah, I got me a few PhDs, but it don't make no never mind. I went out on those sands to get my wallet and my passport.' Suddenly most of the accent was gone. 'I was up on the ramparts, and somebody bumped against me, and they fell out of my back pocket.'

'Fell out?' Alan's voice was full of scepticism.

'Or were pulled out. I felt a bump, and then turned around and saw 'em sailin' down towards the water. I didn't think about anything but goin' after 'em, so I got down all those stairs fast as I could go, tryin' not to lose track of where they might be. Not easy when you're runnin' round 'n' round the island in circles the whole time. But I got down there and started walkin' along the rocks, close to the walls, till I reckoned I was just about underneath the tower I'd been standin' on, but my stuff wasn't there. That was when somebody called down to me from the wall. I looked up, and I couldn't see him, but he said he'd seen a wave take 'em just a minute or two before. "They can't be too far out," he said. "Just out from where you're standing."'

'And the tide was coming in.' Alan's voice was level.

'Hey, have I ever lived near an ocean? Can I tell if a tide's comin' in or goin' out? All I was thinkin' about was my passport and about a thousand euros floatin' away. So I waded out a little way, and then a little way farther, feeling around for my stuff, and the next thing I know I can't move anymore, my feet are caught, and those waves are comin' in higher and higher, and there's people yellin' at me – and then I wake up in a hospital bed feelin' like I've been to hell and back. And I'm here to tell you, whoever threw my wallet and passport down there was tryin' to kill me!'

'And who,' asked Alan, 'rescued you, and reported you as a German? And a woman?'

'*WHAT*!?'

That outraged cry brought on a coughing fit, and brought the nurse back, with a doctor in tow. They made short work of shooing us out of the room and out of the hospital, with what sounded to me like orders not to come back.

'Well!' I said when we got back to the car. 'That answered some questions, but it led to a lot more.'

'Indeed. Fortunately, now we have his story, we do have some trails to follow.'

'But I don't think they're going to let us talk to Sam again, not till he's out of the hospital.'

'And that may be soon. He's really doing much better. He's lucky to be alive, you know. I don't know how long he was under water, but the brain can't survive very long without oxygen, you know. He could easily have died, or turned into a permanent vegetable.'

'Alan!' I put a hand on his arm. 'Someone tried to kill him! What if they try again, after he gets released?'

'That's why we're going to the police station before we go back to the hotel. I need to tell them his story and suggest a guard.'

I stayed in the car while Alan went in and pleaded his case. I spent the time 'given furiously to think', as Hercule Poirot used to say.

The police could do a lot now. Someone must have seen Sam's wallet and passport go flying. Or if not, they must have seen him running down from the ramparts and out onto the rocks at the edge of the water.

Someone did see him. The one who picked his pocket and threw his possessions onto the rocks. The one who urged him out into the water, with the tide coming in. But there must, somewhere, be some person who saw that rat. Why had no one come forth?

The answer to that one was easy. Almost everyone on the Mont on any given day was a tourist. They're intent on sight-seeing and buying souvenirs, and above all, they 'don't want to get involved'. They might get tied up and miss their plane home; what a tragedy. I thought about the quarrelling couple I'd seen on the first day, with their badly-behaved children. I could imagine nothing on earth that would have made them go to the authorities, especially when those authorities didn't speak much English. 'Nothing to do with us, none of our business.' I could just hear either the man or the woman saying it.

Still, the police were going to have to try to find a witness. I wondered how hard they would try. Officers would have to be called in from a bigger force, Caen perhaps, or even Rouen. That would cost money. And, most importantly, there was the risk of offending the tourists, of creating unfavourable publicity, even a scandal. Whatever was bad for tourism was bad for the economy of the Mont, which meant the economy of the region. And what, after all, had happened? A tourist had defied all the warnings and gone wading in the bay when the tide was coming in. He'd gotten wet and taken in some water, but he was all right now. What was all the fuss about?

Maybe I was being too cynical. Maybe.

I had worked myself into a fine sulk by the time Alan came back. He was not in the best mood, either.

'Let me guess,' I said when he'd slid in behind the wheel. 'They're not very interested in Sam's story.'

'They were polite.' Alan pulled out of the parking space, nearly heading for the wrong side of the road until an angry klaxon brought him to his senses. I didn't say a word. Alan doesn't often get into a temper, but when he does, it's best to let him work himself out of it.

'They want us to deal with it,' he said when we were out of traffic and on the way back to the hotel.

'Um . . . deal with it?'

'They don't have the staff to guard Mr Houston at the hospital. Well, he'll be safe enough there, I suppose, at least as long as that nurse is on duty. I pity any malefactor who tries to cross her path. But once he's released, which will probably be tomorrow, the Avranches police want to place him in our custody.'

I opened my mouth, and closed it again. I couldn't think of a response that wouldn't make Alan even angrier. We drove another mile or two.

'The constable seems to think that we've taken Houston under our wing, so to speak. He called him our protégé.'

'Have we?'

Alan considered that for a moment and then smiled. 'Well, hang it all, I suppose we have, in a way. I was inclined to believe him. What about you?'

'I wondered for a while about that folksy-as-all-get-out accent, but I decided it was genuine. When he's under stress he reverts to the university professor. When he relaxes, the Texan comes out.'

'That really is the way Texans speak? I thought it was only in the movies.'

'No, it's real. Some of Sam's accent has been rubbed away, in fact, probably from years in Chicago, where they have their own accent. Not at the University of Chicago, though. Did you know that's one of the most highly-respected universities in America? I'm willing to bet that good ole' Sam makes a whopping big salary.'

'So you take him at face value.'

'Alan, my dearest love, after years of marriage to a cop, I've learned not to take anyone at face value. Well, hardly anyone. But yes, I think Sam's telling us the truth, and he may be the only one in this whole mess. So what does the nice policeman want us to do?'

'Keep an eye on him. Steer him away from risky situations. Though how we're to do that, he didn't specify. Above all, keep him from making a fuss that might scare away the tourists. It wasn't said overtly, but the clear subtext was, send him away.'

'Get him out of Dodge. Right. Somehow I don't think he's going to go anywhere until he's figured out who did the deed. And come to think of it, he can't go much of anywhere without a passport. Are they going to look for it, do you think, now that they know approximately where it might be?'

'I very much doubt it. Once something gets lost in the sands of the bay, it may never turn up again. And in any case—'

'Right. A massive search would be expensive, and might frighten the cash cows. Okay, so where is the guy's hotel? I forget.'

'L'Ermitage, just down the road in Beauvoir. Small, expensive. Looks luxurious; I checked it on the Net. I suspect you're right about his income.'

'Well, if we're to be his sheepdogs, he's going to have to move, or we are. And we can't afford a luxury hotel, so he'll have to deal with the way the other half lives.'

'Which isn't bad at all,' said Alan, slotting the car neatly into our reserved space in the hotel car park. 'Shall we have our nightcap at the bar, or in our room?'

'At the bar, please. I'm not in the mood for bourbon. Maybe some cognac. Or even Calvados. It's getting chilly.'

I popped upstairs to leave my purse and visit the loo. When I came down the stairs I stopped at the landing and thought about turning back. For Alan was sitting at a table with three glasses in front of him, and the man sipping at one of them was A.T. Krider.

TWENTY

Was I ready for a nice, polite little conversation with Mr Krider? I was not. I wanted to have a quiet, peaceful drink with my husband, talking about nothing important, ignoring the things we would have to do and the decisions we would have to make in the morning.

I was greatly tempted to go back up to our room and give him a call on his mobile, saying I had a headache and wouldn't be joining him after all. But there was my drink waiting for me, and the thrifty housewife in me shuddered at the wasted money. Besides, as I stood there dithering, Krider saw me, smiled broadly, and beckoned.

I said under my breath a couple of words that I don't often use, and went on down the stairs.

Alan looked at me with sympathetic understanding, but there was nothing much he could do. I sat down with a false smile pasted on my face and said, 'Mr Krider! What a nice surprise!'

He stood, along with Alan. What a polite little man. 'Well, I saw your husband sitting here all by himself and thought I'd join him. Then you coming down too made it that much better. I ordered Calvados for all of us; Alan here said you liked it, too.'

'I'm getting used to it.' The fixed smile was beginning to make my face ache. I took a sip of my firewater and decided oh, why not? 'I'm a bit surprised that you care for it. The last time I knew you to drink it, it rather did you in, didn't it? Or was it cider that time?'

'Ouch! No, it was just cider, but that stuff has a kick like a mule!'

Looking back on it, I wondered if Krider had really passed out in Avranches. Or was that just another little deception, designed perhaps to make sure Peter and I thought him somewhat ridiculous, a negligible figure?

He went on, 'I didn't cut a very impressive figure that day, did I? Helluva first impression. I'm not really much of a drinker, and that, along with some meds I was taking, knocked me flat. I'm grateful to you and Peter for rescuing me.'

'We put you in a cab headed for the railway station. I take it you decided you didn't want to go to Paris after all?'

'The fact is . . . oh, hell!' He put his glass down with a thump. Normandy's liquid gold splashed on the table. 'Look, I'm tired of telling lies. I get caught up in them, and can't remember what I've said to who, and I'm sick of it. The fact is, I'm here for a very particular reason. And a very private reason, which is why I've been stringing everybody along. Have either of you ever heard of a guy named Abelard?'

It's a good thing Calvados isn't the sort of thing one gulps, or I'd have drained my glass and asked for another. It was too much. I hadn't even begun to sort out what Sam had told us, and now here was another man telling us he was here because of a long dead heretical cleric. A *third* man, now I thought about it. That had been Peter's original story, hadn't it? Looking for missing Abelard music?

I stood. 'No, no, stay where you are, both of you. Alan, I'm really, really tired all of a sudden. I'm going to take this lovely stuff up to bed with me, and I'll bet I'll be asleep before you even come up. Nice to have seen you again, Mr Krider. Night, love.'

I suppose it was rude, but I couldn't bear to hear any more. My mind was full to the top of facts, lies, rumours, speculations, and one bombshell after another. I needed some down time, and I intended to get it, right now.

I did finish the Calvados before I hit the sack, and maybe it has some special properties that stimulate the brain. At any rate I woke up the next morning after a solid nine hours of sleep feeling energized and ready for action. At least I thought it was morning, and the bedside clock confirmed that, but there was no brilliant sunshine. In fact, it was very dark indeed.

And then for an instant there was brilliant light, followed by a long rumble of thunder. A strong gust of wind blew the curtains into the room, and when I got out of bed to go to the bathroom, my feet encountered a puddle. And oh, it was cold! I brought a towel back from the bathroom, mopped up the rainwater as best I could, and closed the window.

And where was Alan? Gone down to get some breakfast for us, no doubt. I snuggled back under the covers for warmth, and listened to the rain and the thunder, counting seconds between lightning flash and thunderclap. The storm was very close.

Alan was taking a long time with breakfast. I wanted my coffee. I could make some in the room, of course, but he'd surely be back in a minute with the real stuff.

And then I remembered. He was going to intercept Peter and take him to the Abbey, and tell him about Laurence on the way.

I got up, put on a pair of warm pants and a fleecy sweater – clothes I hadn't really expected to need in France – and went downstairs in search of breakfast.

Alan showed up before I'd finished my first cup of coffee. 'I phoned Peter to say I'd pick him up and take him to work. I didn't imagine he'd want to cycle in this weather, though the storm wasn't quite so bad then. When I got to his digs, the rain was pelting down and the lightning seemed to be everywhere at once, and they'd phoned him from the Abbey to say several tour groups had cancelled or postponed, so he wouldn't be needed until this afternoon, if then.'

'Did you get any chance to talk to him about—' I looked around and lowered my voice – 'about his friend?'

'Yes.'

'And?'

'He was upset, as you might imagine, but not really surprised. "I knew something had happened," he said, over and over. "He wouldn't have just deserted me."'

'Then why didn't he get in touch with Laurence's parents? Or the police?'

'Those are questions I want to put to him, but I'll wait a

bit. Dorothy, I still don't quite trust the lad, but I have a good deal of sympathy for him. He was truly distressed; I didn't want to push him too far until he's had a chance to deal with the information.'

The policeman with a heart of gold. I could scarcely get up and kiss him then and there, but I could give him the equivalent look. He smiled and touched my hand. Shocking display of emotion from an elderly couple in public!

I poured him some coffee and beckoned to the waiter for another pot. 'Do we have any dates? When Peter came to the Mont, I mean, and when he expected Laurence?'

'I was hoping you knew some of that, from your earlier conversations with him.'

I shook my head. 'It didn't seem important at the time, but let's see what I can remember. I first met Peter on Thursday. Goodness, was that only last week? It feels like years. He talked about Laurence then, said he'd expected him, but that he'd jumped ship. I think he said he'd heard from him about a week before that.'

'Phone call? From where?'

'No, it was an email. I remember that because Peter was peeved about it, thought it was a shabby way to treat a friend, not even giving him a chance to argue about it. And he said he'd been trying to call him, but he wasn't picking up.'

'But he didn't try to reach Laurence's parents. And he didn't call the police.' Alan took a slow sip of coffee.

'Apparently not.'

We both concentrated on breakfast for a moment or two. Then Alan pushed his plate away. 'We need to construct a timeline. That can sometimes show a pattern. And we certainly don't want to leave the hotel until the weather improves.'

'I don't know how great my memory is, but it might improve with more coffee.'

With a fresh couple of cafetières in front of us, I pulled out my notebook and pen. 'I really need something bigger, but this will have to do.' I ran a line down the page, close to the left side. 'Where do we start?'

'With the date Sam fell into the bay.'

'Let's see. I have to work back. Gilly and I left Sherebury – when?'

'On the twelfth. That was a—' he consulted the calendar on his phone – 'a Monday. Two weeks ago. Then you stayed in Paris a few days, and then went to Bayeux, and left on—'

'Wait a minute.' I dove into my purse. 'Ah. Here it is. The train ticket, which nobody bothered to collect, says "21 Mai". And that was the day I talked to Penny, and she told me about the German woman, as everyone thought then, who nearly drowned the day before. So the twentieth.' I wrote that down in the small column on the left, and 'Sam falls in' opposite it. 'I've left some space at the top, because Peter got to the Mont before that, but we don't know exactly when, do we?'

'No, but we will. You'd best leave quite a lot of space between entries, to fill in new information. So you got to the Mont on the twenty-first, a Wednesday.'

'Got to Pontorson. I didn't actually make it to the Mont until the next day, Thursday. That was when I met Peter and he told me that taradiddle about searching for manuscripts. Except it might not all have been lies. Now that we've had two other people mention Abelard, there might be something to it.'

'Agreed. Anything else for the twenty-second?'

'Not that I can think of. But the next day, a lot happened. The best was that you arrived! But that comes near the end of the day. So let me think. I tried to call Peter at the Abbey, but it was closed for the day. Then Peter called me and told me why: the injured young man. We've got to find out his name!'

'I've made a note about it. Go ahead.'

'Okay, so Peter was upset about the guy and wondered if you could come and help. I called you . . . no, first, I decided to rent a car, and met Krider, who drove Peter and me to Avranches and went with us to the Scriptorial. He seemed like a nice enough guy, but he was phony from the word go. Did I tell you what he said about his son wanting to become a Benedictine and all that nonsense?'

'Briefly, yes.'

'And how he lied about not speaking French? Well, anyway,

he went to lunch with Peter and me, and drank too much cider, and we poured him into a cab. And I kept trying to call you, and getting panicky because I couldn't reach you.'

'I was on a plane, love.'

'Yes, when I got your call from Cherbourg, Peter pointed that out and I felt like an idiot. It's just that . . .'

'I know, dear heart. I rather like it that you're concerned about me. But go on.'

'Okay, from here on it's your story as much as mine. Peter told us the injured man had disappeared from the hospital. Then he gave you his tale about what he's doing here – the second version, or third, I've lost count. And you laced into him, pretty fiercely, for you.'

'I don't like being lied to, especially when someone has asked for my help, and then hinders me at every turn. All right, so that's Friday, three days ago. Then on Saturday, Krider tells us his entertaining little tale about being a prospective novelist.'

'And we got away and got in a few hours of holiday. Alan, I want to go back to Bayeux when this is all over. It's such a neat town, and I haven't seen nearly enough of it. And you still haven't been to Gilly's show.'

'We'll do that, and I'll take you to Honfleur, which I think you'll like, and Giverny, which I know you'll love. Monet's garden, you know.' He looked at his watch. 'It's getting on for lunch time, and the rain still resembles Niagara.' He consulted his phone cum computer cum fount of all information. 'There's a full moon tonight. With all this water about, the high tide this evening might be very high indeed. It's something to see, I'm told, when it comes "galloping" in to the bay.'

I shuddered, thinking about Sam. 'I'm not sure I actually want to see it. It's sort of scary. But let's finish our timetable, and then we can decide what to do next. I can't say I'm very hungry, and I certainly don't want to go out. Okay, so we've got to Krider and his novel – fictional in every sense. After we got back from Bayeux, you find out about Sam, that he's an American man, not a German woman. We have to find out what that's all about, Alan!'

'We do. We also need to see if the police have traced that abandoned hire car.'

'And the passport, and the money. And decide what on earth we're to do with Sam when he's dumped on us. And that brings us to today.'

Alan looked out the lobby windows. 'This weather is certainly frustrating. We need to talk to a number of people and follow up a number of trails, but I'm not keen on taking a shower in my clothes.'

There was a flash of lightning, and a thunder peal sounded almost immediately.

'Gosh, that was close! Look, dear. I can only think of one productive thing we can do under the circumstances.'

'A nap?' he said hopefully.

'The elements are making too much of a racket. I couldn't sleep, let alone . . . Anyway, what I want to do is find out everything I can about Abelard. He's a major character in this mess. People have lied about him and pushed him into the background, but he keeps cropping up. What I'd like to do is find a good book about him, but that's impossible at this stage. Even if I wanted to go out in this tempest and find a library, anything they had would be in Latin, or French. But there's always—'

'The Internet!' we said together.

TWENTY-ONE

There was, we found, a good deal of information about Abelard to be found online. Alan let me use his laptop for the search; he logged on to the lobby computer that was provided for hotel guests. After about an hour, we compared notes.

'Quite a guy, this Abelard,' I commented, stretching and twisting my head around to get rid of the tension in my neck. 'From what I was able to gather, the odds were about even of his becoming Pope or being burned as a heretic.'

'I don't think they burned heretics at that stage of the game, but he was certainly convicted of heresy at least once, and excommunicated.'

'But somebody, I forget who – one of his friends – got that decision reversed. I confess I tried to figure out just what was so awful about what he taught and wrote. All that made sense to me was that he thought people should question everything about their beliefs, Let me find what I wrote down . . . ah, yes. "The key to wisdom is this: constant and frequent questioning, for by doubting we are led to question and by questioning we arrive at the truth." I can see how that might have made him unpopular with church authorities. But beyond that idea, I got totally lost. I think maybe abstruse philosophy is not my cup of tea. Speaking of which, I'm finally hungry. How about you?'

'A bit. Do we still have any cheese and biscuits, or other picnic fare?'

'A couple of biscuits, is all. I think we'll have to go downstairs and see what they have to offer.'

There wasn't a lot of choice on the menu. Lunchtime was almost over, and they were out of nearly everything, but a French cook can always whip up an omelette and some '*frites*', those skinny strips of fried potato that resemble what Americans call French fries a lot more than the English version, 'chips'.

As we were polishing off the last of the glass of white wine that accompanied our modest repast, Alan's phone rang. It was Peter. I listened in.

'They're not going to need me at the Abbey at all today. The storm's keeping everyone away. I thought I should let you know. I don't imagine you've heard any more about Laurence?'

'I'm afraid not. My English contacts will phone if they learn anything new.'

I asked Alan to give me the phone. 'Hi, Peter, it's me. Listen, Peter, do you have any books about Abelard? I mean, with you here in France?'

'Yes, of course.' He sounded puzzled and a bit wary.

'I'd like to borrow one. If there's one that uses plain English and doesn't wander off into philosophical jargon.'

'Well, he was a philosopher, you know.' Now the tone was amused.

'I thought he was a theologian.'

'Back then there wasn't a lot of difference. But I do have one book that's written for the layman, and certainly you may borrow it. Why, though?'

'Because Alan and I have trolled the Net and found a lot of information, but almost nothing that gives me a feeling of what the man was actually like. He's at the centre of what's going on here, Peter, I'm sure of it, and we want to know more about him.'

'Umm. Sure, okay. I can drop it off tomorrow if the rain tapers off.'

'Look, you're going to think I'm obsessive about this, but I really want to read it now. It's such a horrible day for doing anything outside. If I sent Alan after it, could you give it to him?'

Alan raised his eyes heavenward, and gave a meaningful look out the window, where one would not have been surprised to see an Ark under construction. Peter acquiesced, somewhat reluctantly, I thought, and we ended the call.

I thought an apology was in order. 'I'd go myself, Alan, but I'm not sure how to find the house. And I'm sorry to be so insistent about it, but something's eating at me about Abelard and the manuscripts, and I really, really need to try to track it down.'

'I know, love. The itch that must be scratched. Let me take a closer look at the weather and see what's possible.'

He left the dining area for the lounge, where the large windows would give him a panoramic view. Just as he reached the door of the room a thunder clap was followed instantly by a lightning flash, and I came to my senses. This was ridiculous! An obsession was one thing. Sending the dearest person in the world into danger was another. I went to call him back, and he met me.

'It's hopeless, darling. Between the rain and the wind and the tide, the roadway will be submerged in places. We'll have to wait out the storm. Meanwhile I'll let Peter know I'm not coming, and then we can work out what we're to do about lodging for Sam when the time comes.'

Still feeling guilty about asking Alan to risk the drive, I went out to the lobby and spoke to Jacques, the concierge. 'I hope you can do something for me. No one seems to be at the desk just now.'

Jacques gave one of those eloquent Gallic shrugs. 'No new guests will come in the storm. François, he takes a little moment for the lunch.'

I nodded. 'So maybe you can help us. Tomorrow or the next day, Alan and I are expecting a . . . a friend to come to stay with us. Is there another room for him? It will be for perhaps a week.'

Jacques was a stout man with a round, cheerful face, but now it fell. 'But, Madame, there is no room at all. The high season, it begins in two, three days. The school holidays, you comprehend. Already we have turned away many, and today more were coming, but for the storm. You and Monsieur are booked in until the middle of next week, it is understood. Your room is reserved for you. But another guest, no. I regret. I am desolated. But what will you do?'

'Oh, dear. No, I do understand. We will just have to try to find another place for our guest.'

'But Madame does *not* understand. There will be no rooms at all, anywhere. This is the time when all the world comes to the Mont. It is very good for business, but me, I do not like it. It is too busy, and the guests sometimes are rude. It is better like now, when we can talk and be friends. No?'

'Yes. Yes, much better.'

Another guest wandered up and asked Jacques something, and I turned away. Oh, dear, indeed! What on earth were we going to do with Sam? He couldn't stay here, and we certainly couldn't afford his posh hotel, pleasant though it might be.

Well, it was a change from fretting over that stupid book, anyway.

After a while I left Alan keeping an eye on the weather and plodded back up to the room to lie in bed staring out at the soggy, dispiriting world. What wouldn't I give right now to be in my own cosy parlour with a cat or two on my lap and Watson at my feet, and a nice fire crackling away, even if it was almost June?

I didn't have long to wallow in despondency. My phone rang. 'Time to surface, my love. Peter is here, and he brought the book.'

'I'll be right down.'

I gave my hair a quick brush and put my shoes back on, and picked a couple of towels in case Peter was dripping, but his rain gear was quite efficient. His sandals were wet, but as he said, they'd dry faster than closed shoes, and weren't too uncomfortable.

'I think you're very brave! I didn't expect you until the storm passed.'

'A tourist in the B & B next door needed to catch a train, so his host gave me a ride.'

'We're having coffee,' said Alan. 'Same for you?'

What I really wanted was about a gallon of hot tea, but I wasn't at all sure what tea would be like in a French hotel. I decided not to chance it. 'Sure. But not espresso. *Café au lait.*'

'I brought you the book, Dorothy. It's not exactly light summer reading.' He reached into his backpack and brought out a heavy bundle wrapped in a plastic bag. 'I'd like it back when you've finished.'

'Oh, my. Well, I doubt I'll get all the way through it, but thank you. It's plainly a lot more comprehensive than Wikipedia.'

Both the men laughed, but Peter looked a little shocked. 'Um . . . I'm afraid . . . that is, you do know that . . .'

'That Wikipedia can't always be taken as gospel. Yes, I do know, and if I were doing serious research I'd turn elsewhere. But for a cursory overview of a subject, it isn't bad, especially if you look pretty closely at the references cited in the articles.' I had unwrapped Peter's book as I spoke. 'This one was cited a number of times, which gives me a useful cross-check. Thank you, Peter. I'll treat it with great care and make sure you get it back.' I put it back in its plastic bag and laid it on the spare chair at our table.

'Peter and I had a little chat while we waited for you,' said Alan, his voice so carefully casual that all my senses went on high alert. 'You know we both wondered, you and I, why he didn't call either the police or Laurence's parents when he seemed to disappear.'

I haven't seen anyone blush for years, but Peter went red from his neck to the roots of his blond hair. 'I said I'd rather talk about it when you were here, Dorothy. That way I'd only have to say it once.' He took a deep breath. 'The truth is, I've never got on well with Laurence's parents. He . . . they still treat him like a child. He's twenty-four, the same age as me, but they keep him in leading strings. He spends almost all his holidays at home, and his mother wants to know every move he makes.'

'He's an only child?' I asked.

'Yes. There were an older brother and sister, but they drowned one summer. The family were in Antibes for a holiday. They're not short of a penny, that family. The kids got bored, so they went for a swim and never came back. It was weeks before their bodies turned up, so of course their mum and dad were frantic. Laurence was home with a nanny, or he probably would have died, too.'

'One can understand why that might make his parents a bit over-protective,' said Alan.

'Yes, and I get that. But he's not a kid now, and they still try to keep him wrapped in cotton wool. I was really surprised when he said he would come here to work with me. I thought Mummy dear would invent some reason he had to stay with her, not go off to some scary foreign town.' His voice was full of sarcasm. 'So when he sent me that note, I just assumed he had succumbed to his mother's wishes, and I was furious. When he didn't respond to emails or phone calls, I just got more and more angry for a while, but then I began to get worried. But I didn't want to talk to his parents. I knew his mother would fly into hysterics, and it would somehow be my fault that he'd vanished. So . . .'

'I see. So you've defended your decision not to notify his parents.' I wasn't happy with Peter just now, and my voice reflected my feelings. 'And precisely why did you not go to the police, once Laurence's absence became prolonged?'

Peter looked around the room. It was half empty and rather quiet, except for the steady drumming of the rain. He swallowed hard and lowered his voice to a thread.

'You see – that is, I'm not sure – it's possible that some of the things Laurence and I planned to do . . . well, they might not be considered quite . . . in short, the police might—'

'Oh, for heaven's sake, Peter, spit it out! You and Laurence are – or were – involved in something illegal.'

He put a finger to his lips. 'No! Not exactly illegal. Or at least . . .' He hesitated.

'Perhaps,' said Alan, getting to his feet, 'it would be better to continue this conversation in a more private place.' He nodded toward the stairway. 'I'll join you in a moment.'

Our room was small, but with a little care it could accommodate three people. I arranged the two chairs for Alan and me. Peter could sit on the bed or the luggage stand. Neither would be particularly comfortable. Pity.

When Alan came in, he was accompanied by a waiter, who put a tray on the table. A bottle of white wine, glasses, little bowls of snacks.

'If I'm to hear a confession, I require some sustenance,' said Alan. 'Perhaps we all could use a little something. Peter, I've no wish to turn this discussion into an interrogation, which is why I'm keeping it informal. But I must remind you that I'm still a sworn police officer, though retired and out of my jurisdiction. If you tell me anything that requires police attention, I am in conscience bound to report it to the authorities in Avranches. Understood?'

'Understood, sir.'

'Good. Hand me your glass.'

I wasn't sure I was quite ready to treat Peter like a friend, but Alan had a point. An informal discussion was more appropriate at this point than a grilling. I held out my own glass to be filled, and helped myself to a handful of little crunchy things. I wasn't sure what they were, but they looked and smelled good.

'Right,' said Alan. 'The floor is yours.'

Peter put his glass down. 'I'm not eager to talk about any of this, but I have realized that I must. As you have guessed, Dorothy, it's all about Abelard and his works.'

'Deduced,' I murmured. I think only Alan heard me; he gave me a little private smile.

'Most of what I've told you both is true. Abelard really did write a number of songs. There are references to them in too many original documents for that not to be a fact. It is also a fact that we don't know what happened to them, apart from a handful of hymns that have survived.'

'Various Internet sites say that some of his work was burned as heretical,' I put in. 'Could that have happened to the songs? The love songs, especially, must have annoyed the authorities, if they were written when both Abelard and Héloïse were in holy orders.'

'No, they were written earlier. But secular music of any kind was held in low regard in twelfth-century Europe, at least by the Church. And you have to remember that, back then, the Church had enormous power, far more than the monarchies that nominally ruled the various states. Yes, the songs probably contributed to the rancour some of the churchmen felt for Abelard. But the real troubles of his life, the "calamities" he catalogued in his autobiography, his serious brushes with authority, came later than the love songs. It's most unlikely they were burned.'

'But you don't know that for certain,' Alan said.

'We know nothing about them for certain, except that they existed.'

'Peter, I'll know when I dig into your book, but where did Abelard live? In Paris?'

'He moved around a lot, often fleeing from persecutors, though sometimes from situations that were simply uncongenial. He compared himself to the "peripatetics" – the students of Aristotle.' Peter raised an eyebrow; Alan and I nodded our understanding.

'He was born in Brittany, not far from here, and later in his life was the abbot of a monastery called Saint-Gildas, again in Brittany. You know Mont-Saint-Michel is right on the border between the two regions, Normandy and Brittany?'

Again Alan nodded. I hadn't known, but in view of Abelard's travels, I was interested.

'And we know the Abbey here had copies of Abelard's works, even though he was regarded with suspicion in many quarters. That suggests a liberal bent among the abbots here.

So it seemed to us, Laurence and me, that it was entirely possible that they had once had copies of some of his music, the hymns at least, and maybe, possibly, some of the other music.'

'And why was that so important to you?' Alan asked gently.

'I'm a student of music and theology. Laurence is a medievalist. None of those fields promise anything very lucrative in the way of a career. But if we could discover a lost Abelard work, our names in academia would be made! We could get good positions at any university in the Western world. It would be a dream come true!'

'And where does the illegal part come in?' I asked. The wine had mellowed my mood a little, but I still wasn't inclined to let Peter off the hook until he'd come clean.

'We were convinced that if we could work out the right place to look, we'd find something here at the Mont. If not at the Abbey, perhaps in a cellar in one of the houses, or even at the Scriptorial, though that was a long shot. It's a museum. Everything they have has been carefully scrutinized and catalogued to a fare-thee-well. Still, it was just within the bounds of possibility that there might be a palimpsest that had been reused. You know what a palimpsest is?'

This time neither of us nodded.

'It's a sheet of parchment that has been scraped or washed clean of whatever was written on it, so it could be used again. With the right techniques, the original writing can sometimes be read.'

'I would imagine that involves destruction of whatever was written on top of it.'

'Not nowadays. There are all sorts of techniques for bringing up the earlier image. The whole idea is a very long shot, though, because by the twelfth century very few parchments would have been re-used. They might unearth some ancient sheet that nobody could read or care about, and clean it and use it, but it's most unlikely that something would be cleaned just because it was deemed heretical. It might be burned, or more likely just stuffed away someplace, for later use if it became necessary. Because by the end of the century, paper was coming in, and as it was far cheaper than parchment, parchment was used less and less.'

'Peter.' My schoolteacher persona was coming to the fore. 'All this is very instructive, but you've taken us off on a tangent. I want to know what you and Laurence were proposing to do that was illegal.'

'Not illegal, exactly. Just a bit dodgy. We were pretty sure we could find something. And if we didn't, we were going to claim we did.'

'But you'd have to produce it!'

'That's where we come to the dodgy bit. We know – well, Laurence knows – an expert in illumination.'

'So you were going to forge a manuscript.'

'Only if we couldn't find a real one.'

'You couldn't hope to get away with it, you know,' said Alan. 'Modern dating methods would give you away in five minutes.'

'This chap has old parchment. I don't know where he gets it. I don't want to know. He makes the inks according to the old formulae. He copies the style impeccably. He ages the things somehow; again, I don't even want to know how. As for getting away with it – he has done. Several times of late.'

TWENTY-TWO

'The trickle of manuscripts coming on the market!' I smacked my head.

'I remind you again, Peter,' said Alan in a voice so cold I almost didn't recognize it, 'that I am a policeman. Are you confessing to being an accessory to art fraud?' His genial, 'informal' manner had vanished.

'There has been no fraud, sir. There is no law in any country in the world against selling original works of art, unless they are represented as being something other than what they are. And Laurence says his friend has been very careful to make no claims about their age or provenance.'

'So Laurence has been involved in this scheme as well?'

'He . . . has had some involvement with the marketing in this part of the world. His friend lives in New York.'

'Peter, you are a student of theology. Perhaps what your pals have been doing isn't strictly illegal, but can you possibly be comfortable with the morality of their actions?' I was aware as I said it that I sounded like a self-righteous old biddy. Tough. Someone needed to call him to account. What I felt like doing was weeping. I had liked Peter, and I was appalled by what he was telling us.

Peter squirmed. 'I don't see anything so terrible about it. They're selling what people want to buy. It's not as if it were drugs, or stolen jewellery, or guns. A manuscript can do no harm to anyone. And the dealers who buy them, if they know anything at all about art, know perfectly well that the pieces aren't genuinely old artefacts. They're nothing like expensive enough, for one thing.'

'And those who buy from the dealers? Are they aware that they are buying modern reproductions?' Alan fixed Peter with a cold eye.

He shrugged. 'That's up to the dealers, isn't it? Laurence isn't responsible for their actions.'

'Oh, Peter! It's the cynical old argument. The Nazis were fond of it. "I didn't know what would happen, did I? I was just acting under orders. I didn't personally hurt anyone. Nothing to do with me."' I stopped talking, afraid that if I kept my mouth open I was going to be sick.

'I'll need the name of your confederate.' Alan picked up his notebook.

'I don't know his name. Laurence thought it was safer that way.'

'I see. Another proof that you both knew perfectly well that what you were proposing to do was a bit more than "dodgy", as you put it. I'm going to have to report this to the authorities, you know.'

'But it's not illegal!'

'Probably not. Not yet. But the fact that he has been engaged in activities that are dubious, at best, puts an entirely new face on Laurence's disappearance. It may be deliberate. It may not.'

'And I,' I said, 'am going to phone Penny and Gilly.'

Alan nodded approval. Peter looked confused. 'Who are they?' he asked.

'Penny is a good friend and an artist,' I said. 'It was she who told us about the manuscripts that had suddenly appeared on the market. She knows a good many people in the art world. And Gilly, Gillian Roberts, is a young sculptor who is beginning to make a name for herself. She has an exhibition in Bayeux right now, though she's gone back home to Shærebury. That's why we came to France, actually. Between the two of them, word will spread very quickly to the art world about this scam. For scam it is, and you know it perfectly well.'

Peter looked away.

'And there's one thing you and Laurence hadn't considered. Once the word got out – and it would have got out sooner or later, even without Alan and me – you wouldn't have a chance of passing off an Abelard manuscript as genuine.' I paused for a moment and then delivered the final blow. 'Even if it was.'

The storm had stopped while we were talking. I hadn't noticed; I doubt the others had, either. Peter murmured something and left the room looking like a whipped puppy, his tail between his legs.

'How will he get home?'

'On his feet, I presume,' said Alan. 'It's not far. At this moment I don't particularly care.' He sat down on the bed.

I said nothing. I was already beginning to have mixed feelings about the conversation.

'He's not to be pitied, Dorothy. He's a manipulative, deceptive young ass, and he deserved to be treated sternly.'

'Yes.' I said it without enthusiasm.

'You don't like being lied to. Neither do I.'

'No.' I busied myself with tidying up the almost-untasted snacks and wine.

'Dorothy, stop fussing and sit down.' He patted the bed next to him. I sat. 'That frustrated maternal instinct is coming out, isn't it?'

'I suppose. I just wonder if we were too hard on him. I

know he deserved it, but . . . oh, darn it all, I liked him. And I guess I still do, in spite of everything. But I'm terribly, terribly disappointed in him.'

'And angry.'

'And angry,' I admitted. 'And still wondering what all the other strange things have to do with his nasty little scheme.'

'Well, it's easy enough to see they all have to do with purported lost manuscripts by Abelard. I think we can now assume the young man who was hurt was down in the lower reaches of the Abbey looking for them. We know Sam was looking for them. And you left last night before Krider could expound on what he said, but it turns out he, too, had heard rumours about Abelard manuscripts hidden around the Mont.'

'You know, I've been wondering. Is it even remotely possible that Krider is in fact Laurence's mysterious friend? He lives in America. He's been studying calligraphy and the like. He's lied to us about quite a lot of things. What if he's much more adept at creating manuscript copies than he's led us to believe?'

'He doesn't live in New York.'

'Not according to what he told us.'

Alan shrugged. 'Anything's possible, I suppose. But I don't believe it. For one thing, he's the wrong sort of age to have befriended a man the age of Laurence. For another, it would be the height of folly for him to come here to the Mont and make himself conspicuous if Peter's scheme was about to come to fruition.'

'Yes. You're right. I'm not thinking clearly. Peter upset me. Let's go down and get something to eat, and then do you suppose there are any TV channels that carry English-language programming? Or even subtitles? I want to watch something absolutely mindless.'

'First I need to put in a call to Derek, and then to the authorities in Avranches. Peter's story has thrown a spanner into several different sets of works.'

It wasn't until I had eaten supper and was having coffee and Calvados (for which I was rapidly developing a taste) that I remembered to tell Alan about the hotel situation.

'Hmm,' he said. 'Another spanner. I've no idea what we're

to do with the chap, in that case. Henri didn't mention him this evening, so I assume—'

'Henri? Who's Henri?'

'The great panjandrum of the police at Avranches. I forgot to ask him about Sam. We were rather occupied with annoyance over Peter and his activities. But I imagine he would have told me if Sam were being released from hospital any sooner than tomorrow morning.'

'Well, we have our room for another few days, but I'm darned if I'm going to let Sam sleep on a cot in there. There isn't room, aside from any other considerations. I had thought, earlier when Jacques first told me, about asking Peter if there was any room in his lodgings, but I'm in no mood right now to ask Peter for any favours.'

'Not to mention the fact that Peter is right in the middle of the Abelard conspiracy, and might well have had something to do with Sam's . . . shall we call it an accident?'

'I'd call it attempted murder, but I don't honestly see Peter stooping to that. He's a man with a monomania, and he's not above pulling an elaborate scam. I think he might in the end have convinced himself that he really had found one of Abelard's songs. I suppose he's studied enough music to come up with something that Abelard might conceivably have written. But he'd draw the line at physical violence.'

'There was no actual violence involved in Sam's near-drowning. It was Sam himself who walked out into the rising tide.'

'Still. I know Peter's a liar, though not a very good one, and his views about the limits of legality are pretty flexible, but I truly can't see him as a murderer.'

Alan sighed. 'You're probably right. But who, then, enticed Sam onto the sands and into the bay?'

And to that I had no answer.

We were not successful in finding any television programming that I could follow. Alan offered, with a twinkle in his eye, to translate word-for-word any material I cared to watch, but I turned him down. I searched the shelves in the lounge, where books that guests had left behind were set out in no particular order. Most of them were in French, reasonably enough. I thought about trying to pick my way through a French translation of an Agatha Christie I knew practically by heart, but decided that sounded too much like work.

'Oh, well,' I said to Alan with a sigh, 'there's always Peter's book about Abelard. I'm not nearly as eager to read it as I was, now that Peter's told us a lot of what I wanted to know, but it might send me to sleep.'

'If the Calvados doesn't do it.'

So I propped myself up on pillows on the bed, adjusted the reading lamp, and began to read about the most famous man of the twelfth century, or so the author of the book claimed.

I found it actually to be pretty good reading. Abelard truly was a fascinating man, full of contradictions, a man both of his time and wildly far in advance of it, a man both pious and vigorously secular. I was just getting to a treatise about his philosophy, which I couldn't follow, when Alan's phone rang. It was on the bedside table, closer to me, so I picked it up and handed it to Alan.

'Yes. Yes? I see.' A longish pause.

I'd given up on Abelard for the time being, so I tried without much luck to hear the other half of the conversation.

'Let me ask my wife, and I'll ring you back.' He ended the call and gave me a look I couldn't interpret. 'That was Sam. He's being released first thing tomorrow, and he's made rather an extraordinary offer. The police have told him they wanted someone to stay with him. "Play nursemaid" was the way he put it. He has a suite at his elegant hotel – a two-storey suite, no less – and he wonders if we would care to share it. Quite private, we'd be, according to him, and he's prepared to deal with all expenses.'

'But Alan, it's the answer! I'll actually be sorry to leave here – everyone's been so nice – but we can't have Sam here, so going to him is really the only way. Call him back and say yes.'

'We may have to pay for the rest of the time we've booked here.'

'That doesn't matter, since we'll be riding on Sam's ticket for that time. And anyway, I'll bet they won't make us pay.

From what Jacques told me, they're turning people away every day. They'll be glad to get rid of us and rent the rooms to someone else at the high season rate.'

'You may be right. I'd best dress and go down and tell them. They'll be more amenable if I deal with it in person, I suspect.'

'Yes, turn on the charm, dear. It's a pity the staff are almost all men.'

He ignored that and had started pulling on his pants when his phone rang again. 'Get that, would you, darling?'

My 'hello' was greeted with a spate of agitated French. I handed the phone to Alan.

This time his side of the conversation was even less enlightening, and of course there was no point in even trying to hear the voice at the other end.

'*Pas ce soir, Monsieur. Ah, oui. D'accord. À demain.*' He ended the call.

'I got that part, I think. Something about not this evening, but tomorrow? What's happening tomorrow?'

'The man injured at the Abbey is conscious, and wants to talk. His name, by the way, is Bruce Douglas. His parents are with him right now, but as he's so much better, they're going back home tomorrow, so Henri and I are going to have a conversation with him in the afternoon.'

'Good. That gives us the morning to move to our posh new abode. I sure wish I could go with you to hear what Henri has to say.'

'But of course you'll come with me? Why not?' He tucked in his shirt and buckled his belt.

'Because, dear heart, I'll be babysitting.' He looked blank. 'With Sam. On whom we're supposed to be keeping a close eye, remember?'

He rolled his eyes. 'If this business gets any more complicated, I'm going to fly back to Sherebury and take you with me, and devil take the hindmost!'

'Yes, dear. Don't slam the door on your way out.'

TWENTY-THREE

The management gave no trouble about our early departure. They were indeed glad to be able to get a higher rate for our room, now that the influx of tourists was about to begin, and said so, all the while assuring us that they would miss us, that we were most welcome to return any time, that we had been delightful and honoured guests. So it was with expressions of mutual esteem that we got ourselves out of the hotel the next morning and headed for the hospital to pick up Sam.

'I hope he's informed l'Ermitage about having us in his suite,' I said as we set out. 'Because if they kick up a fuss, we're homeless.'

'He strikes me as an efficient sort of chap. I'm sure we'll be all right.'

The morning was one to make a person glad she's alive. I won't describe it, because all the beautiful-day words have become clichés. Just picture your idea of absolutely perfect weather, and there you have it.

The storm had washed everything clean. It had also filled the rivers and streams with a rushing torrent of water. I looked toward the bay before Alan turned inland. The tide was high and turbulent, crashing against the rocks at the base of the Mont. I thought about Sam's fate if he'd fallen into a sea like today's. He'd have had no chance at all.

I looked away, toward the sheep grazing peacefully in the salt meadows.

Sam was waiting for us at the hospital door, looking hale and hearty and, as I had suspected, brawny. The starchy nurse was there, too, distributing her disapproval equally between Sam and us. He was in a wheelchair, but he sprang out of it to meet us, and further enraged the nurse by giving her a robust smack on one cheek. 'Thanks, darlin', for takin' such good care of me!'

We got him out of there before the nurse could have a stroke.

'She needs to watch her blood pressure, for sure,' said Sam when he was comfortably installed in the back seat. 'Needs to take life a little easier. I tried to tell her, but she doesn't speak English, and my French . . . well—'

'About like mine, I expect. Sam, your clothes seem to have survived the bay remarkably well.' He was dressed in clean jeans and a plaid shirt.

'Nah, they were pretty well done for, the other nurse told me, the friendly one. Actually, she showed 'em to me. They'd run 'em through the hospital laundry, but they were pretty much rags. When I was sittin' up and takin' notice, I called the hotel, and they ran over a few things for me.'

'Speaking of hotel,' said Alan, 'you'll have to show me where we're going. And do they know we're coming, too?'

'They do, and I haven't got any idea where we're going. You gotta remember I was out of it when they brought me here. But I've got the directions right here on my GPS.'

He handed his phone to me, and since the voice spoke in English (technology can be wonderful – when it isn't driving you crazy), we got to the hotel quite easily.

It was a new experience for me. I've never lived in poverty, but never in the lap of luxury, either. We were greeted at the door, Sam with great warmth and anxious enquiries about his health, Alan and me with courteous hospitality. Our car was taken away and parked, our bags brought to the room. Rooms, rather. A ground floor room was furnished beautifully as a sitting room, and a lovely curved staircase led to the bedroom upstairs. 'Only one bathroom, I'm afraid,' said Sam apologetically. 'And the extra bed is a sofa bed down here.' He gestured. 'But seeing as how you folks are my guard dogs, I'm gonna sleep here and give you the big bed upstairs.'

We both protested, but Sam was adamant. 'Looky here, now. This is a big imposition for you two. I know that. I know you'd rather be in your own cosy room at the other hotel. And Dorothy, ma'am, I've got an aunt about your age, and I hope you don't mind my talkin' about it, but she has to get up a lot in the night, and I don't reckon you'd want to be climbin' those steps three, four times in the middle of the night. And that's a king-size bed up there, better for two people, and I can manage just fine on this one. So I'm sleepin' down here, and that's all there is to it.'

Alan nodded his head in reluctant concession. 'But since you'll be downstairs alone here, mind you keep the door locked. And if you have to go out, tell one of us, and we'll go with you.'

'You all really think somebody's out to get me?'

'We think,' I said firmly, 'that your adventure at the Mont was an attempt at murder.'

Alan added, 'God knows I'd rather the police were keeping a guard on you. But I know all about staffing problems; they're a part of police life everywhere. They don't have the personnel to do it, so they've drafted me.'

'And me,' I added.

'And Dorothy.' Alan smiled.

'Well, ma'am, it's not that I'm not grateful, but—'

Alan didn't let him finish. 'My wife is quite an efficient deputy, Sam, though you mightn't think it to look at her.'

I glowered at him.

He grinned and went on. 'She's also quite touchy on the subject of being protected because she's a woman, as I've learned over the years. I owe quite a few of these grey hairs to her habit of getting into tight spots.'

'And I always got out again, so there!'

Alan rolled his eyes at that.

I ignored him. 'Anyway, Sam, I don't do it on purpose. It's just that, when I see a possibility of finding out something useful, I don't always consider the consequences. Or rather, I'm always sure I'll be all right.'

Alan's response to that would have been a snort, if he hadn't been such a gentleman.

Sam had been looking from one of us to the other, his face growing more and more troubled.

'I sure don't want to put anyone in any danger—' he began, but Alan interrupted.

'Sam, it's not you that's creating the danger. I won't pretend it doesn't exist, but Dorothy and I are confident that you are a victim rather than a villain in the case. We've been delegated the job of protecting you from further harm.'

'And to do that, Sam, we're going to stick with you like ticks on a hound.' That homely simile brought a smile.

'We're also going to ask you a lot of questions,' said Alan. 'That is properly the job of the police, but what with the language problem and the dearth of personnel, I might as well start the process. I'd have to serve as translator in any case. So I'd suggest we find a meal somewhere and then return here to start trying to work out what the—'

'Sam Hill,' I suggested.

'—is going on here.'

We had a pleasant lunch at a nearby restaurant. The prices, as we'd come to expect in this area, were high, but Sam insisted on paying, so I mentally shrugged and ordered what I wanted. We shared a bottle of white burgundy (Sam's tastes belied his folksy persona) and went back to the hotel in a mellow mood.

Alan's eyes had surveyed the area all through the meal and our walk back. He'd looked so much like a Secret Service operative guarding the President that I'd had to stifle giggles. He'd apparently seen nothing to disturb him, though, and we got to our suite unscathed.

'Now, Sam. I may get a call soon. You are aware of the man injured at the Abbey, not long after your . . . incident?'

'Heard somethin' about it. Not much.'

'Well, he's English, for a start, and he's very much better and wants to talk about what happened. And *as* he's English, the Avranches police have invited me to be present at the interview, which they hoped would take place this afternoon. So let's accomplish as much as we can now, before I have to leave. For a start, I want you to tell me every single thing you can remember about the time of your "accident".'

I could hear the quotation marks, and evidently Sam could, too, because he made no objection. He settled back in the very comfortable chair and folded his hands in his lap. 'Not a day I'm wild about rememberin', but I'll do my best. I went up there on the ramparts—'

'No, sorry, I want you to begin at the beginning. When did you arrive at the Mont?'

'Two days before. That'd be . . . let's see, now . . .'

Alan was consulting the calendar on his phone. 'Eighteenth May. A Sunday. Right?'

'Right. Yeah, I fell in on the Tuesday, so you're right.'

'How did you arrive? That is, by car or train?'

'Car. I'd gotten in to Paris that morning, and I was tired and anxious to get to my bed. The train service isn't so great on a Sunday, so I'd arranged for a car and driver to get me here. I wasn't sure I could handle driving myself in a foreign country. Didn't think I could read the road signs. So I got the guy to drive me here, right here to this hotel. Nice guy. Even spoke pretty good English.'

'Did you talk to him at all about why you were coming to Mont-Saint-Michel?'

'Nope. Once I got into that nice comfy car I was out like a light, and I didn't wake up till the driver woke me.'

'You had arrived here at the hotel?'

'Not quite. We were on the road, and the driver thought I'd like to see the Mont. "Rising out of the sea", he said, and I mean to tell you! There's nothin' on our side of the Atlantic like that!'

I felt as proud as if I, personally, had built the Abbey. 'It really is something, isn't it? America has its own spectacular beauties, of course, but this . . .'

'Sorta gets you in the gut, don't it? Sorry, ma'am, that's vulgar, but—'

'But that is exactly where it gets you. I agree. Sorry, darling. I interrupted.'

Alan shook his head, somewhat impatiently. 'Yes. Well. Let's get on. So who did know your purpose for this visit? Your family, I presume.'

Sam shook his head. 'Don't have a family. My wife died a few years ago, and we never had kids.'

My sympathy welled up for the man, childless as I had been childless. And that might explain his near-obsession with the Middle Ages and Abelard. A man has to devote his passion somewhere, and with no family . . . That idea passed through my mind and out the other side.

'Your colleagues, then? Or friends?'

He gave a little laugh, more of a snort. 'Maybe you don't understand about academic competition, Mr . . . Alan. A professor who gets a brilliant idea about somethin' in his field doesn't talk about it to everybody he knows. Even when you're doin' pretty well, you hold your cards close to your chest.'

'Surely you have tenure, Sam?' I put in.

'Sure I do. Still got ambition, don't I? You know how it is in America, Dorothy. Everybody wants to be the first, the best, the biggest. I'd be the brightest bulb in the medieval chandelier if I could find an undiscovered Abelard manuscript!'

I exchanged a glance with Alan. Some things, it seemed, were universal.

Alan's phone rang. He looked at the displayed number, sighed, and answered the call. The conversation was brief.

'That was the police. They want me to come talk to Mr Douglas. I wish you could come, too, love, but . . .'

'But I need to stay here with Sam. Don't worry, dear. Tell me all about it when you get back. Oh, and give the poor man my best wishes, and tell him I really hope he's feeling much better.'

'You know the guy?' asked Sam when Alan had left. There was a hint of suspicion in his voice.

'Not at all. I know very little about him. But he's had an awful time, and I'm sorry for him.'

'Okay, right. Sorry if I sounded kinda . . . but there's been too much funny stuff goin' on around here. I guess I don't trust much of anybody.'

'Very wise of you. We'll establish a friendly, mutual mistrust between the two of us, shall we?'

He started to laugh at that, and that brought on a cough that sounded a bit alarming, and by the time I'd administered sympathy and a glass of water and phoned room service for bottles of both cognac and Calvados, we had both forgotten the 'mistrust' part. Or at least, it had retreated to a shadowy background.

'Now, ma'am,' he said as he sat back, exhausted from the coughing fit, 'how did you and your husband come to be messed up in all this? I know your husband's a cop, and all, but what about you?'

'Alan is not exactly a cop anymore. He used to be a chief constable – that's sort of like a county sheriff in America – but he's been retired for a while now. Of course he's still interested in crime, in all kinds of nefarious doings really, and with the police force here so badly understaffed, and with his French so good, he was glad to lend a hand, and they were glad to accept his help.'

'And you're his sidekick.'

'Sort of.' I wasn't in the mood to get into the long explanation of my gradual evolution into a kind of American-born Miss Marple.

'Okay, but what I really meant was, how'd you find yourself in this particular problem? All the goin's on at the Mont, I mean.'

'Happenstance. Alan and I can't seem to take a vacation these days without something cropping up. What interests me a good deal more is how you came to be here. I know, I know, you're a medievalist and you came here to look for Abelard manuscripts. You said there were rumours about the possibility of finding some here. I'd love to know about those rumours. Where did they come from? Who started them?'

'Hmm. Who told me?' He thought back. 'Don't think it was one of the faculty. They'd keep a thing like that to themselves, y'know? So it musta been a student.' I could see him running through a roster of students in his head. 'Not one of my doctoral students; I'd remember that.' He thought some more and smacked his forehead. 'Got it! I had to teach an intro history section last semester. The whole history faculty has to be in the rotation, and my turn came up. Most of 'em hate it, but I don't mind. Sometimes a kid'll come along knowin' next to nothin' about history, and you can get him turned on, y'know? That almost makes up for readin' a whole lot of terrible essays. So we were givin' the Middle Ages a once-over-lightly, and this kid comes up to me and says he's been readin' a little about Abelard. Well, that got my attention, seein' as how he's my favourite boy, and most undergrads've never heard of him.'

'Most people, period,' I interjected. 'In America, anyway.'

'Lady, you ain't just whistlin' Dixie! So when this kid tells me he's been readin' about the old boy, I'm pretty happy about it, and I tell him so. So then he says, "You know about the music he wrote?" and I says I do, wonderin' what's comin' next, y'know? And that's when he says somebody told him they'd heard there might still be some, hidden away in France somewhere. "Mount San Michelin, or somethin' like that," he says. And that's when I started plannin' this trip.'

'On the unsupported word of an undergraduate you didn't know well.'

'Didn't know, period. It's one of those big lecture classes, maybe three hundred students. But I found out his name and looked him up. He was gettin' along okay in the class, and in his other classes. No Phi Beta Kappa, y'know, but a decent student, and never been in trouble, at least that the university knew about. So I reckoned there might be somethin' in it, and I started nosin' around. See, I was really excited about the possibilities, but I'm not stupid enough to jump in with both feet until I figure I maybe know what I'm doin'.'

'No, I wouldn't have said you were stupid. Impulsive, maybe.'

'Yeah, but I can hold myself back when I need to. So, anyway, I know a couple of guys in the music department, and I invite 'em out for a beer and start talkin', just casual-like, y'know. How come there hadn't been any concerts of ancient music lately, or even Renaissance? I ask. And after a lot of talk about there's not a whole lot of good medieval music around, and it's hard to perform it right on modern instruments, and the audience is pretty sparse anyway, I make 'em an offer. "You put together a concert of the best medieval music you can find, and I'll tell my students they all have to come and bring a friend. That'll give you enough to fill that new little recital hall. I don't s'pose anybody's found anything new lately, have they? Some mouldy old twelfth-century chant lyin' around in somebody's attic, or somethin'?" I says. And ma'am, I'll tell you they both went so quiet I thought I'd gone deaf.'

'Hmm. Interesting. And Sam, I do wish I could get you to

call me Dorothy. In these parts – well, in England, anyway – "Ma'am" is the way you address the queen.'

He gave a seated bow. 'Your Majesty. You know, in Texas we call any lady ma'am. But I'll try to remember. Anyway, I knew that minute, when they couldn't think what to say, that they'd heard the rumours, too. And these guys really know about music.'

He casually mentioned a couple of names I'd been hearing for years; I owned some of their recordings. I hope I didn't look as impressed as I felt. I wanted to try to keep control of this conversation. 'So that was when you decided in earnest to come over and see for yourself?'

'Yes, ma— Dorothy. I brushed up on what I knew about the Abbey and got me a plane ticket and a hotel reservation.'

'And what did your colleagues think about this sudden whim?'

'I'm the head of the department. I can pretty much do what I please. And I didn't have any classes or seminars this summer, so it didn't matter.'

I continued with the matter at hand. 'Sam, there's one thing that still puzzles me. No, two. Your story hangs together and makes sense, right up to the point when someone tried to kill you. But then there's a detail that doesn't make sense at all. When the news reports about your accident – yes, I know, but we'll call it that for lack of a better word – when the news came out, you were identified as a "German woman". Of course the minute you landed in the hospital they got your gender straightened out, but since you couldn't talk and had no identification, your nationality was still in question. Do you have any idea how that odd mistake could have happened?'

'Ma'am—'

'Dorothy.'

'Dorothy, I ain't got no more idea than a new-born dogie! Do I look like a woman? Do I sound like a German? When your man said that to me in the hospital, it made me so mad – well, you were there. Guess I upset that nurse some.'

'I guess you did.' We both smiled at the memory. 'But to answer you, no, you certainly don't look like a woman. I suppose it's just barely possible that English spoken with a Texas accent might sound like German to a Frenchman, though it doesn't seem likely. So that suggests to me that someone misidentified you on purpose.'

'Why?'

I shrugged. 'It must have been the person who rescued you who gave the media the wrong information. And you don't know who that was, right?'

'I was plumb outta this world when they saved me. And woulda been for good if they hadn't, so the doctors told me. It was a mighty close shave.'

'And you might have had permanent brain damage even then. So you're really lucky. Well, the police will presumably know who fished you out of the drink, so we'll have to shelve that one for a little while. The other thing I wondered about was the car.'

'What car?'

'A car was abandoned in the big parking lot, the one where the shuttles start. It was there for several days, and when the police checked it out and discovered it had been rented by someone from Germany, they assumed it was yours.'

'Like I said, I got a car and driver in Paris, or at the airport, anyway. Sent him back once he'd delivered me here. I reckoned I could get a cab to take me from here to the shuttle stop, and if I wanted to go somewhere else, there'd be a way to get there.'

I sighed. 'So we don't know any more about the car, or the misidentification, or . . . or anything, really. Every thread seems to lead either nowhere, or into a worse tangle.'

'Dorothy, I've been doin' some thinkin', and I'll tell you what's got me bamboozled. These attacks, the one on me and the one on that poor kid at the Abbey. They were nasty and all, but neither of us died. I might've, except somebody rescued me. That boy might've, only somebody found him in time. So I'm thinkin' maybe we weren't intended to be killed, only roughed up some. Maybe enough that we'd hightail it outta here and head for home. Now why would anybody be fool enough to risk a jail sentence, or worse, just to get us out of here?'

TWENTY-FOUR

I didn't have an answer to that one, either, so I was glad when my phone rang. It was, of course, Alan, telling me he was pulling into the car park and would be knocking on the door in a few moments. The fact that he thought it necessary to warn us of his arrival told me that he took very seriously the possible threat to Sam. He even gave me a code knock so I'd know it was him. It all felt a little like the Hardy Boys. And yet – Sam had nearly died; so had the guy at the Abbey. Precautions might seem ridiculous, but my husband is a sensible man, not given to panic. If he thought all this was necessary, I was prepared to take his word.

Alan looked very tired. He came in and plopped down in a chair in a manner very unlike his usual sturdy, unflappable self. I poured him a glass of cognac and started the kettle for coffee, and waited for him to begin the conversation. When Sam opened his mouth and took a breath, I gave him a school-teacherish look, and he subsided.

When the coffee was brewed, I gave it to Alan and ventured, 'Bad, darling?'

He shook his head wearily. 'Just confusing, and I do not welcome more confusion just now. The story Mr Douglas told me is very much like yours in general outline, Sam. He has no idea who his assailant was; never saw him, and remembers very little before waking up in hospital with, as he put it, "the great-grandfather of all headaches".'

'Did he tell you why he was down in the catacombs, or whatever they call it, the lowest level of the Abbey?'

'That's the truly confusing part. He says he was never there.'

'But . . . he was found there.'

'He was unconscious, Dorothy. The last thing he remembers is climbing the many stairs up to the Abbey with his tour group. He had gone ahead of the rest, he says, because he was so fascinated with the structure and wanted a little time to have a good look before the tour actually started. He is an architecture student, and could hardly believe the ingenious ways the medieval builders had solved the formidable problems presented by the site. He had moved off the path and around a corner to study a detail – and that's all he remembers.'

'Someone attacked him and took him into the crypt,' I said.

'Apparently. Though the other possibility is that he slipped – it was raining, remember, and the rocks would have been wet and treacherous – slipped, fell, hit his head, and wandered in a daze into the first door he saw.'

'All right, I'll tell you the reasons I don't believe that for a moment.' I ticked them off on my fingers. 'First, I'll bet you anything you'd like to risk that his injuries aren't consistent with falling and hitting his head.'

'Pathologists' opinions aren't always reliable,' Alan murmured.

'Aha! So the doctors agree with me. Second, even in the rain, the Mont was swarming with tourists. Not as many up near the Abbey as down in the town, I admit, but still enough that someone would have seen a man "wandering in a daze" and done something about it.'

'Um . . . not to cause trouble, ma– er . . . Dorothy, but if the poor guy was hit on the head, wouldn't someone have seen that, too? Or seen him being dragged away?'

'Not necessarily. If Mr Douglas was "around a corner", as he said, he could well have been hidden from the view of the foot traffic, behind a buttress, or a bush, or whatever. It takes only a second or two to bring something heavy down on someone's head, and not a lot longer to conceal the body, at least temporarily. Did he show signs of having been dragged, Alan?'

'The hospital, most reprehensibly, threw away his clothing. A nurse I talked to said it was beyond repair and, when pressed, cited rips and abrasions and ground-in dirt. His skin also suffered some abrasions. None of that is evidence, Dorothy.'

'Not police-court evidence, no, but an interesting indication, wouldn't you say? I suppose the police talked to whoever found him at the Abbey.'

'Of course. It was one of the monks, a somewhat unworldly

person whose sole concern was to get help for the man, rather than to take any notice of his surroundings.'

'Pity. Understandable, but how much more useful it would have been if Brother Cadfael had been there. A fictional twelfth-century monk and amateur detective,' I said to Sam.

'Hey, give me a break! I'm a medievalist! I know about Brother Cadfael; been to Shrewsbury and seen what's left of his abbey.'

I turned back to Alan. 'And did Douglas tell you why he ran away from the hospital?'

'He says he doesn't remember doing that, only waking up in an alley somewhere feeling awful. Whoever found him called an ambulance and he was taken back. My own idea is that someone drugged him and slipped him out.'

'But why—'

'Dorothy.' Alan dropped his hands on his knees in an irritated gesture. 'I'm tired, and I'm hungry, and I've had quite enough of circular conversation that gets us nowhere. Do you think we could find dinner somewhere and talk about something else?'

Alan and I both hate to admit that we're getting old, but it's true that we tire more easily than we used to. Sam looked us over and made a suggestion. 'Look, I don't know about you two, but after a century or two of hospital food, what I want isn't terrific French cuisine, but a really good big hamburger. Do you know of any place around here where we could get some?'

Alan actually laughed at that. 'My dear man, I read only a little while ago, in the *Telegraph*, that "le burger" is the fastest-growing food fad in France. I'm sure we can find them in Avranches.'

'Real ones? Not fast food?'

'Real ones,' Alan assured us. 'If you're ready, we'll go and ask the concierge where to find the best ones near here. He's sure to know.'

We found them. We found that they taste even better washed down with some good Beaujolais than with a Coke. Sam had two, along with a mountain of *frites*, and was a changed man. 'This is on me,' he said, when Alan picked up the bill and looked a trifle startled at the total. 'You're my guard dogs. Need to keep you fed and happy.'

'I think I'd better walk back to the hotel,' I said, getting up with a groan. 'I've consumed about three days' worth of calories, and I can barely move.'

'Climb in, old girl,' said Alan, opening the car door. 'It's close to ten miles by road. You can go for a nice walk in the morning.'

'Assuming I'm ambulatory by then,' I grumbled.

When we got back to the hotel, though it was early, I was more than ready for a nightcap and bed. 'Sam, do you like Jack Daniel's?' I asked.

'Sure do.'

'Well, Alan found a bottle in Avranches the other day, and there's a little left. We might as well polish it off, since we're having a very American evening.' Glasses filled, I raised mine. 'And here's to a happy issue out of all our afflictions.'

'That sounds like poetry,' said Sam, 'but I don't recognize it.'

'*Book of Common Prayer*,' said Alan with a grin. 'Poetry indeed, by a sixteenth-century archbishop. And an appropriate toast, my dear. Hear, hear!'

There is a theory, especially popular among the often lazy (like me) that going to bed with a problem in one's mind will produce a solution by morning, by some alchemy of one's subconscious. The theory doesn't usually work for me. I go to bed thinking about the problem, I have trouble falling asleep because of it, I toss and turn and keep Alan awake, and we both wake up in the morning out of sorts and no nearer a solution.

This time I'd consumed enough alcohol before bed that an earthquake might not have kept me awake. The morning found me, rather than suffering the hangover I deserved, actually somewhat refreshed and in reasonably good spirits, if no nearer to answers to any of our questions. Alan, however, was so merry and bright as to be distinctly annoying.

He did not, however, expect me to respond in kind until I'd had some coffee. Good coffee, in fact. I surfaced after the second cup. 'You never made this in the room.'

'No. Sam ordered it in. He woke up early and had them bring us enough to float a battleship and keep the sailors awake into the bargain.'

'Sam has Texas-sized ideas, bless him. I do feel as though he's looking after us, rather than the other way round. And I certainly never heard him come in to use the bathroom. He moves lightly for such a big man.'

'He has many remarkable qualities. There are croissants and brioches as well, and fruit, and so on. Shall I go down and fetch some?'

'No, I'm still full from last night. I could maybe face some fruit after I've showered and dressed. Do we have any plans for the day, so I'll know what to put on?'

'Not yet,' he said mysteriously. 'Put on whatever's comfortable, and we'll decide later.'

All right, let him have his fun. I finished the last few drops of my coffee and disappeared into the bathroom.

Alan and Sam were comfortably ensconced in our lounge when I went downstairs. There was still a large pile of pastries and a large basket of fruit on the table, and an urn of coffee big enough to destroy my sleep for the next week. It smelled wonderful. I recklessly poured myself another cup and took an almond croissant I certainly didn't need.

'We been havin' us a nice little chat, Dorothy. Alan told me all about your friends Peter and Krider, and we've come up with some real interestin' ideas. Have a sit, and tell us what you think.'

'Alan, is this what you've been dying to tell me ever since I got up?' I demanded.

'It is, with some embellishments provided by our friend here. I awoke this morning with an idea. Now those early morning ideas often prove to be illusory, vanishing like the morning mist in the strong light of day, but this one seemed to have some substance, so when I heard that Sam was awake, I came down to talk it over with him, and we're agreed. At last we may be about to make some progress.'

'That'll be a nice change. I'm all ears.' I absent-mindedly took a banana and began to peel it.

'Right. For a start, then, the thought that woke me this morning was that Bruce Douglas is a student of architecture.'

'Yes. You told us that last night.'

'Architecture, Dorothy. Not medieval studies. Not music, or art. Nothing to do with manuscripts, or Abelard.'

'Hmm. That's a bit odd, then. It falls outside the pattern.'

'That was what I thought, until I had a cup of this excellent coffee and my brain started to function. Then the picture began to form.'

I looked around the room. 'I only see a picture of the Mont, in a tasteful frame.'

'Ah, but I have an advantage you have not. I have seen Bruce Douglas.'

'Alan, you're being utterly maddening! Spit it out, dear heart, or I'm going for a walk.'

'Sorry, love, but I had to spin it out a bit. It's seldom enough that I know something you don't. I took a picture of Douglas yesterday. I don't know why, except that something was teasing at my mind even then. Have a look.'

He took out his phone, did some poking, and handed it to me.

'Wrong picture, dear. Look some more. This is Peter.'

'No, love. It's Bruce Douglas. He looks enough like Peter to be his brother.'

'But that means – wait.' I paused to think it out. 'No,' I said slowly, 'it doesn't make sense. My first thought was that someone attacked Bruce by mistake, thinking he was Peter. That would preserve the Abelard connection. But the prime suspect for all the attacks has to be either Krider, only we can't figure out a motive, or the mysterious missing Laurence Cavendish. And they both know Peter.'

'Krider didn't know him until he met the two of you last Friday. But if he had attacked a young man looking like him only the day before, he would surely have reacted at the sight of Peter. And he didn't, I take it.'

'No, not at all. I would have noticed. Okay, so we absolve Krider, of that crime at least. And we have to absolve Laurence on the grounds that he would have known he wasn't assaulting Peter. Not that he would have, anyway, if they're such friends as Peter's said. To tell the truth, I've been coming

closer and closer to the certainty that Laurence was behind
the whole ugly mess. But you've just destroyed that theory!
So honestly, Alan, I can't agree that we're making progress.
It sounds like we've just tied the whole thing into a Gordian
knot.'

'But if you remember your mythology, there was a way
around that little problem. And there's a way around ours.
We're not going to try to untangle the knot; we're ignoring it.
Sam?'

'Well, y'see, once we got to figgerin' it all out, an' figgered
it couldn'a been Krider who lured me into the drink, on
accounta he wasn't even around here yet—'

'Wait a sec. That's what he told us, but do we know it's
true?'

Alan nodded. 'He entered France on twenty-one May. I had
Henri check with passport control at de Gaulle airport. That's
the day after Sam's little swim.'

Sam grinned. 'Little slog, y'mean. I reckon I know how all
those mammoths felt at La Brea. Anyhow, so we knew it
wasn't Krider, and we'd already worked out he wasn't the one
who attacked the poor kid Douglas. So then there's this missing
Laurence What's-is-name, who's maybe a no-goodnik, and
maybe could've gone for me – except why? – but for sure
wouldn't have bashed Douglas, cause he'd've know he wasn't
Peter.'

'If Peter was the one aimed for,' I murmured, but nobody
paid any attention to me.

'So if it wasn't Krider and it wasn't Laurence, then it had
to be somebody else.'

I refrained from the scatological remark that sprang to mind.

'And before you say what you're thinking, dear heart, listen
further. We have not, as you believe, opened up the field of
suspects to all the humans in the area at the relevant times,
not unless we posit that the attacks were random.'

'Okay, okay, we don't think that. We're pretty sure they
have something to do with those elusive, perhaps mythical
Abelard manuscripts. How does that help?' I picked up the
last brioche and spread it with jam.

'Who else is deeply concerned with the manuscripts?'

'Well, Peter, but he was the one who got you involved, Alan. To my mind that clears him.'

'Probably. Who else?'

'Nobody – oh. Oh!'

'Exactly. The shadowy third figure in the scam. The one Peter won't name, claiming Laurence never told him. The artist from America. And where is he at this juncture? We haven't the slightest idea, have we?'

'So what's the odds he's right here, tryin' to get ever'body else outta the way so there's only him and Laurence to share the take?'

I shivered. 'Or maybe – only him.'

TWENTY-FIVE

The men decided breakfast was in order, coffee and pastries being insufficient for masculine appetites. They also decided not to order it in, and I heartily agreed. I was already getting cabin fever. How long, I wondered, would it be before this whole mess was cleared up and we could stop spending all our time with Sam? Not that I didn't like Sam, but I had a feeling I was going to get very tired of being joined at the hip.

The hotel served an excellent breakfast. Alan and Sam tucked in, but somehow I wasn't terribly hungry. I couldn't resist another cup of coffee, though, and by the time the men had finished eating I thought I could probably fly to the top of the Abbey and back. 'Look, I need a walk,' I said, scraping back my chair. 'Come with me, you two, and we can talk on the move. I've had enough caffeine to fly into little pieces if I have to sit still.'

'Well, we can't have that, can we?' Alan turned to Sam. 'Are you agreeable? It's both of us, or neither, I'm afraid.'

Sam sighed. 'Walkin's not my favourite thing, y'understand, but can't let a lady out all on her lonesome. Sure. I'll just poke my head out the door to see if we need jackets.'

Alan said, 'Wait, I'll go with you,' but Sam was already out of the dining room. Alan tried to follow, but a young couple with a little boy were just coming in, and by the time Alan got around them Sam had gone out the front door of the hotel.

It happened so fast. A car was parked right in front of the door. Two men got out; Sam stepped aside to get out of their way. Then there were shouts and sounds of a scuffle. Alan ran faster than I'd known he could. More shouts. The sound of a car roaring away.

By the time I got there, the hotel staff were gathered around something lying on the ground. I pushed my way through.

Sam lay sprawled on the concrete, Alan bending over him. I think I cried out. Alan was speaking to him.

'Sam, can you tell me your name?'

'You know damn well my name's Sam Houston!'

Alan turned briefly to me. 'He's all right, love. Right, friend, is anything broken, do you think?'

Sam is built roughly along the lines of a Texas longhorn, and he looked quite a lot like one as he got slowly to his feet, shaking his shaggy head. 'What's gonna be broken is some guy's head, soon's I find him, the no-good, low-down son of—'

'Ladies present, Sam. Come on back in, and we'll find some plaster for those scrapes.'

'You just gonna let those bastards get away?'

'They're long gone, Sam,' I said soothingly. 'No point in chasing them now.'

'We'll find them,' said Alan, sounding very grim. 'Come, now.'

He was bleeding a bit from several scrapes, his lip was cut, and his pants were torn, but he seemed to have suffered no real damage. We got him cleaned up, with considerable help from a shocked staff – this sort of thing simply did not happen at l'Ermitage. We sat down then in our sitting room, closed and locked the door, and put a glass of cognac in front of Sam, who by that time had calmed down a little.

'Don't want that stuff,' he said petulantly. 'Want you to catch the b— rats who did this.'

'Alan called the police while we were nursing your wounds. Drink it; it's good for shock.'

'How you gonna catch 'em? I didn't even get a good look at 'em. Got in a good punch, though!' He smiled reminiscently, and then winced and touched his lip.

'I saw the licence plate,' said Alan. 'Though it may be a stolen car, or hired. Looks as though one of them punched you, too. Drink your medicine.'

'Huh! Little tap, is all. Took me by surprise, or he wouldn't have landed that.' He moved his jaw from side to side, experimentally. 'My daddy taught me how to defend myself, and I learned a little more on the streets of Chicago. If you catch up with those . . . er . . . crooks, one of 'em's gonna be nursin' a pretty sore jaw. Broken, maybe. I hope.' He sipped at his 'medicine' and put the glass down. 'Okay. What I want to know is, what's the point to all this . . . er . . . stuff, and who's doin' it?'

'Which brings us back to where we left off yesterday,' said Alan, 'when I had to go talk to young Mr Douglas. Who knows what you were hoping to find here at the Mont?'

'Nobody! I didn't tell a livin' soul.'

'Then who could have guessed?' I asked. 'Your musician friends at the university? You were asking some pretty pointed questions.'

'Dorothy, they're musicians. If I laid one of Abelard's songs down in front of 'em, they'd get all excited about doin' an arrangement of it, and puttin' it in proper notation, and writin' an accompaniment, and maybe translatin' the words – but they'd never even think about askin' me where it came from. They just plain wouldn't care.'

'Your travel agent, then. Or did you book the flights and so on yourself?' That was Alan.

'Had my secretary do it. She can do anything on a computer, and she's used to me goin' all over the place. Only worries if it's someplace hard to get to, but not a normal place like Normandy.'

'And she wouldn't have been curious about why?'

'She's travelled some. She's never been here, but she knows about it. She would've figgered I was comin' here for the same reasons everybody does, plus a little extra because it's so old.'

I had run out of ideas.

'All right,' said Alan. 'After you got here. Your driver brought you to this hotel. Then what?'

'They brought in my luggage. I checked in. They showed me my room.' Sam's patience was wearing thin. 'I asked 'em where was the best place to start lookin' for hidden treasure.'

It took us both a beat to start laughing.

'Okay, Sam. One for you!' I chalked it up in the air. 'But there's still a point to the exercise. We have to try to find out why someone's trying to kill you.'

'Not kill me.' He was sober now. 'We worked that out before. Even those b– those thugs just now. They were tryin' to take me away, but they didn't aim to do me much damage.'

'To get rid of you, then. You must have mentioned to *someone* what you were doing here, or hoping to do.'

'Yeah, I get it.' He closed his eyes. 'So first thing, once I was settled here, was take a nap. I never get any sleep in a plane, and it's a long flight, Chicago to Paris. I'd slept some in the car, but I crashed for sure when I hit that bed.

'I didn't sleep more than a couple hours, though. I know enough about jet lag to want to get on a regular schedule as soon as I can. Besides, by then I was hungry. It was past lunchtime at home, and almost suppertime here, so I went out and got me a sandwich and a beer. And no, I didn't talk to anybody, except to ask at the desk where to find food. Couldn't talk to anybody much, come to that, unless they spoke English. And then I came back and read the book I'd brought with me, and went to bed early.'

Alan considered that. 'And the next day, Monday, I imagine you went to the Mont?'

'First thing. The shuttle doesn't come this far, but the bus from Pontorson does, so I caught that to the shuttle stop. Sat next to a couple who spoke English, so we talked about the Abbey; they'd been there before. Just chit-chat, y'know, nothin' important.'

'Was this on the bus or the shuttle?'

'Both. We both caught the same shuttle.'

'Ah.' Alan didn't quite rub his hands together, but his face conveyed satisfaction. 'And did they accompany you to the Abbey itself?'

'No, we got separated in the village. A real crowd, y'know, even first thing in the mornin', and that street is sure narrow! Last I saw of 'em, they headed into some shop, and I wanted to go straight up to the Abbey.'

'What shop?' asked Alan.

'Dunno. They're all kinda alike – tourist stuff, souvenirs, T-shirts.'

'Some of them have quite nice things,' I said. 'Overpriced, of course, but you expect that in a tourist trap. There's one with some lovely tapestries.'

Sam shrugged. 'Can't say I noticed. Don't care a lot about that kinda thing. My wife, she was one for fixin' up the house. Looked real nice back then. Now, just doesn't seem like it's worth the effort. So anyway, I went on up to the Abbey and paid my money and toured around with the audio thing. Just sort of a once-over, so's I'd know what I wanted to see when I came back. Took most of the mornin', so I had me some lunch there in the village. Talk about tourist trap! The food wasn't bad, but it set me back as much as a fancy dinner back home – and Chicago's not what you'd call cheap.'

'Did you encounter the couple again, the ones you chatted with earlier? What did they look like, by the way?'

'You do keep harpin' on them, don't you? I never saw 'em again, and maybe wouldn't've reckernized them if I had. They were just ordinary. American, by the way they talked, or maybe Canadian. Nothin' special. Didn't talk to anybody over lunch, either, or on the shuttle or the bus back to the hotel. I was runnin' outta gas by then, so I had me another nap, and then walked to a little grocery store. Bought some stuff for a snack-supper, brought it back here, had a bite to eat, went into the bar and had a drink or two, read some more, went to bed. And the next day you know.'

'Not quite. We know most of it from the time someone picked your pocket on the ramparts, but get us to that point if you will, please.'

Sam held up his hands in the classic gesture of frustration.

'What's the point? I'm telling you, nobody knew what I was up to. Nobody cared. I'm no dumb bunny, y'know. I didn't speak to any sinister strangers, I didn't drop any notes from my research. Didn't bring any with me, in fact.'

'And yet someone has tried to run you off. Twice. The next time they might consider a more permanent solution to their problem. So I want you to tell me what you did that morning, the Tuesday of your accident, from the time you got up, please.'

Sam wasn't happy, but he complied. It was the same story. Chatted to a few people who spoke English. Said nothing of any importance. Decided to see as much of the Abbey as he could from the outside, and climbed up onto the ramparts to do so. Walked part of the way round the island, studying the various levels of the Abbey buildings. Was trying to take a picture when he was nudged and his wallet and passport went flying.

'And then I ran down as fast as I could. Wasn't real fast. There was a crowd, and I'm not as young as I used to be.'

I groaned sympathetically. 'We've noticed that ourselves. You do slow down, don't you?'

'Ain't it the truth! And then those cobbles aren't great for runnin' on, and I got lost once or twice, what with ever'thin' goin' round in a circle on that dratted island. An' before you ask, no, I didn't talk to anybody except to ask once what was the best way down, and that didn't get me anyplace, cause the lady I asked didn't speak English.'

'But you got down to the bay eventually. And you say someone called to you about your missing possessions. Called in English or French?'

'English, o' course. I wouldn't've known what they were sayin' otherwise, would I? But say! That's kinda funny. How'd they know to speak English?'

'How, indeed?' Alan's tone was dry in the extreme. 'Plainly this was someone who knew you, or knew who you were, at any rate. A man or a woman?'

'I never saw whoever it was. Sounded like a man, but when somebody's yellin' . . .' He shrugged.

'And the accent? English or American?'

Again Sam shrugged. 'Don't remember.' He looked at the

wall, plainly seeing not a hotel room, but a place in Mont-Saint-Michel, hearing a voice calling to him. 'English, I think, lookin' back, but I'm not sure.'

Which got us exactly nowhere. Alan made one last attempt. 'That picture you took?'

'On my phone. Went into the drink along with me. Deader'n a doornail.'

So that was that. We sat and looked at each other with blank faces and, at least in my case, a blank mind.

Alan's phone rang. He looked at the number displayed. 'Avranches'. He answered, listened, said a few words, clicked off. 'The car was hired two days ago by a harmless family from Rome, who reported it stolen yesterday afternoon. It was found abandoned a few kilometres from here. They're checking it for fingerprints and so on, of course, but they don't expect any joy. Neither, I must say, do I.'

TWENTY-SIX

After a few moments of depressed silence, I got up. 'I still need that walk. More than ever, in fact. I didn't notice earlier what the weather's like; I was sort of worried about other things. So I'm taking a sweater. I can always take it off. Who's coming with me?'

Of course they both got up, since they didn't want me walking alone. I would have been happier by myself, actually. I wanted to think, and chatting doesn't allow thinking. I doubted I was in any danger from whatever maniacs were wreaking havoc in the vicinity. But I knew my two chivalrous escorts weren't about to let me off the leash, so I resigned myself to company.

The weather was actually perfect for a walk. There was a little haze to keep the sun from being too hot, along with a light breeze from the sea. I've lived inland all my life, so I don't know where my love of the sea comes from, but the tang of salt air always raises my spirits.

We couldn't walk far. Alan's ankle was much better, nearly healed, but a long or too-brisk walk would set him back again. And Sam, as he'd told us, was anything but an enthusiastic walker. The refreshing air had quickened my pace as well as my mood, but when the others lagged a bit I slowed down.

It was a good thing I did. Just around the corner I'd been approaching came a bicycle ridden at speed. I'd come *that* close to stepping right into its path.

'*Sorry*!' said Peter, nearly falling off the bike. 'I didn't hurt you, did I, Mrs Martin?'

'Never touched me,' I said. I didn't sound very friendly. I was still annoyed with Peter. 'You're a bit out of your normal orbit, aren't you?'

'I was coming to find you and your husband. They told me at the hotel you'd moved over here.'

Oh, dear. We hadn't thought to tell the hotel people to keep quiet about that. No help for it now.

Alan came up, making sure Sam was right next to him. He didn't entirely trust Peter, either. 'You were looking for us, Peter?'

'Yes. There's amazing news!' He looked from Alan to Sam.

'Mr Cummings, Mr Houston. Mr Houston is a friend from America, Peter,' said Alan somewhat deceptively. 'Sam, we've told you about Mr Cummings, who volunteers at the Abbey.'

They shook hands with all the cordiality of two strange cats meeting each other. Tails bushed, hackles rose. I stood back to watch the fun.

'Um . . . I have some news,' said Peter.

I thought he wasn't eager to talk in front of Sam. I ignored the hint. 'Oh? It must be exciting, to bring you all the way out here. Do tell!'

Alan smiled and cocked his head attentively. Sam, who could see just as well as we could that something was up, said nothing.

Peter gave up. 'Well, you'll hardly believe it, but Mr Krider came to the Abbey a little while ago to tell me. A manuscript has been found!'

If he'd wanted to create a sensation, he succeeded. Three mouths dropped. Peter's attention was focussed on Sam, who was the first one to speak.

'You're talking about a work by Abelard?' he said, in the crisp, standard-American accent that meant he was on edge.

'Why do you ask that?' Peter sounded just as tense.

'Look,' I said, suddenly tired of the game, 'we don't have to stand here and spit and hiss at each other. Besides, Alan's been on his feet quite long enough. Let's go back to l'Ermitage where you two can brawl in comfort.'

Both Sam and Peter gave me sharp looks, but they turned toward the hotel, Peter walking his bike.

I wasn't sure they'd let Peter in. He'd ridden quite a distance this morning, and the day was warm. His clothes were not what our hostelry expected, either. But we could go to Sam's suite and be quite private. Fortunately our door was quite near the main door of the building, so we snuck in (as I was sure Sam would have put it) and sat in our lounge.

'Now,' I said, before hostilities could begin, 'it's getting on for lunch time. I'm not hungry, myself, but I could do with something cold to drink. Cider? Beer? Something else?'

The men chose beer; I opted for plain tonic and ordered them on the phone.

When I re-joined the group they were still sitting in a charged silence. Alan, who knew well how uncomfortable that could be, was waiting for someone to say something indiscreet. Peter and Sam were both waiting for the other to speak first.

'Oh, for heaven's sake! This is ridiculous! Peter, you're wondering why Sam jumped to the conclusion that the manuscript you found, or somebody found, has a connection to Abelard.'

'It had occurred to me to find that somewhat odd,' he said stiffly in his most intimidating accent.

'Come off it. Do you really not know that Sam is the person who nearly drowned in the bay a little over a week ago?'

From the look on his face, he had not known. 'But . . . that was a woman. A German woman.'

'No, son, it was me, all right. And I've been wonderin'—'

'One moment, Sam, if you will.' Alan stepped in smoothly. 'Peter, Sam is also interested in old manuscripts, particularly anything pertaining to a certain medieval philosopher, of whom, I may say, I am becoming extremely tired. Sam is in fact Dr Houston, a distinguished professor of medieval history at the University of Chicago. He is here on much the same quest as yours, looking for original works by Abelard.'

'Not original, exactly,' said Peter. 'They'd be monkish copies—'

Alan waved that away. 'And like you, Sam is hoping to gain academic acclaim by such a discovery.'

Peter looked petulant. I could guess he was thinking that a distinguished professor at a distinguished university had as much academic acclaim as he needed, whereas he, Peter, was young and unknown and in search of recognition. He said nothing, however.

'He came here,' Alan went on, 'because he had heard rumours that such manuscripts might exist. I wonder,' he said, looking Peter straight in the eye, 'if you would happen to know how those rumours got started.'

I didn't know young men, in this day and age, could still blush, but Peter's fair skin turned fiery from the neck of his T-shirt all the way up to his hairline. As for me, I was mentally smacking myself on the head. Of course! All that probing to try to get from Sam the source of the talk, when all the time . . .

'Well, sir . . .' Peter paused to swallow. His Adam's apple seemed to be obstructing his throat. 'We – that is, Laurence and I – we thought that . . . that is, if the ground were prepared ahead of time—'

He stuck there, so I finished for him. 'You two started the rumours yourself, so when you came up with something, people would be more inclined to pay attention. Just out of curiosity, is this newly-discovered manuscript real, or one of your friend's ingenious forgeries?'

Sam's jaw dropped again, and Peter's colour receded as fast as it had come.

'I suppose I deserved that,' he said in a low voice. 'But I swear to you all that neither I nor anyone I know had anything to do with this manuscript. And I was not the one who found it. I don't know who did, or anything about it, really. It was Mr Krider who came to me at the Abbey with the news. He was coming here to tell you all about it, after he discovered you weren't at the other hotel. He had to find transport – didn't care to share my bike – but he should be here soon.'

The phone rang. Alan picked it up, said a few words, and replaced the receiver. 'He's here. That was the desk asking if we wanted to see him.'

And the knock sounded on the door.

No one could call Mr A.T. Krider a sensitive soul. Though the atmosphere in the room was electric enough to produce at least a minor flash of lightning, Krider showed no sign that he felt it.

'Dorothy, Alan, has Peter told you the news? I can hardly believe it! I've lived a long time, and this is the most exciting thing that ever happened to me! Me, of all people – an old duffer from Cleveland. Just wait till I tell you all about it! I was – oh. Excuse me.' He had spotted Sam.

'Mr Krider, this is Mr Houston, from Chicago. Sam, A.T. Krider from Cleveland.'

Krider did a double-take. 'Sam Houston?'

Peter had no idea why this was odd, and Sam had seen the reaction too often to be more than slightly offended. 'Yeah. For real. Blame my Texas daddy. I was born within spittin' distance of the Alamo. Now, what's this about you findin' an Abelard manuscript?'

'Abelard? Good grief, no! And I didn't find it. And it's only a fragment, anyway. And may I ask what your interest is in the matter?'

'And I'd like to know the same about you, bud!'

They glared at each other. Peter opened his mouth to join in the fray, but Alan held up a hand. Apparently he thought it was time to intervene before tempers got out of hand. 'Order, please, gentlemen. By coincidence or design, we have three people here near Mont-Saint-Michel, all vitally interested in a man who died well over eight hundred years ago, and in his work. Peter's interest is commercial, Sam's academic. And about yours, Mr Krider, I'm not quite certain.'

'Call me A.T. Everybody does. And I guess with me it's mostly just . . . well, an adventure. I've raised a family, made money, done pretty well in life, but I've never done anything just because I wanted to. But a lot of what I've told you two is plain truth.' He nodded at Alan and me. 'I read that book. I wanted to come and see this place for myself. And then I read something about this guy Abelard, and . . . well, Peter, I heard you talking about maybe finding something he wrote, something that's been lost for hundreds of years, and . . . I guess it just set a match to something inside me.'

'So you, with only a passing interest in the matter, you, with no background whatsoever in the subject, you have to be the one to come across what scholars have been seeking with all their souls these past many centuries.' Sam was furious. His face didn't show it, but all trace of his Texas accent and attitude was gone; he was suddenly all professor.

Krider made an exasperated sound. 'I keep telling everybody I didn't find anything. I haven't even seen the manuscript! I went to the Scriptorial as soon as they opened this morning, and nobody was talking about anything else. Great new discovery! Amazing! Marvellous!'

'Ah,' said Alan, pouring a little more oil on waters that were threatening to boil over. 'Then suppose you tell us all about it.'

'What have I been trying to do?' But he sat down, accepted the beer Alan offered him, and began his story.

'I told you I went to the Scriptorial this morning, early. I wanted to look at some of the manuscripts. I can't read Latin, not medieval Latin, anyway, but it doesn't matter. I just like to look at them, and think about how old they are, and how beautiful, and how long it took those old monks to write them out, and . . . well.' He cleared his throat and looked embarrassed. The successful businessman getting all sentimental about a piece of old sheepskin! I'd never liked him so much.

'I didn't get to see anything, though. Everyone in the place was in the front lobby, shouting and waving their hands around and talking French a hundred miles an hour. I thought at first the place was on fire! I finally found someone who'd take the time to slow down and tell me what was happening. He said the museum would be closed today and maybe for several days, to give the staff time to decide how to deal with their incredible gift. Except the guy was so excited, and he kept lapsing back into a French I couldn't follow – a local dialect, maybe – so I had to ask around until I found a woman from the gift shop who's English, or maybe Scotch, who could tell me just what was going on.'

'Yes, but—' I began.

'Okay, I'm getting there. This lady said someone had brought them a book, said he'd found something in it that he thought they might be interested in. It looked really old, he said, and maybe it was in Latin, but he couldn't really read it, the printing was peculiar. And she, the gift shop lady, had thought it looked pretty interesting, so she called the curator in his office, and when he saw it . . . well, she said she thought for a minute he was having a heart attack. He went all white, and almost had a fit when the guy – the one who brought it in – went to touch it, to point at something. He – the curator – whipped out his white gloves and yelled at somebody to bring some pieces of glass to protect it, and then he asked the guy where the thing had come from. And the guy said it was slipped into a book, this book he had right here. And where had the book come from?'

Mr Krider might not be destined for a career as a novelist, but he did have a fine sense of the dramatic. He let the pause lengthen for a beat before he went on.

'It came, the guy said, from the library at the Abbey.'

TWENTY-SEVEN

Peter was the first to recover. 'The Abbey!' he cried, sounding anguished. 'It was there all the time, and I never even thought to look in the library!'

'Krider, you said the document – whatever it is that was found – has nothing to do with Abelard. What is it, then?' That was Sam, still being very, very starchy.

'They don't know. The people at the Scriptorial, I mean. It's just a piece of vellum, a page of a book. From what the gift-shop lady told me, they think it's very, very old.'

'How can they possibly tell, without carbon-dating?' Sam sounded exasperated.

'They can't, of course. But from what I was able to piece together, it has to do with the language it's written in and the style of the calligraphy. And before you ask, I don't know what the language is, except I'm guessing it isn't Latin, or they wouldn't be making such a fuss over it.'

'What of the book it was found in?' asked Alan.

Krider spread his hands. 'Dunno. Nobody said anything about it. Just an ordinary book, I guess.'

'It wouldn't be anything very special,' said Peter dully. 'The Abbey library has no old books anymore, only those for the use of the Community. Mostly twentieth-century works of theology, and mostly in French.'

'So the person who brought the manuscript to the Scriptorial was a member of the Community?' asked Alan.

Krider shrugged. 'I suppose so. I didn't ask. Anyway, by the time I got there he'd left.'

'*Left?*' Alan hadn't allowed his voice to rise until now. 'The entire staff of the Scriptorial was in a frenzy about this apparently important find, and they allowed the finder simply to *leave?*'

'Maybe somebody got his name and address,' said Krider doubtfully.

'Wait a minute.' I was finally able to organize my thoughts. 'Of course they would have taken his name. If this thing is genuine, and as important as the ruckus over it seems to suggest, the Scriptorial people are going to have to start an intensive search for its origins. They, of all people, would know that the provenance of an artefact is of supreme importance.'

'Mr Krider.' Alan had his voice back under control and was sounding like a policeman. 'When did this happen? How long ago?'

Krider looked at his watch. 'Maybe two hours, two and a half?'

'Then there has been time for the initial excitement to die down a bit. Does anyone here know the Scriptorial phone number?'

I had one of the brochures on the bedside table. I handed it to Alan; he made the call. After a brief conversation in

French that seemed to consist mostly of *oui* and *non*, he turned back to us. 'Apparently everyone thought someone else was taking the information. The chap I talked to was a bit cagey about it, but reading between the lines, I'd say the bloke simply faded away in all the fuss, and no one has the slightest idea who he is, or where he can be found.'

'And that means,' I said grimly, looking at Peter, 'that there's something really fishy about the whole thing, and I'll bet money that your friends *are* involved, whether you know it or not.'

Alan let the silence grow. Just when it threatened to become unbearable, he said, very quietly, 'Gentlemen, it's time to put your cards on the table. All of them. All of you have pieces of information, pieces, as my wife has said, of a puzzle – if I may mix the metaphor. There may be only one puzzle. There may be several. But it's time, and past time, that all of you stopped hiding what you know and what you suspect. If you will not agree to that, I will go to the police in Avranches and request that they call in the next level of authority to interrogate you all.'

The men looked at each other with varying degrees of suspicion. Finally Sam spoke. 'I got nothin' to hide, and I shore as hell want to know what's goin' on around here. Beggin' your pardon, Dorothy, ma'am. I'm in.'

'Me, too.' That was Krider, who did, I was pretty sure, have a few things to hide. We'd see.

We all looked at Peter. 'Oh, for . . . all right. Yes, there are things I haven't told you. Ask your questions, Mr Nesbitt.'

No more 'Alan', I noted. Peter was addressing the policeman, not the friendly new acquaintance.

'Then, Peter, I'll begin with you. I want you to tell us, first, exactly why you came to Mont-Saint-Michel this summer, and second, what you've been doing while you've been here. No editing, please.'

'You know, sir, but maybe these . . . gentlemen don't.' There was the faintest hesitation before the word. I thought I could guess what noun he'd thought about using. 'I came to the Mont to try to find at least one of the missing Abelard songs, and if I couldn't find one, my friend Laurence was going to help me forge one.'

The frowns on Sam's and Krider's faces grew blacker, but at a sharp look from Alan, they said nothing.

'Laurence has a friend in America who can do that sort of thing very well, well enough to pass all but the most searching tests. He uses . . . well, you don't need the details, but his work is very, very good.'

'You've told us, Peter, that it was you and your friends who put about the rumour that such manuscripts might be hidden here. Knowing that the story was fabricated, did you actually do any searching, or did you simply wait for your American colleague to deliver his forgery into your hands?' Alan sounded severe.

Peter winced at that, but he replied calmly enough. 'The story wasn't entirely a fabrication. I had done a good deal of research into the matter. The Abbey here, back in Abelard's day, was much more sympathetic to him than some elements in the Church. It might have been because he was a Breton, and back then they thought of themselves as more Breton than Norman. For whatever reason, there have been hints for centuries that the monks might have hidden some of his work to prevent its destruction. All we did, Laurence and his friend and I, was bolster those hints a bit and start spreading them in the right quarters. The rumour mill did the rest.'

'I see.' Non-committal.

'So I wangled a volunteer job at the Abbey. They always need guides, and I speak several languages, along with knowing a lot about the buildings, so I was an asset. And I want to say here, to all of you, that no one at the Abbey, either members of the Community or volunteers or paid staff, has had anything to do with my activities.'

'Right. Point noted. Now let's go on to your involvement in the two attacks, on Mr Houston here and on Bruce Douglas. One moment, Sam. Let Peter tell us his side of the story.'

'That won't take long.' He made a face. 'I had nothing to do with either of them. But I admit that when I heard of them from the Abbey people, I was horribly afraid that Laurence or his artist-friend might have been behind them. Laurence is . . . not always the most well-balanced person. And I know nothing about the other man at all, except that he does a thriving business in art forgery. That's not a crime in itself!' he added defiantly. 'If he sold the copies as copies, that is. Good copies can bring good prices.'

'But you're not sure he always did make the distinction clear.' I couldn't keep the schoolteacher out of my voice.

He was silent, but his face spoke for him.

'And you said earlier,' Alan pursued, 'that you knew nothing about the forger except that he was American. Yet you leapt to the conclusion that both he and Laurence might be here in the area, might have assaulted Mr Houston and Mr Douglas. Why?'

Peter squirmed. His eyes focussed on the far wall. 'I didn't really think that. I just . . . wondered. I . . . to tell the truth, I've had my doubts about Laurence for some time. When I last saw him, he seemed . . . evasive. I had a notion that he had his own agenda, and it wasn't quite the same as mine. And this friend of his – oh, all right, the more I heard about him, the less I liked the idea of working with him.' He looked back at Alan and took a deep breath. 'You don't have to believe me, any of you, but that's why I told all those lies from the very beginning. I wanted a way out, just in case. I was on the verge of walking away from the whole scheme when all the frightful things began happening, and then it would have felt like . . . like letting the side down.'

Against my will, I was moved to pity for this very young man. He looked and sounded so much like a schoolboy hailed up before the headmaster.

'A bit out of your depth, are you? Very well. Let's move on. Mr Krider, what do you have to tell us about your visit to Normandy?'

Here was a very different sort of person. Middle-aged, verging on old, a successful businessman, and an American, with all that implied about his character. Say what you will, a person's nationality is an important factor in his approach to life, and the cliché of the brash American is not entirely without basis (I admit to my sorrow).

Krider cleared his throat. 'First of all, I wish you'd all call me A.T. Everybody does. It isn't just that I dislike my names; I've always hated them, so as soon as I could, I dropped them.

I'm now A.T. legally. Okay? All right, then.' He cleared his throat again. 'Well, it seems I'm not the only one in the room who's been telling a pack of lies about why I came here. I don't know why, exactly, except the idea of a man my age travelling a few thousand miles on a treasure hunt is so blamed ridiculous I didn't want to admit it. For the benefit of you two—' he nodded to Sam and Peter – 'who haven't heard the real story, or not all of it, it all started years ago when I read a book I guess everybody but me had heard of, by a guy named Henry Adams.'

Universal nods.

'Well, that started it. I wanted to see those two places, but especially Mont-Saint-Michel, but there never seemed to be a good time to come, and my wife wasn't enthusiastic. So the notion just lay there in the back of my mind until another book brought it to the surface. And I guess everybody here knows about that one, too: a book of hours made for the Duke of Berry.'

'Oh, my, yes! I have a copy of it, a modern reproduction, I mean. Gorgeous illuminations!' The mention of the book brought it to my mind's eye. It was the only limited edition book I owned, bound in dark blue leather, the spine faded now to a dull green, but the rest still pristine in its slip-case. I'd had to leave many of my books behind when I moved to England, but I couldn't give up that one – one of the most beautiful things I've ever possessed.

'Which one?' demanded Sam. 'He had six, and they all still exist.'

'This one is called the *Belles Heures.*'

'Ah. The best, in my opinion.'

Thus spake the expert. A.T. bowed his acceptance. 'Well, it sure blew me away. And I was getting ready to retire at the time, so I decided to take some art classes to learn how to do stuff like that. Well, of course I was no good at all. I'm an accountant, not an artist. But the more I learned about it, the more I wanted to see some of the real thing. And that brought me back to good old Henry Adams and Mont-Saint-Michel, and I decided, by golly, I was going to go and see for myself. So I read up about the place and heard about the Scriptorial, and that did it. I started making travel plans, and I kept on reading. And that's when I came across Abelard. Sure is a coincidence, huh? I mean, you two know all about him. It's your field. But I'm just a bean-counter. Weird that we'd all come together here, all looking for the same thing.'

I shook my head. 'I don't believe in coincidence. I think things happen for a reason. Either God's pulling the strings, or . . . Mr . . . um . . . A.T., how did you come across Abelard's name?'

'Lemme see. It was when I was looking for some manuscript libraries in the States. I did an on-line search and came across this store that sold what they said were excellent copies of illuminations. I went to the site, but I wasn't really interested in copies; I wanted to see the originals. There aren't a lot in the States. Oh, lots of digital ones, but the actual vellum ones are mostly in New York, and I've never liked New York much.'

'But you did visit the site that was peddling copies,' I persisted.

'Yeah.' He looked puzzled. The others all sighed.

'A.T., surely you know by now that there is no privacy on the Internet. You visited that site. And I'm willing to bet that it wasn't more than a day or two later that a little "news" item about Abelard appeared in your inbox.'

He looked at me as if I were a witch, or a soothsayer, or something. I sighed. 'Let someone else tell you about "cookies" and the Web. I don't know enough about it to get it right. I wouldn't know anything at all, except I have a young friend who's an expert on these things and has taught me to be careful. But it's plain to me that Peter's forger runs that site you saw, and that he's going around sending interesting little hints to people who show interest. It's easy, and doesn't cost him anything, so if nobody bites, he hasn't lost anything but the time it takes to hit send. But you bit.'

'I didn't go back to that site!'

'No. You came here instead, and started looking around for anything to do with Abelard.'

'And lying about it.' That was Alan, sounding neutral.

'Well – yes. See, if I did find something, I wanted it to be my own discovery.' He looked abashed, as well he might. 'And

I guess . . . oh, hell, I guess I was just too much of an amateur for the bad guys to worry about me.'

'Very well. Sam, it's your turn.'

'You're lucky, A.T. I'm not an amateur, and I got half-drowned and almost kidnapped. And to tell the truth, I'm wonderin' why. These guys want somebody to find their forged manuscript, right? Why were they drivin' me off?'

Peter shook his head. 'They wanted *me* to find it. That was the whole point of the thing. See, if I could find a genuine Abelard, there'd be every sort of glory in it for me – and Laurence, as we'd planned it. If someone else found it, it would all fall flat for us. And if someone like you, sir, found a forged one, there would be too good a chance that you'd recognize it for what it was. That's why they wanted you out of the way, but killing you would have brought the police in with a vengeance. I'm nearly certain that whoever enticed you onto those sands was also the one who rescued you.'

I shook my head at the convoluted criminal mind and let Sam continue.

'There's nothin' secret about why I came here. Except I didn't broadcast it to my colleagues, 'cause I didn't want 'em to get here ahead of me. I heard the rumours – I guess you and your pals planted 'em, son – and I came to see if I couldn't find me a long-lost Abelard song or two, and I've had nothin' but trouble ever since.'

'And you still say you told no one about your plans?' asked Alan.

'Not a livin' soul.'

'Then I don't understand how the villains apparently knew who you were and what you intended.'

I gasped. 'But I do. I just this minute figured it out.' I was almost scared, because it meant we could all be in danger. 'Sam, you told us you brought a book with you, from home, and you've read it out in the public lounge. Is it this book?' I pointed to the volume lying carelessly on the coffee table. It was a dull-looking paperback entitled *Historia Calamitatum*. 'I don't read Latin, but this is pretty easy. It's Abelard's story about his life, isn't it? *History of Calamities*, or something like that?'

'*The Story of My Misfortunes*, it's usually translated,' said Sam. 'And I was idiot enough to leave it lyin' around where anybody could see.' He smacked his forehead. 'I guess as a cloak-and-dagger type I make a pretty good bus driver.'

'But, Alan . . .?'

'Yes, love.' He gave me a reassuring look. 'What my wife has just grasped is that someone with access to this hotel is the one who knew why Sam was here. Unless you read the book anywhere else?'

Sam shook his head. 'I didn't wanna leave it someplace. I'm bad for puttin' things down and forgettin' where, and I don't wanna lose this. Cheap paperback, but I've made lotsa notes in the margins.'

'So someone saw you reading it. Someone who knows enough about Abelard to recognize one of his principal works. In Latin, so the person reading it must be something of a scholar.'

'It ain't,' said Sam with a wry smile, 'your usual vacation reading.'

'No.' Alan wasn't smiling. 'So. This hotel does not serve any meals except breakfast, and that only to guests. There is therefore no casual traffic. The person who saw this, and acted upon the knowledge is either an employee, or a guest.'

'Or the guest of a guest,' I added, looking at Peter and A.T.

'Right.' Alan ran his hand down the back of his head in his favourite gesture of frustration. 'And this would have happened before you were attacked, which was on . . .'

I consulted my notebook. 'Tuesday, the twentieth. A week ago yesterday.'

'Great Jumpin' Jehoshaphat, is that all it's been? A week? Feels like years.'

'Yes,' said Alan wearily, 'and the point is: how many guests have been in and out of this hotel in that time? And how are we going to trace them?' He stood and pulled his phone out of his pocket. 'Time for another call to Henri.'

'No,' I said firmly. 'I'm tired and I'm starving, and we need a break. We're going to the best restaurant anyone can recommend and have a thumping good lunch, and we're not going to talk about anything medieval or criminal while we do it.'

TWENTY-EIGHT

I t was rather a silent meal. Several times someone opened his mouth, thought better of it, and resumed eating. I imagine the food was good; it's hard to get a really bad meal in France. I don't remember a single thing I ate.

We jammed ourselves back into Alan's car, since we had become wary of separating, and drove back to l'Ermitage, where we sat around in the small lounge of Sam's suite and looked blankly at each other.

I'd been mulling over an idea all through lunch, and now, I decided, was the time to air it.

'Have any of you ever watched a magician do card tricks?' I asked, throwing the remark into the silence.

Four heads swivelled my way. Three faces looked bewildered. Alan's looked speculative.

'No, I haven't suddenly gone round the bend. There's a technique called forcing a card. A friend of mine who used to do parlour magic explained it to me. When the magician tells you to "pick a card, any card", a skilled operator can be sure which one you'll pick, and of course he already knows what it is. I can't do it; it takes some skill and practice. But I know it can be done.

'I'm beginning to wonder if our villain, probably Laurence or the mysterious forger, or the pair working together, hasn't been forcing a card on us – the Abelard card. "Calamities" keep on happening, à la Abelard. Every time we turn around, there's that medieval monk disappearing just around the corner – and we keep on chasing him. Come to think of it, maybe the analogy I want isn't the card trick but the good old familiar red herring. We're all concentrating on Abelard – his connection with the Abbey here, his lost music, his manuscripts. What if, like "The Flowers That Bloom in the Spring, Tra-La!" he has nothing to do with the case?'

'But everything we've seen and heard—' Sam began to object.

'Exactly. And who was it who first brought the name of Abelard to our attention?'

'Peter, I suppose, to you and Alan. But I was following the trail much earlier than that, and so was A.T. here.'

'Yes. But I remind you that you, Sam, were led in by rumours, and you, A.T., by an anonymous email. And we know who started those rumours, and we think we know who sent that email.'

Peter looked utterly miserable. 'You're saying it's me, that I'm the one responsible for the whole mess.'

'No, Peter. If I've understood my wife correctly, she thinks it's your colleagues who are up to some hocus-pocus.'

'Especially the unnamed American forger. And now you've used the word, I want to change my analogy again. What we have here is hocus-pocus, all right, but it's in the form of misdirection – the heart of all illusions. Make the audience look elsewhere while you're switching the hat, or the bowl, or whatever. And somehow I have the feeling the rabbit that's going to come out of this hat will be a particularly ugly one. Alan, Laurence and his pal have *got* to be found!'

Alan's phone rang. The call was brief. Alan's responses were in French, so I assumed he was talking to the Avranches police. '*Oui. Immédiatement.*' He ended the call.

'Laurence has in fact been found,' he said heavily.

Peter caught the implication first. 'It's bad, isn't it?'

'Yes. The police responded to a call about a man in the ditch near the shuttle car park. He wasn't drunk, as the people who found him had assumed. He had been assaulted with something large and heavy. I'm sorry, Peter. He's dead.'

After a silence that filled the room, Peter said, 'I think I knew it. He wouldn't have just disappeared.'

'But he did, I'm afraid. He has been dead for only a few hours. Twenty-four at most, the police think. We still know nothing about where he's been since he was last seen in Paris.'

Laurence's death meant that the full powers of the police were invoked. Peter was interviewed extensively, as were Alan and I as potential witnesses to a plot. Sam, A.T., and even poor Bruce Douglas had their turns. Everyone who might have seen or heard or known anything was questioned, including the staff at the Scriptorial and at the Abbey, as well as a few members of the Community and most of the shopkeepers in Mont-Saint-Michel and the surrounding villages.

Henri, in Avranches, asked Alan to convey the bad news to the English police, so he called Derek, who had the unenviable task of telling the parents. Derek reported back that, predictably, Laurence's mother had hysterics and blamed Peter for the whole thing, 'luring my boy to his death' and so on. Alan didn't feel obliged to pass that along to Peter, who had troubles enough. The police finally decided he could go back to England. They weren't entirely happy about it, but there was no evidence that he had any involvement in Laurence's death, and quite a lot of indication that Peter was damaged, both emotionally and otherwise, by the event.

The authorities took pictures of Laurence, taking care not to show the back of his head, and showed them around. They took his fingerprints and, from that piece of routine procedure, got their first lead.

'The car,' Alan told me a couple of days later. 'The one we connected at first with Sam? It was hired by Laurence at the airport in Paris. He used a false name, of course, but his fingerprints were all over it, and the hire firm is, fortunately, a small one. The agent recognized his picture. He was a good-looking chap before . . . um. And the agent is a young woman. Our first bit of luck.'

Well, it was nice to know that much, but I didn't see that it got us much further. 'Okay, so we know how he got here. And when, I guess, if he came directly here. But we don't know where he was staying, or what he was doing, or – or *anything*, really!'

'The police are working on it, Dorothy. It won't be too hard to find where he was lodging, now that they have a picture. Even if he was staying in a private house, someone will have seen him about. It's just a matter of time. As for what he was doing, we can hazard a guess that he was up to no good with his partner in crime.'

'And we still don't know who the partner is. "An American" isn't worth much, what with the hordes of tourists around here. And lots more coming, according to Jacques at the other hotel.'

'Yes,' said Alan absently, 'it's the beginning of school holidays for much of Europe, so families will be coming here *en masse*.'

'And here we are, pretty well stuck in the role of babysitter.' I looked around our little lounge to make sure Sam was still upstairs shaving, and lowered my voice. 'Alan, I hate to say it, but much as I like Sam, I'm getting awfully tired of this arrangement. Don't you suppose Sam could afford to hire a bodyguard?'

Alan sighed. 'Nobody thought it would drag on this long. For myself, I wish the bloke would decide to go home.'

'He won't,' I said. 'He's stubborn. He's not going to leave until he knows exactly what's been going on and who's responsible.'

'Well, then, let's take him on a sightseeing tour.' He waggled his booted foot. 'I can walk a lot farther on this than I could a week ago. Why don't we go to the Mont? We haven't seen much of it together. I might even be able to climb up to the Abbey, if I take it in easy stages.'

I wasn't terribly enthusiastic. The crowds would be awful, I pointed out. It was a hot day. What I really wanted to do was get some answers to the mess we'd become embroiled in. In short, I was feeling, and acting, like a sulky three-year-old.

'Love, there's nothing we can do at this stage. The police have it well in hand. Our role just now is to stay out of their way. Snap out of it and come along. We'll get Sam to buy us omelettes. He can certainly afford it.'

'I refuse to eat an omelette that costs thirty-five euros, no matter who's paying for it! But we might as well go to the Mont, I suppose. There's nothing much else to do.'

'We can decide after breakfast.' There was Alan's favourite ploy again. Feed her and she'll feel better. Oh, well. I took his hand to get me out of the squashy armchair, and, Sam returning just then, the three of us went in to breakfast.

Sam was all in favour of the little expedition to the Mont, and I felt better about it once I'd had a good breakfast – drat it all! I was genuinely uneasy about Alan climbing all those stairs, but it wouldn't do any good to tell him so. Within certain limits, we don't tell each other what to do. It seldom works, anyway!

I did insist that he take along his cane, just in case. And of course Sam would be along to provide assistance, if needed. I thought about suggesting a wheelchair for Alan, but one look at his face when he saw me thinking about it made me change my mind. And it was true that the going was pretty tough on the cobblestones. I put on my sturdy walking boots, the better to negotiate those cobbles, and brought my own walking stick. Thus armed against any hazards I could foresee, we set out for the shuttle stop.

It was a really lovely day. Streaks of soft cloud floated in a sky of that indefinable 'French blue' that I've never seen anywhere else I've travelled. A gentle breeze kept the sun from feeling too hot, and it must have been too early, in the day or in the season or both, for an objectionably huge crowd of tourists.

Sam was eager to get up to the Abbey, but he took it slowly in deference to Alan's ankle. I was watching my husband closely for winces or other signs of pain, which is probably why I didn't notice the man striding out of the shop door straight into our path.

We were moving at a stroll. He was in a hurry, and he wanted to go back down the street as we, and most of the other people, were going up. He ploughed straight into Alan and almost knocked him off his feet. His cane went clattering to the cobbles, entangling itself in the hurrier's feet.

I was furious. Fright on Alan's behalf mixed with wrath over the man's rudeness, and I lost my temper completely. 'Idiot!' I cried. 'Do you have to bang into— oh! It's you! I should have known! You never do watch where you're going, do you? You just barge along your own way, never mind who you might knock down, never mind about anybody else's welfare—'

'Listen, lady, I never saw you before in my life, and if I never see you again—'

'Oh, yes, you did! Your little boy ran his stroller into me a while ago! He must take after you! And then you pushed me aside last week, and said it was my fault. You must injure so many people you forget who they are!'

'*Will* you get the hell out of my way!'

By this time Sam had restored Alan's cane to him and come up behind our attacker, looking very solid and formidable. 'Pal, you want to watch your language to a lady! Seems to me you owe these people an apology.'

'I . . . oh, for God's sake! Okay, okay, so I apologize. *Now* can I go about my business?'

'Not much of an apology,' observed Sam, not moving an inch. 'This gentleman has a broken ankle. If you've made it worse, you might be looking at a lawsuit, mister.'

The man rolled his eyes. 'I was in a hurry. You were just standing there in front of the door. I didn't see you. I didn't hurt anybody.' He reached in his breast pocket, and Sam moved in a little closer. 'Here!' He'd pulled out his wallet. 'Maybe you'll think this is a little better apology.' He handed Sam a wad of banknotes. 'Have a drink or two on me. Now, let me through!'

He pushed past. The other tourists had scattered, as people will to avoid unpleasantness, so he was able to go down the street at a near-run. I tried to suppress my wicked wish that he would trip on the cobbles and fall headlong. He didn't. He was sure-footed as a goat, and was gone around a corner before any of us had quite recovered our wits.

'Waall, I'll be hornswoggled! Lookee here!' Sam held out the handful of money. 'The little skunk don't maybe got manners, but he sure is generous!'

With a sense of shock, I saw that most of the notes were pinky-purple and bore the large numeral 500. 'But . . . but there's thousands of Euros there!'

'Yep,' said Sam.

'I would be interested to know,' said Alan, 'first, whether they're real, and second, how that miserable specimen came by them. And I would like to sit down.'

There was a café just across the street. Alan and Sam headed for it, I paused a moment to pick up some debris that had fallen out of the man's pocket when he pulled out his wallet. 'He's a litterbug, on top of everything else,' I said, laying the oddments on the table Sam had managed to snag. 'Is there a rubbish bin somewhere?'

'Wait.' Alan laid his hand on the little pile of paper. 'I'd like to keep this.' He held up a business card. 'It probably isn't his. People give these things away, and one tucks them into a pocket and forgets them. But just in case . . .' He looked at it carefully. 'Hmm. Pretentious. The type is so very elegant one can hardly read it, but I can just make out a New York address. It could belong to the boor, at that. You said he was from New York, Dorothy, after our last encounter with him.'

'Yes. The accent, and the attitude. Not only the tearing hurry and the rudeness, but that insulting assumption that money can solve any problem. I don't want his money, Alan. Where shall we donate it?'

'Oh, the Abbey, I think, don't you?'

We had our coffee, at an exorbitant cost which Sam insisted on paying, and then Alan pronounced himself fit and ready for the climb to the Abbey.

We took it slowly, and made Alan sit at every possible opportunity, by the simple expedient of claiming a need to rest ourselves. It wasn't much of a fib, at least for me. I was still shaken by the nasty little encounter. It wasn't the sort of thing one expected in a place like the Mont. Granted, it was now more tourist attraction than holy place, at least down in the village, but many of the tourists had come on a pilgrimage of sorts. Why on earth had that man come here? And stayed – I counted back – over a week?

As on my first day, the crowds thinned considerably as we neared the stairs up to the Abbey, and the higher we climbed, the more people gave it up, so that when we finally got to the entrance and the gift shop, we had plenty of room to rest.

As we were catching our breath, I saw Peter slip away from a small group of employees. He came over to us.

'Peter! It's lovely to see you, but I thought you were going home.' He looked awful, grey and tired and about twenty years older than he really was.

'I was. There didn't seem to be any reason to stay here. I'll never find anything now, even if there's anything to be found. But there's nothing much for me in England now, either. My job was only a stop-gap. And it's high season here; the Abbey needs me. So I'm staying on for a little while at least. I really do care about Abelard, and this way I'll be close to the Scriptorial and his work.' He smiled, a wry smile with no pleasure in it. 'The police will be happy. If they decide I'm a murderer after all, they'll know where to find me.'

'Peter, my dear—'

'I'm sorry I can't give you a tour, but I'm booked solid for the rest of the day.' He waved and hurried off to lead his group.

'Collateral damage,' I said to Alan.

He nodded. 'Always. From every crime, but murder is the worst. Everyone involved is hurt. And of course he's not blameless himself. What seemed almost like a prank to begin with led in the end to Laurence's death.'

Sam shook his head, and we sat thinking about the unhappiness in the world.

TWENTY-NINE

I stood, eventually. 'Well, we're here. We might as well take the tour, with those audio things. We don't have to do the whole nine yards, Alan, if you're not up to it. Promise you'll admit it if your ankle starts to hurt?'

'Yes, nanny,' he said, but the smile robbed the remark of its sting. He allowed Sam to give him a hand with standing up, while I went over to get the audio devices.

Without Peter's helpful and witty comments, the tour was pretty bland. Oh, the place was amazing, but somehow, for me it was just a complicated pile of rock. We moved at a faster pace than the group Peter was guiding, so they came in to the refectory just as we were going out.

I clutched Alan's arm. 'Look,' I said in the lowest tone I could manage. I had remembered just in time how whispers can carry, especially in such a 'live' space as this high, vaulted chamber. 'At the end of Peter's tour group.'

Alan took a quick glance and frowned back at me. 'Let's get out of here.'

The door led to a staircase leading down. I didn't know where it would take us. I didn't care. Sam, after looking back, took the lead and moved rather faster than was really safe on the steps. He beckoned urgently and mouthed 'C'mon!'

After a few steps there was a turn, with a niche, with a convenient stone bench. We moved into it. 'What's that guy doing here?' asked Sam, and his voice, though quiet, was belligerent.

'I don't know, but I don't like it one bit. I saw him look at Peter . . . anyway, Alan, give me his card, will you?'

There was a window in our little niche; lots of light poured in. I held the over-elaborate card up to the light, trying to read it. When I deciphered the lines of small print, I gasped.

'What is it, love?' asked Alan urgently.

I read part of the card to him: '"David Grant Gallery, Fine Manuscripts, Tenth to Sixteenth Century, New York and London". And, Alan, he's up there with Peter!'

'And a crowd. Don't forget the crowd, my dear.'

'Crowds are slow to react. We have to go back up there!'

'You two stay here,' said Sam, in a voice that he must have used back when he was a Marine. 'I can take care of that sidewinder!'

Alan started to object, but I shook my head. 'Sam's younger than we are, and a lot more fit now that his lungs are more-or-less back to normal. And he has a pretty good grudge against Mr Grant, if the man is who we think he is. I'm betting he can cut him out of the group as slick as a cowboy going after a troublesome calf.'

'And what precisely is he going to do with his calf when he's roped him?'

'Who knows? I suppose we'll find out.'

'And what, incidentally, is a sidewinder?'

'A rattlesnake, I think. Some kind of snake, anyway. Appropriate.'

We were chatting mindlessly, I knew, to keep from running upstairs to join Sam in the fray. But it didn't work. The voices echoing from the refectory were growing louder and more raucous by the moment. Alan and I stood up in the same split second. 'Yes,' he said, and we started to move.

It's a good thing we didn't move far. The man we'd identified as David Grant came pelting down the stone steps, heedless of their danger, with Sam right behind him, bellowing like a bull, and Peter bringing up the rear. On up the stairs we could hear sounds of distress and confusion as Peter's abandoned tour group wondered what on earth was going on.

Alan had pushed me back in the niche, out of the way of the chase, but once they had passed, we followed – much more slowly. Alan had already broken his ankle once, and though I'd suffered nothing more than scrapes and bruises on these ancient staircases, I remembered very well how hard they were. It wouldn't help anyone if we were to fall and require aid ourselves.

'I hope they don't kill themselves,' I said, almost to myself, as we felt our way gingerly down the worn treads. Alan didn't feel the remark required a response.

They were well out of sight when we heard a series of thumps and clatters and cries of anguish or fury – I couldn't tell which.

I wanted to run. I didn't dare, and Alan couldn't. We moved as fast as we could, though, and a couple of turns later came upon a shambles.

Sam and Peter were both getting up off the floor, slowly and with grunts of pain. Blood was streaming down Sam's face; one elbow of Peter's white shirt was rapidly turning red. Papers were scattered about them, and in the midst of the papers, something that looked like a brown leather sheath.

The other man was nowhere to be seen.

Alan took control. Pulling a large handkerchief out of his pocket, he pressed it to Sam's head, just above his right eye. 'Have you another, Dorothy? This one will soak through.'

I didn't, but I had a packet of tissues in my purse. I handed them to Alan and then turned to Peter. 'Anything broken?'

'I don't . . . no, I don't think so.'

'Then take off that shirt. We can make it into a bandage for Sam's head. Scalp wounds bleed like crazy.'

'But he's getting away! We need to—'

'You need to get yourselves patched up. We'll deal with the rest later. How far away is the nearest first-aid station?'

He led us there, limping and bleeding. With a few fifes and drums we'd have looked quite a lot like the Spirit of '76.

While we cleansed and bandaged them, they tried to tell us what had happened.

'I went up to him just as he was moving toward Peter,' he said, his accent nearly vanished. 'He was carrying a book in both hands. I didn't like the look of it, or of him. He was planning something, but I couldn't tell what. Ouch.'

'Sorry.' I went on dabbing with the alcohol-soaked cotton. 'I didn't want to use peroxide so close to your eye. Go on.'

'So I got between him and Peter, just casual-like. He said something I'm not going to repeat. We're still inside a church. Then he tried to shove me aside, but I don't shove all that easy. So he shoved at one of the tourists, who didn't like it much, and Peter saw what was going on and told him, pretty sharp-like, that it was a closed tour group. And that was when he pulled the knife out of the book.'

'Knife!' said Alan and I in horrified unison.

'So I went to tackle him, and he broke away.'

'And you both followed him, and both fell,' I said, nodding. 'We saw that part.'

'You didn't see all of it,' said Peter grimly. 'Sam was getting really close to him, so he threw the book at us. Literally. It hit Sam on the head, and then I tripped over it, and over Sam, and by the time you arrived on the scene he was gone. Who *is* the maniac, anyway?'

'We think he's the mysterious forger.' That was Alan. 'We need the police.' He pulled out his phone.

'I'm afraid there's no signal in here, sir,' said Peter. 'The walls are too thick. I can sometimes get one if I step outside – but the terrace isn't very near.'

Alan held up his hands in frustration. 'Take us there. I'm moving pretty slowly, though. My ankle's playing up, drat it! No, look, you go with Sam and Dorothy, and I'll try to find someone who can phone from the landline here. One of us will get through. You'd better make the call, Peter, because of your good French.' He gave him the number. 'Tell them the man is named David Grant, and that he's suspected of murder and theft and any number of other charges. Can you give them a good description?'

'Between the three of us, we can,' I said firmly. 'Let's get going.'

The Abbey was rapidly filling up with tourists, who gave us curious looks as we made our way to the terrace. Peter knew the back ways, of course, off the main route, but there was still a lot of 'sorry' and '*pardon*' and once or twice a brief 'no, it's nothing' or '*ce n'est rien*' when Peter met other guides who knew him and were taken aback not only by his T-shirted informality but by the damaged appearance of two of our party.

The terrace was swarming with tourists. Peter pulled out his phone, checked for a signal, and entered the number Alan had given him. I expected a good deal of bureaucratic hassle, but Peter was savvy enough to mention '*Monsieur Nesbitt de la police Anglaise*', which apparently smoothed the way. I couldn't follow Peter's end of the conversation past that point, but from his expression and the many repetitions of '*merci*' at the end, it was satisfactory.

'So now we wait,' I said, sounding, and feeling, dispirited.

'And now I go try to make my peace with the Community,' said Peter, and he didn't sound much happier.

'Dorothy,' said Sam after Peter had left, 'I got two questions. First, where the Sam Hill are we?'

'I don't have a clue. But we'd better stay here, because Alan can find us here.'

'Right.' He sighed. 'And second, what's this all about? We thought we had an idea, but now I'm just about as confused as a chameleon on a plaid blanket.'

'Me, too. I'm only certain that we've gotten ourselves mixed up in something criminal, and I'm pretty sure that that nasty guy Grant is at the bottom of it all. Other than that . . .' I shrugged. 'Want some ibuprofen? I'll bet you've got one doozy of a headache.'

Peter re-joined us after a time. 'Alan's a bit rocky,' he said. 'Two of the Community are helping him down to meet the police at the entry gate. They're planning to comb the place for Grant, but you know what a warren it is. Not just the Abbey, but the whole island. They're also going to post a guard at the gate, but with the tide out at the moment, the bloke could walk across the sands.'

'He'd be fairly conspicuous,' I pointed out.

'And damn stupid,' growled Sam. 'Sorry – confounded stupid.'

'It would be poetic justice if he got caught in quicksand,' I said. 'And I should apologize for that remark, too, Sam. Most unkind and unforgiving.'

He grunted.

'How did you do with the Community, Peter?' I asked.

'They're not happy. They do realize I'm not entirely to blame, but they don't like disruptions here. This is a house of prayer, even though they're not cloistered. They will consider whether I will be allowed to continue to volunteer. But I'm leaving, in any case. I've done nothing here but create trouble.'

I sighed. The young can be so unbending, so inclined to black/white judgements. 'Think about it, Peter. You said yourself there's nothing much waiting for you in England. In any case, I doubt the police will let you leave for a while. You're a material witness in today's affair, and probably in a good deal more involving Grant.'

Sam looked at Peter in an odd way. I wasn't sure what was going on behind that speculative gaze, and I was too tired to try to work it out.

We made our way down through the labyrinth of stairs and passageways, out into the brilliant sunshine of a very hot day.

I was very cross by the time we reached the gateway at the bottom of the street. I, who love the old and quaint, was heartily sick and tired of cobblestones and a narrow street thronged with tourists and foreign languages being spoken all around me. All I wanted at that moment was my big old house and spreading green lawn back in Indiana, with some hamburgers on the grill and a pitcher of iced tea in the fridge. And no sound louder than the quarrelsome chatter of the squirrels.

Failing that, I wanted Alan. And he was off with the police somewhere.

We left a message at the gate telling Alan we were going back to the hotel, in case he came back looking for us, and I climbed aboard the shuttle in no sweet mood. Peter, sunk in his own misery, was silent, and Sam prudently left both of us to our thoughts.

'Shall we find some lunch somewhere?' he ventured when the shuttle had dropped us off in the village-cum-shopping-mall.

I shrugged. 'If you want. I don't care. Everything is over-priced here.'

'Of course it is. How about I buy us a picnic? We can get some bread and cheese and wine over there.' He pointed across the parking lot. I nodded wearily and followed him, Peter trailing behind, looking like a lost sheep dragging his tail behind him.

The food was probably excellent. This was France, after all, and it's hard to go wrong with crusty bread and aged cheese. I used it as fuel, not noticing what I ate, but it did perk me up a little. I'd refused the wine in favour of apple juice, knowing anything alcoholic would send me right to sleep. When we got back to the hotel, though, I thought I'd have a glass of wine at the bar and then take a nap. I was more than ready for one, and there didn't seem to be anything more useful to do.

Sam had other ideas. 'Did you leave your bike here when you went up to the Abbey this morning, Peter?'

'Over there.' He jerked his head toward a crowded bike rack.

'Locked, I hope?'

Peter just gave him a look.

'Good. Then let's find a cab and go back to l'Hermitage for a pow-wow. We've got a powerful lot of thinking to do.'

There went my glass of wine and nap.

THIRTY

S am was right, of course, but I resented it all the same. I wanted to drift way and forget all about this place and our troubles, forget about a young man lying dead, forget, especially, about a medieval monk named Abelard.

But I knew, somewhere in a still-functional part of my brain, that I wouldn't be able to forget, nor would I be able to sleep. Might as well get on with it. I pulled up my figurative socks, ordered a pot of strong coffee from room service, and sat down in the least squashy of the armchairs in our little lounge.

'It's your agenda,' I said to Sam.

'No, ma'am,' he said firmly. 'No agenda. Brainstormin'. We're goin' to think about all this sh— stuff that's been happenin', and we're goin' to figger out what to do next. Peter, you've been in on this from the git-go. You start.'

He spread his hands. 'I don't know what you want me to say. I never knew Grant. Laurence was close-mouthed about him. I had the feeling there was something dodgy about him.'

'Well, yes,' I said in some exasperation, 'if he was forging manuscripts.'

'More than that, I mean. And don't ask me what. I don't know. It was just a sense that perhaps there wasn't much the chap would stick at.'

'Like murder.'

'No! I never thought that! Who would? I just had the idea that he wouldn't be too worried if our plan, Laurence's and mine, turned into something illegal.'

'And Laurence?' I asked. 'How did he feel about that?'

'I don't think he liked it much, but he wasn't – I shouldn't say it – but he wasn't a very strong character. He . . . sort of drifted, you know?'

'With parents like his, I don't wonder,' I said, rather tartly.

Sam cleared his throat. 'Any other impressions about Grant? His interests, his way of life – anything?'

'I don't think Laurence actually knew him too well. They'd met when Laurence visited New York and popped into his gallery. He sold genuine medieval artefacts, Laurence said. Or at least he – Laurence – thought they were genuine, though I suppose . . . anyway, I had the impression Grant was doing quite well for himself. New York's almost as expensive as London, you know, to live, I mean, or do business. Laurence said it was quite a nice gallery, not large, but well-appointed and in a posh part of town.'

'So.' Sam leaned over the coffee table with an air of concentration. 'It seems that Grant's been hangin' around here for a while now. I'm guessin' he hasn't been stayin' in some cheap motel. Not that there are any cheap ones in these parts! But you know your way around here. Where would you think he's been holin' up?'

Peter almost smiled. 'Well, this is the best hotel.'

Before he could go on, Sam had picked up the house phone. 'H'lo, this is Sam Houston. I'm lookin' for one of your other guests, name of Grant. David Grant. Which room – oh. Yeah, okay. I'll do that. Thanks.' He scowled and turned back to us. 'Not here. Never been here, 'cordin' to the guy at the desk.' I opened my mouth, and he put up a hand. 'Afore you ask, the guy said ever'body 'ceptin me come in couples, or families. I'm the only single for the past month.'

'Scratch that, then. Okay, Peter, what are the other possibilities? The most likely places, I mean.'

Peter shrugged. 'If he has a car, almost anywhere. Caen isn't all that far away, even Cherbourg or Rouen.'

'And there would be plenty of deluxe hotels in any of those big cities, and an American tourist wouldn't be noticeable. But wait a minute! I'd forgotten! The first time I saw him, that first day I visited the Mont, he had a wife and two kids with him. Real little brats,' I added.

Peter shook his head. 'He isn't married. I know that for certain. Laurence once called him . . . er . . . well, he hinted that the fellow had a good deal of success with women, and wasn't hampered with a wife.'

'Peter, I *saw* him with a wife and children. Two boys, one in a stroller and one about five, and both having temper tantrums. And the two adults were arguing, too. Something about . . . oh, I remember now. No, you're right, Peter. At least the children aren't his, because he was complaining that she had brought them, and she said something about not wanting to leave them with their father.'

'D'you reckon he met up with the woman somewhere when she didn't have the kids with her, and they hooked up, and then he dumped her when he found out about the kids?'

'Well, that could be. I've seen him two or three times since, but he was always alone.'

''Cause if we could find her and the kids, she might be mad enough to rat on him. And a couple little monsters that age should be easier to track down than one man. I'll bet they made themselves unpopular enough to be remembered.'

'You're right. I'm going to call Alan. That's a police job; they have the manpower for it.'

Alan, when I reached him, was at the police station in Avranches, talking with some pretty exalted officials from Caen. 'No, they haven't tracked him down yet,' said Alan wearily. 'Unfortunately there's nothing really distinctive about his appearance.'

I told him about the kids. 'We thought that might help. And the older boy has a shock of really red hair; I just remembered that. Pure carrots, long and unruly. Maybe that would be useful?'

'Indeed, love! They might not still be around, but any hotelier would remember children like that. Thank you, my dear.'

'When will I see you?'

'No knowing. I'll phone when we leave here.'

When I clicked off, Peter was looking – not excited, exactly – less apathetic than before. At least some spark of something stirred in his eyes. 'You didn't say that before,' he said. 'About the kid's red hair.'

'No, I just thought of it.'

'Because I think maybe I've seen him.'

'Where? When?' Sam and I spoke in chorus.

Peter held his hands up. 'Wait! I have to think. It was when I was cycling to the Abbey one day. Not today. Yesterday, maybe? Or the day before? I was trying to get past l'Auberge de la Baie – that hotel there on the corner – but they were taking the sheep to pasture and I had to wait. And a redheaded boy was trying to catch one of the sheep and causing general chaos. Someone finally caught him and he started screaming. But by then the sheep had passed and I could go on.'

'Definitely the same boy,' I said. 'Appearance and behaviour. Who caught him? Man or woman?'

'A man. Not Grant. He's tall, and this chap was short and sturdy. Oh, and he was speaking French. I think. There was a good deal of noise, what with the sheep and the dogs and the shepherds and all.'

'So musta been one of the farmers, or somebody from the hotel.'

'Or a tourist,' I said.

'Don't think so,' said Sam. '"Don't want to get involved", y'know. No, pretty sure it was somebody local.'

'So maybe they were staying at—what did you say the hotel's called?'

'L'Auberge de la Baie.'

'And maybe they're still there.'

'Better tell the police,' said Sam.

'No! No, they have enough to do without chasing any wild geese, and this is something I can easily do myself. After all, I know what these people look like, and they don't. Sam, you'll come with me, of course. I guess I'm still your guard dog. Peter, are you in?'

'Might as well.'

He was back to the hangdog expression and attitude. A little hunting expedition would be good for him. And for me, as well. I no longer wanted that nap.

'Right. Let's go.'

We headed out of the room, and nearly collided with the man who was about to knock on the door.

'Sorry, folks. Looks like you're leaving.'

'A.T.! Yes, we're on our way to . . . um . . .' How much did I want to tell this man who just might be involved, somehow? It was unlikely, but still . . .

Sam had another idea. 'We're off to chase an idea, and we could use your car, if it's okay with you. Save us having to call a cab.'

'Sure, sure, anything! I was just coming to see if you'd learned anything lately.'

'It's been quite a morning, A.T. We'll tell you all about it on the way.' Sam winked at me and murmured, 'And we'll have him under our eye, just in case.'

So the four of us squeezed into A.T.'s small rental car. Peter told A.T. where we were going, and off we went.

I sat in back, leaving the front passenger seat for Peter, who had the longest legs. I was behind A.T. in a good position to give him a brief recap of the morning's activities. 'So we're helping the police look for this guy Grant,' I concluded. 'They can't be everywhere at once, and we think we may have found some people who were with him a couple of weeks ago, and might know where he is.'

'Count me in,' said A.T. 'He's not only a murderer and thief, but he's spoiled this place for me forever. I know that's petty, but it matters to me. I'd like to have a minute or two alone with him before the cops close in.'

On a warm, sleepy summer afternoon, very few people were around the hotel when we got there. That made sense. The locals were going about their business; the tourists were at the Mont or headed for it. Very few would yet be coming back. I gave myself a mental slap on the forehead. This was a poor time for a visit. Our little family would probably be elsewhere.

But we were in luck. A.T. parked the car and, as we walked toward the front door, we heard a well-remembered scream.

'Ah! That's Red. I'd know that pitch and volume anywhere.'

We went in, and there was the miniature monster, with his mother and brother, apparently checking out. The look on the face of the desk clerk told me how he felt about the situation.

There seemed to be some trouble about the credit card. The woman was raising her voice to be heard over her son, who screamed louder than ever. Peter stepped in.

'You,' he said to the child. His voice was quietly menacing. 'Stop that right now.' He gave the boy a basilisk stare, and the child was so surprised at being disciplined that he choked in mid-scream.

'And what seems to be the difficulty?' he asked the woman. She began to rant in English. The clerk chimed in in French. Peter quieted her as he had the child and dealt with the clerk in fluent French. The problem was solved in minutes.

'Now, then,' he said to the woman. 'Are you taking the train from Pontorson?'

'Yes, but this stupid man says I can't get a taxi from here, and I don't know how—'

'We'll take you. Or rather, this gentleman will. He has a car. When does your train leave?'

'Not for an hour, but I want to leave now. I have lots of luggage.'

'Right. Not to worry. We'd like a word, first. Shall we go out to the terrace?' He said a few words to the clerk, who lifted one eyebrow, but apparently agreed.

'I've ordered ice cream for the kids,' he said to me as we moved outside. 'I hope somebody can pay. I haven't a sou.'

I grinned. 'Cheap at half the price if it keeps them quiet.'

The desk clerk was efficient. He desired peace at least as much as we did. The ice cream appeared even before we had settled at one of the pleasant, shaded tables. Red (whatever his name was) dug in messily at once, and the baby began eating with his fingers. It was chocolate; they would both soon look like Uncle Remus's Tar Baby. Never mind. Their manners were their mother's problem, not ours.

'Well, what do you want? I've got a train to catch!'

'Yes. You won't miss it, I promise.' I tried an encouraging smile, which had no effect whatsoever. I soldiered on. 'What we want is very simple. You visited the Mont, a couple of weeks ago, with a man named David Grant. We're eager to talk to him. Do you know where he's staying?'

Her face hardened, bringing the angry woman to life in my memory. 'I don't know what you're talking about.'

'That may not be his real name. I'm talking about the man who was with you when your little boy pushed the stroller over my foot, up in one of the shops.'

'Oh. Him. No. We hardly knew each other. He'd offered to help with the boys. Fat lot of help he was! I never heard his name, and I haven't seen him since.'

'You spoke as though you knew each other quite well and had been together for some time.'

'You need your ears cleaned out, lady. I didn't know the guy.'

Red's ice cream was all gone, much of it transferred to his person. He snatched at the baby's. The baby set up a howl and threw the dish to the ground; Red screamed in fury. The mother stood and glared at all of us. 'Okay, where's that car of yours? It's time to get going. Shut *up*, brats!'

I shrugged. She was lying, but there didn't seem to be much point in pursuing the issue. She wasn't going to say any more. I picked up one of her suitcases to carry it to the car, hoping to get a glimpse of the ID tag.

'What the hell are you doing with that?' A harsh voice sounded behind me. I turned around and gasped.

It was Grant, and he was trying to grab the suitcase out of my hand.

'*Do* you mind!' I was hopping mad, and the schoolteacher in me came out. 'I am assisting this lady with her luggage. Keep your hands to yourself!'

'Oh, it's you! I might have known. You keep turning up where you're not wanted, don't you! That case happens to be mine!'

He tugged. I held on. He pulled harder. Sam and Peter joined the fray. A.T. was shouting something. The children screamed.

I'm not sure how it happened, but somehow my feet slid out from under me and I fell, landing on the suitcase. It was stuffed full to bursting, and with my added weight on top, it burst. The zipper gave, and clothing scattered over the terrace.

'Damn it to hell, woman, if you've destroyed . . .' Grant pushed me roughly away and rummaged frantically in the suitcase. He pulled aside the last of the contents, a large, flat package, and began to pull at the fabric of the case itself.

'What's this, then?' said Peter, picking up the package.

'You leave that alone! I – it – you could damage – but where—' Grant was incoherent with rage, trying to take the package from Peter while still doing something to the suitcase.

The children still screamed, and now their mother screamed with them. I sat on the stone floor of the terrace and watched as the desk clerk and a couple of other people came out of the hotel. The clerk was positively dancing with anger. His cries were in French and were almost inaudible over the rest of the confusion, but I could guess he was deploring such behaviour at his hotel.

Peter moved away and began, slowly, carefully, to unwrap the package. Grant let him go, concentrating on the empty suitcase, for no reason I could imagine.

'Oh, dear God!' The exclamation from Peter was almost reverent.

The action at that point seemed to me to go into slow motion. Peter let the loosened paper slip from the package to reveal a large sheet of paper wrapped in clear plastic. He held it up so we could see the brilliant colours, the ruled lines, the black circles and squares marching up and down on the lines, the closely-written text beneath.

Grant gave a cry of anger and despair, made a move to snatch the paper from Peter's grasp, and then seemed to change his mind. He stood, battered suitcase in hand, and ran toward the parking lot.

There were shouts, sounds of a struggle, and then, distinguishable to me even over the mass confusion, the most welcome sound I've ever heard: my husband's voice.

THIRTY-ONE

Hours later, we sat around the table in the bar at l'Hermitage, glasses in front of us. After disposing of Grant, children, mistress, and the police, we'd eaten an excellent meal at what we'd been assured was the best restaurant in Avranches, and returned to our hotel for a post-mortem.

'I don't know what we would have done if you hadn't thought to call Alan,' I said to A.T. 'That was brilliant.'

He spread his hands in disclaimer. 'Looked to me like the situation was getting out of hand. Seemed to be the thing to do. We're just lucky they were already on their way here.'

'They nearly got away with it,' said Alan, who was still a bit shaken. 'Why didn't you call me at once when you thought of talking to the woman?'

'We thought you were busy tracking down other leads, and this one might not pan out anyway. And what trouble could we get into, four of us against one woman?'

'We didn't expect Grant to make an appearance, sir,' said Peter. 'We'd never have let Dorothy—'

'Son,' said Alan heavily, 'when my wife makes up her mind to something, she's approximately as stoppable as a force-ten gale. She sweeps all before her.'

'Anyway, we got him,' I said with satisfaction.

'And we got this,' said Peter. The piece of music was resting in honour on the next table. The police had let him borrow it for the evening. 'Of course it's a fake, but I still don't want drinks spilled on it. It's so beautifully done!'

After his moment of sheer elation, Peter had realized that the music couldn't be a medieval manuscript. Something about the Latin text – I couldn't follow it. 'He got everything else right, though. The parchment is old, the style is right, the inks are right, even the music would sound authentic. He probably copied the text from something of about the right period and didn't realize that there were various dialects. Abelard wouldn't have used this one. Grant was an artist, not a scholar.' He spoke as though David Grant were dead.

'There isn't a death penalty in France, is there?' I asked.

'No,' Alan answered. 'Nor in New York, Grant's residence, nor of course in England, Laurence's residence. There will no doubt be endless bickering about where the case will be tried, but in any event, Grant will not be executed.'

I tried not to think that was a pity.

'And what about the painting?' Sam changed the subject. 'What d'you s'pose he was plannin' to do with that?'

For the police had found a false lining in the suitcase, and behind it, a small but exquisite Renoir.

'Oh, didn't I tell you?' Alan polished off the last of the wine in his glass. An attentive waiter appeared with a refill. 'He wouldn't say a thing about where he got it or what his plans were, but when the police found a description of it on a list of looted Nazi art, his girlfriend was only too eager to talk. Apparently he had bragged about finding it deep in the cellars of the Abbey, when he was looking for lost Abelard manuscripts. As an art dealer, of course he knew what it was, and knew that it should be turned over to the commission entrusted with restoring such things to their rightful owners, when possible. But you can guess that Grant was more interested in the fortune he could make from it. He told Mary Anne—'

'Oh, is that her name?'

'No idea. She wouldn't say, but until the police find her passport, we have to call her something. Grant told her he had a private buyer waiting in the States, ready to pay him a king's ransom for the thing. By that time she wasn't so keen on him anymore, so she told him he was a fool to think he could smuggle a thing like that out of the country.'

'So that's when he came up with the idea of using the faked manuscript to hide the real thing?' I suggested.

'More or less.' That was Peter. 'He told me a few things while he was waiting for the police to interrogate him. He'd done the fake ages ago, in New York, and brought it *into* the country to use in Laurence's scheme, if necessary. He didn't even have to smuggle it. As a fake it's of little interest to the customs people. But when he found the Renoir, he realized he could hide it in the suitcase, keep it stiff and safe with the wrapped manuscript, and let his luggage be searched by anyone who wanted to. They'd see the manuscript, he'd tell them he painted it and was selling it – *as* a reproduction, of course – and show them the purchase order from a Paris gallery. That was real, too, incidentally. Some art dealer in Paris is going to be quite upset when the piece doesn't turn up.'

'Who knows, they might get it yet,' said Alan. 'Once the police have finished with it as a piece of evidence, they may put it up for sale. Hard to know what they'd do with it at the station.'

'I wish I had the money to buy it. Ah, well.' Peter gave a long sigh.

'What about that genuine manuscript he "found"?' asked A.T. 'The one he gave to the Scriptorial. That doesn't seem to fit anything.'

'He told me about that, too,' said Peter. 'He was gloating, almost as if I should be awed by his cleverness. It was his. He'd found it years ago in somebody's attic and paid them for it. Probably not what it was worth, but he didn't steal it. He brought it with him to . . . I can't remember the expression. Something about salt.'

'"Salt the mine", probably,' I said. 'Comes from gold- and diamond-mining days, when someone would strew a few chunks of gold or diamonds around a worthless piece of property to convince a naïve buyer that there was a fortune to be found there. In this case Grant "found" the manuscript at the Abbey to prepare the way for his "finding" the Abelard music. So that's one good thing to come out of this, anyway – another medieval artefact saved for posterity.'

'The only good thing,' said Peter. 'Laurence is dead. He wasn't maybe the world's best scholar, or the most honest chap, but he was my friend.'

'I suppose Grant killed him because he got too close to the truth,' I said.

'That, or he wanted to go halves on the Renoir. That would have been like him. Oh, there was such a lot I didn't like about him, but we'd known each other a long time, and we had some hopes for the future. Now . . .'

'I've got some ideas about that, son. We'll talk tomorrow, okay?'

The party broke up after that. We were all exhausted. I plodded up the stairs to our bedroom in Sam's suite and wished I could just drop into bed in my clothes.

'You heard what Sam said to Peter?' Alan asked as I was trying to kick off my sneakers without untying them.

'Hmm?'

'He's going to offer him a job. Sam is, to Peter, I mean. He told me earlier. He thinks the boy has what it takes and just needs proper supervision. Nice chap, and it would do Peter good to get out of England.'

'Mmm.' I'd given up on the shoes and bent down to untie them.

'Love, you haven't heard a word I've said. Poor dear, it's not been much of a holiday for you, has it? Tomorrow I'm going to take you to Paris and show you the place properly.'

That roused me. I sat up, one shoe in my hand. 'You are going to do no such thing! You are going to take me home, and I'm going to cook chili, or meatloaf, or something as American as I can think of. And we're not going to mention France or speak a single word of French till Christmas!'

'Right, dear heart. Go to bed.'

I was asleep before he turned out the light.